The Metal Heart

ALSO BY CAROLINE LEA

The Glass Woman
When the Sky Fell Apart

The Metal Heart

A Novel of Love and Valor
in World War II

CAROLINE LEA

HARPER PERENNIAL

NEW YORK • LONDON • TORONTO • SYDNEY • NEW DELHI • AUCKLAND

Dear Reader,

While inspired by real events and the construction of the Italian Chapel in Orkney during the Second World War, this is very much a work of fiction. As such, characters and places have been invented and the names of locations and timings of events have often been changed.

Within this book, I wanted to give voice to the people who find themselves caught up in war, swept along by love and transformed as a result of circumstances beyond their control.

While editing the story, I found myself in the midst of a global pandemic and months of lockdown, watching the world close in on itself: people confined to their homes, yet still reaching out to each other, supporting each other, offering love through everyday acts of kindness. I was struck, once again, by the ways in which people under pressure seek escape, the ways in which we create beauty through art and the places where we find love and light.

Thank you for reading this book. I hope you enjoy it.

If the earth shook and the sea swept over the fields, it was the Stoor Worm yawning. He was so long that there was no place for his body until he coiled it around the earth. His breath was so venomous that when he was angry, every living thing within his reach was destroyed. People grew pale and crossed themselves when they heard his name, for he was the worst of the nine fearful curses that plague mankind.

From *Asipattle and the Stoor Worm*,
an Orkney folk tale

Prologue

The girls, Selkie Holm, Orkney, September 1942

Of all the ways to die, drowning must be the most peaceful. Water above, sounds cushioned, womb-dark. Drowning is a return to something before the knife-blade of living. It is the death we would choose, if the choice was ours to make.

It is the death we would choose for others too – if we loved them enough.

The sea is cold, filling our noses when we surface. We dive back beneath the water to tug the foot free. Everything is blurred as the waves crash into the barriers. We clutch each other, kicking furiously to stop ourselves being smashed into the rocks, watching the pale body drift back and forth with each tidal tug. Above the waves, the storm churns – people on land will be smothering their lights, shutting out the lashing rain, the threat from passing planes and unseen monsters. They will believe the Stoor Worm is in a fury.

The body is silent now; motionless, apart from the movement of the waves. Our lungs burn. Moments ago, scrabbling nails had clawed at us and fingers had reached for our hands. A fierce, desperate tug. A final watery shriek. Then sudden stillness – the eyes fixed open, as if the body was alive and breathing brine, like some creature of myth.

We help each other from the water, both sobbing. And then we work to get the body from the sea, to free the clothing where it has snagged on the rocks. We dive in again and again. Our lungs ache. Our muscles shudder. Our hands grow numb and our fingers slip from the body's slick skin.

Finally, it comes free.

We drag it upwards onto the barrier that the prisoners built. We'd watched them laying down stone, unspooling barbed wire, changing the shape of our island and bringing chaos to our doorstep.

Even before the war arrived here – before the guns and the guards and the iron huts full of foreign prisoners – Orkney hadn't been a safe place. People have their own beliefs this far north: their laws are ancient and quick and brutal. These islands teeter on the edge of the world. Once, Orkney would have been a blank on a map. *Terra Incognita* – some skinny-shanked sailor's drunken dream, the land rising out of the fog and disappearing again before he could set foot on the shape his finger traced on the murky horizon.

There are a hundred sunken tombs on these islands where we could hide the body – deep pits in the ground, covered with rock and earth, surrounded by the ragged incisors of standing stones that rear skywards – but they are too far away. Instead, we begin to drag it towards the quarry, where there will be shelter from the wind's bite, and rocks enough for a burial.

The walls of the quarry rise dark around us; the wind snaps our hair over our faces, whipping tears from our eyes. We scrabble in the rubble, our hands wet and numb, until we find seven stones of a good size. We place them on the body, according to the ceremony. One on the forehead to still the beating thoughts; one on the chest to quiet the hammering heart; one in each hand and one on each foot, to end all movement; and a final pebble in the mouth to stop the breath. Without such precautions, the dead are restless and tormented and have been known to haunt the living. We say the rhyme:

'Take blood and breath and flesh and bone,
take all between these seven stones.'

Finally, we take the metal heart from our pocket and place it on the chest, above the space where the living heart used to beat. We turn away so we cannot press our lips to the cold skin: the feel of that cooling flesh will be too much.

It is finished. We can do no more to say farewell.

The ground is rough beneath us as we sit next to the cold body, waiting for the last of the storm to die down.

After they find us, we won't see the sky again. It'll be a private hanging in a dark cellar, last used to string up smugglers and fish thieves. Or perhaps we will see sunlight when they take us out to a quiet field at dawn, before they blindfold us and take aim.

The clouds drift away, revealing the last of the stars, their signs and warnings unread by those islanders hiding in the blackout or sleeping in their beds. This is the time of salt laced outside doors to warn off sea spirits. The land, pockmarked by dropped bombs and groaning under skeins of wire, smells of doused fires and explosives from the quarry. Had we knocked on any of those darkened doors tonight, we'd have found it barred.

We wait.

'How long, do you think?'

We draw a shuddering breath. It doesn't matter now: the unseen days and weeks and years unravel blankly ahead of us. Light will bleed out over this water nightly; day will settle in again and again. We won't know.

The first glimmer of sunrise brightens the sea, picking out the skeletal shadows of the wrecks from the last war. We used to swim down to them: ships full of dormant bombs and bleached bones. When the tide shifts, the jaws on some of the skulls clack open and shut, as if there is something they still want to say.

A figure finally walks along the barrier – Mr

4

Cameron, with his rope-tied trousers, his grey skin, his hacking cough.

He is ten paces away before he sees the body.

'Christ! What have you . . . ? Christ!'

His face pales and he stumbles back along the barrier, not towards the houses of Kirkwall, just across the water, but up towards the camp, with its spiked fences and metal huts.

Now would be our chance to escape.

We don't move. The cold from the ground seeps up into our bones, rooting us.

This is where we belong.

We squeeze our hands together as if we could become a single being. As if we could return to the time before the war. Before we knew about love and death and envy.

We count two hundred shared breaths before they come for us – not the police, but one of the guards from the camp, black-booted and in a pressed uniform of dark green: a practical colour to hide mud and bloodstains.

We stand and turn, face him and hold up our hands – the blue-white skin on our wrists identical, indistinguishable, even to our own eyes.

And with one voice, we say, 'She didn't do it. I did it. It was me.'

PART ONE

Friday I held a seaman's skull,
Sand spilling from it
The way time is told on kirkyard stones

From 'Beachcomber', George Mackay Brown

October 1941

Midnight. The sky is clear, star-stamped and silvered by the waxing gibbous moon. No planes have flown over the islands tonight; no bombs have fallen for over a year. The snub noses of anti-aircraft guns gleam, pointing skywards. The cliffs loom like paper cutouts, hulking shadows above the natural harbour of the bay. Everything is flattened by the darkness, as if the sea around Orkney is a stage set, waiting for an entrance.

The German U-boat glides between the rocks that lead to Scapa Flow. It is alone, on a mission that cannot be accomplished.

People have told Commander Pasch that he is mad, that he is risking his crew, his vessel, his own life. His men snap commands to each other in broken sentences. They touch the pictures of wives, children, lovers.

One of the men whispers, *'Vater unser in Himmel...'* Our Father in Heaven.

Around the boat, the water shifts and sighs: so close to winter, the sea temperature would shock the air from the men's lungs. Inside is safety. This boat has carried them through enemy waters, past icebergs and monsters of the deep. Their living home, snug, bullet-shaped, fuggy with their breath, thick with their laughter.

The submarine slides past the clean-picked bones of ships long-sunk. A maze of broken-ribbed vessels, stretching steel to snag them. Beyond, the navigator can make out a dark mass of ancient rock. Beneath the waves, one land looks much like any other; friend and enemy soil are the same in the darkness. But the man has studied this land, this route, these remote islands.

Orkney.

And above their heads, floating like ghosts in the moonlight, are the massed ships of the British Royal Navy. They will be full of men at ease: sleeping, dreaming of home. Their portholes will be open. No one will expect an attack.

But it is best not to think of the men. Best to focus on the instruments, on loading the torpedoes, on setting the sights on the largest boat at dock. HMS *Royal Elm*. It hangs, suspended in the water above them, bobbing like a bloated corpse.

The Orcadians sleep in their beds with half an ear open for bombers, which might still whine overhead for all it's just past midnight. It's rumoured that the Germans are developing a new plane, which can fly entirely silently, and they'll be testing it on Orkney first. It's been said that the Germans will overrun them.

'Hush, you,' the mammies whisper, when their children repeat the horrors they've heard in the schoolyard.

'The Germans will peel off our skins, Mammy!'

'We'll no have Germans here.' But their brows are creased as they smooth covers flat and kiss foreheads and press the blankets more closely around the windows to block out any light that might call to a passing plane.

There are many different islands, some clustered closely enough that you could swim from one to another, or shout insults across the water. The only safe secrets are concealed under the ground or beneath the sea.

They are a cold, closed people here. Hard-faced and with a single lonely beating heart. They survive as one. They weather storms and winds and bad harvests together. They know each other's middle names, whose baby is teething, or whose children are in need of a sharp slap and some manners. They know when a couple has fallen out, or when someone has taken ill, and they deal with both problems the same way: a loaf of bread on the doorstep, like a promise, and an expectation that the matter will be resolved.

They have their own names for people from different

islands: folk from Flotta are called Fleuks or Flounders. People from Hoy are Hawks. South Ronaldsay dwellers are called Witches. Nothing sinister in that – it's an age-old name and no one asks for reasons.

There's another, smaller, island too, Selkie Holm, named so for the creatures that are rumoured to swim in its waters: half woman, half fish. Until recently, no person had lived there for more than a hundred years. The only building is a broken-down shepherd's bothy, which squats on the hill like a decaying tooth. It was uninhabited by anything except sheep until a few months ago, when the Reid twins moved in.

The inlet of Scapa Flow, which runs between the island of Selkie Holm and that of mainland Orkney and Kirkwall, has been used as a naval base since the Great War. No one is happy to see the ships come back, but what's to be done? The English sailors are loud when they come ashore. There is less food for everyone and the small town of Kirkwall is crammed with young men, who drink too much beer, then whistle at the local girls. Only last week, a sailor grabbed a woman around the waist and tried to kiss her. She shrieked and cuffed him about the head. There was talk later that a group of Orcadian men were going to storm one of the boats and teach the sailor some manners. Nothing came of it – just old men and flat-footed youngsters making threats – but, still, the air has a frayed-rope feel, close to snapping.

Most of the young Orcadian men have gone off to fight. The islands are full of grandfathers, women and children – or young men unfit for combat. Those who remain feel raw and exposed, and huddle together against the gathering storm of war.

In the warmth of a Kirkwall pub, five men crouch around a table. They should have gone home an hour before, when the pub closed, but they have paid the barman well to lock the doors and keep the beer coming. They have cards and stories, which they share by the light of a single candle; they would barely be visible to anyone passing outside.

The old tales are told, one by one, as the cards are dealt: the mists that have been seen around the shores of Hoy, and the shapes stirring within them that one fisherman took for selkies; he steered closer, only to have his boat hit a rock.

'He had to swim to safety. Spent the night clinging to the cliffs.'

The men laugh, but huddle closer to the fire.

Then Neil MacClenny looks over his shoulder and tells them he's seen something else, something that doesn't make sense, and just tonight too, when he was walking to the pub. The moonless sky was lit by the flare of the aurora – the Merrie Dancers – and Mac-Clenny saw something moving just beneath the water out in the bay.

A dark shape. Like some beast, he whispers, leaning forward.

But MacClenny, with his drinker's nose and his bloodshot eyes, is a gullible fool, even when sober, so the other men clap him on the back and buy him another whisky.

All the same, the story sobers them, quiets their chatter. There is something stirring – they can all feel it. They bid each other farewell quickly and quit the warmth of the pub soon afterwards, running past the sea, hardly daring to look at the water. They arrive home gasping, rushing upstairs to check on their children, and on their wives, who are indignant at having been woken and roll their eyes when they hear Mac-Clenny's tale. The men look at their sleeping families and laugh softly at their own foolishness. All the same, they snuff out their lights, check the bolts on their windows.

So, after midnight, the ships are silent in the bay and no one is watching when the periscope of the German U-boat snakes above the water, just long enough for Pasch's trembling crew to load four torpedoes and fire them.

Dorothy

I am nearly asleep when the world catches fire.

I had been lying awake for hours, blinking at the

grainy darkness, wishing for sleep, but every time I closed my eyes, I found myself counting: we had enough oats to last two weeks, but only enough butter for one. The meat might last ten days, if we were careful. But many of those things could only be found in Kirkwall, and returning there always sets Con to shaking, and stirs nausea in my gut.

Earlier that day, Con and I had rowed across from Selkie Holm to Kirkwall to buy supplies to repair our new home — an old shepherd's bothy. The door is coming off its hinges and we need wood to repair the broken beams. We also have to find slate for the roof — it would be bearable sleeping half under the stars in the summer, but we'll freeze this winter.

The war has made it a struggle to find anything for sale. But we had some wool and eggs to exchange, and another supply of washed and rolled bandages to be taken back to the Kirkwall hospital, so I was hopeful, as we moored in Kirkwall — or I was trying to be hopeful. Con's mouth was downturned, but she wouldn't argue with me again.

She climbed out of the boat and I squeezed her shoulder. She smiled reluctantly and I could feel her thinking, *You wee bampot!* It was something our parents used to call us. We both laughed, as if she'd said it aloud. Impossible to argue with someone when you know their every thought.

There were fewer motor-cars than there used to be,

because of the rationing of petrol, and most people walked with their heads down. It was still strange to see the streets empty of young men – they'd left gradually, at first, but then in a flood, as the war came closer and the rumours of the horrors and violence elsewhere grew. With the streets half empty, you'd expect the shouts of children to be louder, but the mothers kept them close to their sides and shushed them. It was as if everyone was waiting for the next blow to fall.

The stonemason, Andrew Fulton, was stacking slates in his warehouse. I tapped lightly on the door and he looked up. He scratched his wispy grey hair, then walked towards us, wiping his hands on a rag. 'Ah, Constance,' he said.

'It's Dorothy. Con's there.'

'Of course it is,' he said, his gaze flicking back and forth between me and Con. 'And how can I help you, Dorothy?'

'We need slate for the roof. And help laying it, I think. The bothy beams are crumbling.'

He scratched his head again. 'Aye, well, that bothy's in a poor state altogether. But I'm afraid this slate is all spoken for. It's going south, you see.'

'Along with everything else,' Con muttered darkly.

'True enough,' Andrew said. 'But we've to do our bit for the war. Even those of us too decrepit to fight.' He laughed. When we didn't join in, he let the noise trail off. 'Now look, girls –'

'We're twenty-three,' said Con.

'Of course. *Ladies*. Selkie Holm isn't the best place for you – for anyone. It's a bad-luck island. Would it not be better for you to come back across to Kirkwall to live in your old house? It's what your father would have wanted, I'm sure – two young women living alone in that place, it's not right. And it seems a shame for your old Kirkwall house to be sitting there, locked up and empty –'

'No,' we said, in unison, as if we'd planned it.

His eyes darted between us, and then he used the rag to wipe his forehead, smearing slate dust across his brow.

'I see, I see,' he said. 'Well, just you take care of yourselves, then. War isn't the time to hold grudges.'

I could see Con was about to snap something at him, so I pulled on her hand, dragging her further into town.

It was the same when we went to buy rope, and when we enquired about new wooden beams: nothing was for sale; everything was being sent south. Wouldn't we be much better off coming back to Kirkwall, rather than living alone and putting ourselves at risk? Shouldn't we let the past lie and leave that dreadful island?

Night was falling when we rowed back to Selkie Holm, in silence, Con slashing the water with her oars. She's always thrown herself into arguments – it's as if, at birth, we were given enough anger for one and

Con took all of it. At least, I used to think it was anger, or bravery. But of late I've realized that Con was never brave: she simply chose not to show her fear to others. What a gleaming thing the world seemed for her, pretending to have no fear.

Lately, she seems frightened of everything.

The temperature was dropping as we dragged the boat off the beach and turned to walk up to the broken-down bothy. We'd covered its single window with an old sail, but the wind still winnowed in through the gaps and funnelled out of the gaping hole in the roof.

Con tried to slam the door, but I caught it before it banged off the wall and loosened the hinges further.

'I'm not going back,' she said, throwing herself face down on the double bed, which we'd shoved into the corner that didn't get wet in the storms.

'All right.' I tipped water from the jug into the single pan and set it on the stove to boil. The gas wouldn't last long, with rationing pulling all our belts tighter, but I'd worry about that another day. At this moment, we both needed tea.

'I'm not.' Her voice was muffled.

'All right,' I said again.

'Don't try to placate me.'

'All right.' I grinned, then ducked as she flung the pillow at me. I threw it back and laughed when it hit her squarely on the head. Her face crumpled and her blue eyes filled with tears.

I swore and put my arms around her. Her body was stiff against mine.

'Don't make me go back,' she said, into my neck.

I reached under the bed and pulled out the bottle of brandy.

She shook her head. 'We're saving that. For when we've got something to celebrate.'

I uncorked it and took a swig. 'We're celebrating staying.'

She fell asleep quickly, her face set in a frown, and now I am awake and alone, remembering Andrew Fulton's words. The way his laughter had choked in his throat. There's a hum of fear across all the islands — especially for us here on Selkie Holm, with all the rumours of bad luck and curses. But Con won't go back. So I listen for engines; I scan the broken patch of sky through the hole in the roof, searching for the light or movement that might be a plane. I hold my breath, waiting. Nothing. Silence, except for Con's sleeping breath.

A thud and a roar, the noise like a punch. Both of us bolt upright with a gasp.

What is it? What was that? Are you hurt?

The bothy is still standing, neither of us is injured but that noise can only have been one thing.

A bomb. The Germans. We tug on sweaters and boots, and step out into the night, blinking.

A ship in the bay is on fire.

Across the bay, lights appear on the hill one by one, along with the sound of whistles and a high-pitched alarm signalling for people to find safety. In Kirkwall, there is an old air-raid shelter from the last war, but its walls are crumbling — for years it's been clambered over by children playing war games. Con turns to look back at our crumbling bothy, its broken walls, its missing roof. There is nowhere for us to hide. I scan the sky for a plane, but can see nothing, can hear no engines. Still, the desire to find shelter and curl up into a ball sets my knees shaking. My teeth chatter. A chorus of dogs howls, their voices threading into the black sky, like the rending cries of wolves.

Con grabs my shoulders. 'We need to go back inside. We can hide under the bed, barricade the door.'

I shake my head, brushing her hands away and stare at the flaming ship in the middle of the bay. Smoke plumes upwards and, in the orange glow, I can see bodies writhing. From this distance, they might be dancing.

Another blast shakes the earth beneath us. Thunderous *roar* of water being thrown skywards, then crashing back to the sea, and the shrieking echo of twisting, bending metal.

The ship lists to one side and, even at this distance, we can see the speed the water is taking it.

'Oh, Lord,' I say. 'It's going to sink.'

The vessel groans. A chorus of cries and splashes as some of the crew jump into the water. I watch as a man in flames stands on the side of the ship and flings himself off, arms flailing.

'How many men aboard?' I ask.

There are more lights on in Kirkwall and the alarm shrieks through the air, its pitch rising and falling with my breath.

'We must get inside,' Con says, her eyes wild.

'Five hundred men? A thousand?' I demand.

She looks away. Both of us are remembering our parents. We'd never found their bodies. And Con had always blamed herself.

'We can't let them drown,' I say.

'Dot, *please*.' She reaches out. 'The bombs, the Germans. And –'

And I know she is thinking about the people in Kirkwall. The ship will bring them out this way. But we can't think about that now. I grab her hand and pull her down the hill towards our rowboat, towards the water.

Towards darkness and death.

We can't think about that now.

'Dot, stop!' she calls.

But I ignore her, throwing my whole body at the little boat. It won't move. I grunt and smack the wood.

'Stop, Dot!' she says. 'We're not doing this.'

The rowboat is still stuck in the sand. The sinking ship in the bay squeals again and I scream with it: 'Come on, you bastard!'

The boat shifts forward, gaining momentum as I shove it towards the water.

'We're staying,' Con calls. She nods across to the opposite bay in Kirkwall, where the whistles are still calling and torches bob among dark shapes on the beaches. They are a mile further away from Scapa than us: we are close enough to smell the smoke from the ship, to hear the screams. Con doesn't move.

'*You* stay, then,' I snap, climbing into the boat and dipping the oars into the water. The boat pulls away.

The dogs are still howling. The alarm is still wailing.

Please, please, I think, looking at Con. And I picture her dead in the bothy when I return. And I picture myself dead in the water without her. And I don't want to leave her like this. But I can't watch those men drown.

She must be thinking the same: she covers her face with her hands.

'Stop!' she growls, and she throws herself into the water and wades out to the boat, pulling herself in. I try to help, but she slaps my hands away.

I give her an oar.

'At least if the world is caving in, we'll die together.'

She sounds, for a moment, like her old self, not the terrified creature I'd lived with over the past months.

'Don't be so bloody foolish,' I say. 'No one's drowning.'

Except those men are.

We begin to row.

She gasps as we're thrown sideways by the huge swell from the bombs. Inky blackness below us. Above, the sky yawns.

I imagine a German ship skulking somewhere in the harbour, taking aim.

Thick black smoke balloons, and the ship lists further, her guns pointing almost vertically towards the star-hammered sky.

'There!' We speak at the same time. Mirrored expressions, tight-lipped and trembling – even Con, for all her bluster when she'd joked about dying, is full of fear.

A man in the water, face down, floating. And holding onto his arm, another man, floundering and spluttering.

I lean down and start to haul the man from the sea. His skin is slippery-slick; his mouth stretches wide and noiseless.

We heave him into the boat, where he lies coughing and retching. I pat his shoulder. He blinks, shakes his head.

We row on. How can we choose which life to save?

How can we know the difference between a good man and a bad man? Rich man, poor man, beggar man, thief.

Bodies bob in the water, belly up. Their faces wear the wide-eyed blankness of sudden death. An expression that is almost acceptance.

We fish two more men from the sea, both barely alive. The boat rides low in the water and tilts sharply to one side when we pull the last man in. He huddles with the other two, grey-faced and shaking. One groans; the noise is an animal cry. Other men wave in the water, crying weakly for help.

We must leave them.

'There are other boats coming,' I call. Then I have to turn away, in case I see a man sink when I can't save him. The Kirkwall boats are closer now – close enough, I hope.

Con is shaking and rows with her head down, without looking towards the Kirkwall boats.

The men in our boat stare at us, saucer-eyed, open-mouthed. They think they are mad or dreaming, or that their vision is playing tricks.

'Are you . . . ?' one of the men says, accent unfamiliar and English: vowels flat.

'Death's boatmen,' Con says. 'Rowing you to the Land of the Dead.'

Con's always had a black humour when distressed.

'We're twins, yes,' I say. 'You're seeing straight.

We'll have you to safety soon.' Other boats from Kirkwall have finally drawn level, with the old fishermen shouting to each other, pointing out men in the water, tugging them into the boats.

Oh, God, what if the noise and the lights draw another bomb?

I glance at the sky. Starlight clear as a struck bell. No bother for a German pilot to see us and finish the job. My breath is tight in my throat again.

'It wasn't planes,' one of the men in the boat says. He speaks quietly, so that we have to lean closer, our faces millimetres from the man's wild eyes. His breath smells of metal; when he coughs, a dark ribbon creeps down his chin and drips onto his white shirt. He groans and clutches his chest.

'Not planes,' he whispers again. 'German submarine.'

We stare at each other. *Surely not.* These waters are safe – half the British fleet is moored here. The rocks around Scapa Flow make it impossible for an enemy ship to sneak through. And there is an entire barrier of sunken craft from the Great War.

'How did it get through?' Con asks.

The man shrugs and coughs again. Another plume of blood. He cries out in pain and the man next to him tries to say something, then pats him on the back. The other man's hands are badly burned, the fingers blackened. He holds them up near to his face, examining them as though they don't belong to him, as though they're objects he's found and he's wondering where they've come from.

'How . . . ?' he says. And it is difficult to give a reply because there are so many questions with no clear answers.

'What shall we do with them?' Con hisses. 'We can't take them back to the bothy – they need proper medical care.'

'Kirkwall,' I say, ignoring the way she flinches from the suggestion, ignoring the fear in her eyes.

We row towards the shore that is still busy with lights and shouting people, but then, at the last minute, Con pulls more strongly on her oar, giving three good strokes that redirect the boat to a small rocky cove.

'It's closer to the hospital,' she says, without looking at me. There are no torches here, no moving shadows, no other boats.

The man in the white shirt wheezes. Darkness mushrooms on his shirt. I take one hand from my oar and place it on his shoulder. Con does the same. He shivers convulsively, his teeth chattering.

'We're nearly there,' I murmur.

'We'll get you help,' Con adds. 'Not long now.' We pull past the rocks and the boat crunches up onto the sand.

Behind us, the ship is disappearing beneath the

waves. We turn to watch, along with the men. Then, at the last, one by one, we turn away. All except for the man with the hole in his chest, whose eyes are fixed and staring. For a moment, I think he must have gone already – must have died, right there, sitting up in our boat.

I lean in closer and can hear the rasp of his breath.

All the men are shivering now. I take off my shawl and wrap it around the two who have climbed down onto the sand. 'We'll take you to the hospital in a moment. Just . . .' I nod towards the boat, towards their comrade. Con has laid him back so that his head is in her lap.

'Not long,' I say to the men.

They flinch, then collapse onto the wet sand. The man with the burned hands is sobbing quietly, still holding them in front of his face. Out on the water, the sounds of oars and the shouts of injured men, and rescued men, and drowning men, who will not last the night.

I climb in alongside the dying man and place my hand on his chest, near the gaping hole where some shard of metal has found a home. He coughs. Blood splatters our dresses.

'Oh, God,' he gasps. 'Oh, God. Make it stop.'

I've never been religious. But, still, there is a Bible on our shelf, swollen with damp, crusted with salt, like everything on these islands. And I know the stories it contains: sacrifice, suffering, peace, eternal life. Sometimes death can be a gift that you offer to another. Sometimes death can be a thing that you take for yourself.

Con looks terrified as she leans close to the man. Is she thinking about our parents too? Is she wondering, as I am, how much they suffered? I feel sick.

'Do you have a sweetheart?' she asks.

The man draws a pained breath. 'Fiona,' he wheezes.

'I'll write to Fiona for you, and I'll tell her you fought well.'

He closes his eyes and his mouth twitches into something that might be a smile.

The sea slaps the sides of the boat.

'It hurts,' he says. 'Help me. Please help me.'

Such a flimsy door between life and death. Such a thin skin.

Con puts her mouth close to his ear.

'You want it to stop?' I hear her ask.

A pause. The man shivers, then gives the slightest of nods. 'Make it stop. Please.'

Con takes off her coat. 'Lie down.' He hesitates. 'Go on,' she says. 'It'll be quick.'

The man glances at his comrades on the beach, who are both frozen, gaping. All of us waiting.

I watch as he shifts his weight and lies down on the floor of the boat. He coughs and another streamer of blood spatters onto his shirt. I imagine the sour metal of it, like the taste of fear in my mouth. I swallow.

The man groans, then whispers, 'Please.'

Con bunches up her coat and presses it over his face, cupping her hands over his nose and mouth, closing her eyes. The man doesn't struggle at first, then he kicks his legs.

Behind us, the men yell and Con lifts the coat free of the man's face. He draws in a breath and then coughs again, catches Con's hands in his and presses the coat against his own face. Con's face is rigid as she holds the coat against his nose and mouth. Her cheeks are wet.

'Help me,' she says. And I know what she means: the thought of a slow, lonely death is monstrous. The idea of leaving this man to die alone would torture us both. I imagine the nurses in the hospital, watching him labouring for breath. And I know that, if we let him go now, he will stay like this in our thoughts: not fully alive but not quite dead. Struggling. Fading. He will haunt us, like our parents, whose bodies must be out there somewhere. Whose bones must be beneath these waters.

A heat rises in my throat – nausea or a scream. But the blood on the man's shirt gleams in the moonlight and his limbs are trembling with cold and fear and pain.

And I put my hands over hers. The wool of the

coat is rough and the man's breath is warm. Again, he kicks his legs and a tremor runs through my body and Con's, but we press down harder. The other men on the beach are silent, their heads bowed as if in prayer.

I count to thirty, to a hundred.

The man has been still for a long time when we lift the coat from his bloodied mouth. Sobbing, Con dips the wool into the sea and wipes his face clean. He could be sleeping.

At the hospital, they will wrap him in a sheet and send him home to Fiona.

Afterwards, as we row back across to our island, and tuck ourselves into our bed, I can't help feeling that something has crumbled or broken.

I can still feel the rough wool under my fingers and I know that Con can't sleep either. I can tell from the shallow, broken rhythm of her breathing that she is awake, that she is crying. My own tears are hot on my cheeks. I want to reach for Con, want to take her in my arms, but every time I do, I can see the man's face; I can hear his laboured sobs. And, as I drift in and out of sleep, his face blurs with our father's face, with our mother's. I remember the last time I saw them, when they pushed their boat out towards the darkening horizon. Mother was failing fast, and they needed medicine from a bigger hospital than Kirkwall's. But the sea was too rough by the time they left; it was too much of a risk. They should have waited.

I remember the way Con had shrieked at them to go, her whole body rigid.

I remember her silence when they didn't come back. The way she had taken herself down to the shore, day after day, watching the sea. The way she had blamed herself. The days when she had gone swimming and had held herself below the water, trying to cut off her own breath.

I'd seen the expression on her face today, as she held the coat over the soldier's face. Along with grief, and fear, I'd seen something like longing. Something like envy.

I hold my trembling hands against my face in the darkness, trying to rid myself of the damp scratch of that wool, warm from the man's breath.

The next day dawns bright, the light blinding as it reflects off the still sea.

Con is quiet as she scatters grain for the chickens, as she stirs the porridge on the stove.

'Are you all right?' I ask.

She tells me she is; she flashes a quick smile at me. But as soon as she turns away from me her smile fades. She looks grief-stricken.

I watch her from the corner of my eyes as she scrubs the man's brownish bloodstain from her shirt sleeve.

'Let me do that,' I say.

'I'm fine.' She pushes me away, her face like a waxwork.

'For Heaven's sake, Con!' I snatch the shirt from her. 'What's wrong?'

But I know what's wrong: we both do. Con had gone into the sea to rescue the sailors; instead, she'd held a man down and cut off his air to save him. I can see her thoughts in the way she looks at her hands, the way she rests her fingers on the pulse at her neck when she thinks I'm not looking. The pulse that tells her she is still alive; the hands that tell her she can end a life, if she wants to.

Early January 1942

The town hall in Kirkwall is packed with people: every seat taken and all the standing room besides. Whole families huddle at the back, with mothers anxiously rocking babies and shushing their children's questions. The windows are misted, the air hot and close. All eyes fix on the table at the front, where John O'Farrell, Kirkwall's mayor, is shuffling papers and avoiding eye contact.

He is a big man, broad across the shoulders, with a shock of red hair – greying of late. On a normal day, he wears an easy smile, although his face now is serious as he clears his throat and looks out at the murmuring crowd.

'Thank you for coming,' he says, and the chatter in the room fades. 'I know it's a cold night and there are those of you who'll want to be getting back to your beds. Myself, for a start.'

A series of polite titters, and everyone waits.

He continues: 'Now, you'll all have noticed the ships coming in and unloading materials and I know there's been some talk and speculation. But I want to tell you that the main priority is to keep these islands safe. The sinking of the *Royal Elm* has hit all of us hard. The Germans coming so close – it's a worry.'

A sob from the back of the room, quickly stifled.

O'Farrell coughs. 'Over eight hundred lives lost that night, but many men saved – hundreds of English sailors – and that's down to the heroism of the people on these islands. Still, we need to be sure that such a thing never occurs again. We're in agreement with the English about this –'

A shout from the back: 'Is it true Churchill himself came here?'

'Don't be ridiculous, Donald,' someone replies. 'You wouldn't know Churchill from your own –'

O'Farrell holds up his hands. 'Aye, it's true. He came.'

Whispers hiss around the hall.

O'Farrell waves for quiet. 'Mr Churchill has discussed the matter with myself and the Kirkwall Parish Council, and we're all in agreement that these islands need fortifying.'

Fortifying? An uneasy mutter rises. What does that mean? Does it have anything to do with the shipments of cement over the past weeks? The sheets of metal, the spools of wire?

'So,' O'Farrell holds up his hands again, 'to that end, we've decided to build barriers in the bay, between the islands. Four of them, made of rocks and cement, and strong enough to withstand the currents –'

Shouts ring out: 'Barriers?'

'Blocking off the sea?'

'You must be mad!'

'What'll it do to the tides?'

'The fishing?'

'It'll cause floods and all sorts.'

'*Enough!*' John O'Farrell bangs a fist on the table, and there is immediate quiet — he isn't known for his temper, after all.

'Enough,' he repeats, more quietly. 'The barriers must be built: it's an order from Churchill himself.'

Stephen Alexander, with the windswept hair and the red-veined cheeks steps forward. 'With due respect, it could be an order from God Almighty Himself, it still wouldn't make it right.'

There is some muttering at this blasphemy, despite the nerves.

Stephen apologizes and agrees that he needs to keep away from the bottle, these days.

John O'Farrell clears his throat. 'In order to facilitate the building of these barriers, a workforce will be needed. So I must tell you that, in two weeks' time, a large number of foreign prisoners of war will be arriving on the islands.'

A stunned silence.

'*Foreign?*' someone says.

'Aye, Italian men, currently being held in North Africa. A thousand of them.'

Uproar.

'A *thousand*?'

'You're jesting,' someone calls.

O'Farrell stands, his face impassive, but his hands brace against the desk in front of him. His fingers press down hard, whitening under the pressure.

'The men will stay,' he says, 'on Selkie Holm.'

'No!' Two voices from the back of the room, speaking together.

Every head in the room turns towards them – those Reid twins, so rarely seen in Kirkwall, these days.

'No, you can't,' one of them says. Her voice is shaking; the other girl's breathing is loud, as if she's been running.

'I'm sorry,' O'Farrell says, 'but it's already been decided.'

A collective held breath, as everyone waits for them to answer.

'Jesus Christ,' Stephen Alexander declares loudly. 'Selkie Holm. That's a bad omen.'

And in the silence that follows, no one scolds him for his blasphemy.

Everyone files out of the hall, whispering. You've heard what happens there: the disappearances, the odd lights and noises, aye. People driven mad by the sight of some creature in the waters there, as beautiful as it is repulsive.

Bad enough, people agree, that those girls are

living on the cursed island, let alone a thousand prisoners. Who knows what horrors will be dredged up?

John O'Farrell has sat down at the desk, and doesn't look up at the girls.

'You can't do this,' Dorothy says.

'I'm sorry.' He piles the papers and begins stuffing them into his briefcase. 'I argued against it.'

'But . . . it's our *home*.'

'I know. But things are changing.' He spreads his hands, gesturing to the piled papers.

'So we should just bow down and do whatever the English say? Are messages from London to be our laws now?'

He looks away, tucks the remaining papers into the briefcase, locks it and stands. 'I wish you'd come back to live in Kirkwall,' he says. 'It's not right, the two of you being out alone on that island —'

'Surrounded by a thousand men?' Dorothy says, her face rigid. 'And after everything that's happened . . .' She glances at Constance, who is holding a hand up to her neck, as if she's struggling to breathe.

Dorothy drops her voice to a whisper. 'You know she wanted to be away from men, after Angus.'

O'Farrell's expression is pained. 'I wish I could change it.'

'You know she has nightmares?'

'I'm sorry.'

'So am I,' Dorothy says.

The girls turn and walk together from the hall, out into the cold night.

There is some talk, among those who've been eavesdropping, about following them, trying to talk some sense into them. Those girls have had enough bad luck already, and being on that island can only stir up more misfortune. It's said that anyone living there will go mad. It's said that misfortune will follow them. Enough people have died or vanished there, over the years. Surely the girls should be reminded of that.

But then it is agreed that there is only so much you can do. Some people are determined to go their own way, and all you can do is watch and hope.

Mid-January 1942

Dorothy

It is raining when the Italian prisoners arrive.

Con and I had been watching for a ship all morning, peering through the net of mist and drizzle. The cold had wormed its way inside us, so that we shuddered on every breath, but still we didn't walk back into the bothy.

'There!' Con had said, but she didn't need to point it out: I'd spotted the grey shape at the same moment. There was something monstrous about the sight of that warship, so much bigger than any of the others in the bay.

On the hill, just out of sight of the bothy, was the camp that the prisoners would be living in – we'd watched it being built over the past weeks. A huge rectangle of land had been sectioned off with wire fencing, topped with toothed rolls of barbed wire. Within this yard were flimsy corrugated-iron huts that looked as though they'd be swept away in the next storm. There were bigger huts too: a large building with tables and benches for the men to eat at, and a slightly smaller structure with desks and chairs – we'd seen the English guards bringing them across. There was another hut, tiny, really, which, when the door blew open in a strong gust of wind, revealed a set of manacles chained to the wall.

Con and I had looked at each other in wonder: what sort of men were they expecting that they had prepared chains and manacles? We'd heard rumours in Kirkwall of the awful things that soldiers did elsewhere: Michael Dalton had parachuted from his burning plane over occupied France; it had taken him weeks to escape enemy territory, over the Alps and into Spain. The French women were starving, he'd said. They'd been beaten, shot at. Some of them had been forced to bear German children.

'These are *Italian* prisoners,' Con had said to Michael, 'not German soldiers.'

'They're all Fascists.' His eyes had been wild. 'Just listen to the news reports.'

We'd gone home and Con had twisted the aerial on the radio so that the news reports blurred into a static hum.

'No need to terrify ourselves,' she'd said. 'And over rumours and stories.'

I'd nodded, thinking about the older men on the island who'd fought in the trenches in France: the way Mr Mackenzie's hands trembled; the way Mr Greenwood wept if he heard a car engine backfire. He didn't seem to notice the tears, but sat staring, wet-cheeked and frozen, until his daughter took him by the hand

and led him home. I thought of our own father, who'd woken us all at night, screaming in his sleep.

We'd seen what war could do.

And now, the ship is here: huge and grey, like an approaching wall.

I stand on the clifftop and watch silently as the prisoners are led off it and up towards the huts. So many men, an army of strangers, soldiers. Unarmed, but still – do they carry violence beneath their skin? Have they killed men? Watched them die? Do they support Mussolini and Hitler?

Sometimes, when Con is sleeping, I twist the aerial until it picks up the news reports, then wish I hadn't.

Capture. Bombardment. Slaughter.

'It's not too late to go back to Kirkwall,' I murmur.

I don't need to look at Con to know she is shaking her head.

Half of Orkney has come out to see the men arrive. Some of the people are far-off specks on the hills on the mainland; others have taken to their boats and watch the huge battleship weigh anchor. They are watching us too, the Selkie Holm islanders. We see them, bobbing on the water, staring, as if waiting for a performance to begin.

Sometimes, at night, I think of the curse on this island. The talk of madness. The story about the girl who had lived here long ago and, driven to the point of insanity by the curse, and fearing that her husband meant her harm, had stabbed him in his sleep. To live here is to risk killing a lover.

But Con doesn't have a lover and neither do I. And we don't believe the old tales.

Hundreds of men begin marching down the gang-plank onto our island. Identical, at this distance.

Swarm, I think. *Shoal. Flock.*

Our father's old gun is back in the bothy. Just in case.

'They're handsome,' I say, 'and they look . . .' I nearly say *ordinary*, but it's not quite true. 'Well, they don't look frightening.'

'Best to be wary, even if they're not murderers,' Con says.

Even a dangerous man may look like an angel. Our mother had told us that long ago and, of course, she'd been right. But by the time Con discovered what Angus MacLeod was really like, our mother was gone.

A thin, pale sunlight breaks the clouds; some of the prisoners stop and gaze out at where the water is a shifting mirror. One smiles and points at a fulmar wheeling overhead. The bird swoops, dives, smashes into its watery reflection, then emerges with a fish flapping in its beak.

The two prisoners cheer, then grin at each other. They don't look like foreign soldiers, for a moment. They could be dark-haired young men from anywhere.

They're just like us. The thought is sudden and surprising.

The guards shout, stepping forward with their batons.

The men flinch, then move on, heads down. The gangplank is crowded now, the guards chivvying the men to move faster. They bump into each other and stumble.

There is a sudden cry from the ship. As I look up, I see that one of the prisoners who had cheered is teetering on the edge of the overcrowded gangplank, his arms flailing, clutching at the hands of his comrades, who reach for him.

Too late.

He plummets into the water and disappears.

There is a gasp and the Italians stop walking and stare at the spot of water where the man fell. The sea is green-grey, moodily shifting, but there is no sign of the man.

'Oh, God,' I whisper.

In their boats, some of the islanders are crossing themselves. I can imagine the stories: the prisoner who disappeared, the sacrifice taken by the sea before she would allow foreigners safe passage to the island. The superstitions about Selkie Holm will grow.

Death. Murder. Sacrifice.

On shore, the guards shout to each other and pace up and down, watching the water.

'We have to do something.' The words emerge before I'm aware of thinking them. How can I let the man drown? I remember the men from the ship sinking, their fading cries. I remember the stillness of the man's body as we lifted Con's coat from his bloodied face.

'We have to do *something*,' I say again.

'Don't even think of it,' Con replies. 'It's not like before. The water's rough. You'd never find him.' Her face is tense, her jaw clenched. Con has barely slept since the sinking of the boat and the death of the poor sailor. She refuses to wear her coat – I found it stuffed under the bed, a black bloodstain on the blue wool.

She shivers.

I remember the feeling of the man's face under my fingers. The way his body had fought for air, even when he'd decided he wanted to die.

We wait. Nothing. A body can survive for three minutes without air.

The guards pace, watching, waiting. Not one will jump in to save him. Again, that heat rises in me – the nauseating panic and dread.

He is gone.

He is drowning.

He is under those waters, fighting for breath, his lungs burning.

'*Lay salt upon his chest.*' Con murmurs the beginnings of the old funeral rite.

'He's not dead yet,' I snap.

Ten paces in front of me is the cliff face.

I let go of Con's hand and run.

Whistling wind, then the smack and cold shock of the water.

Stupid to do this in January. Brainless. Foolhardy.

I hear a cry above me. Con's pale face, like a coin. I can see her running down towards the harbour, the gangplank, where she might try to reach me. But by that time, it will be too late for the man.

I dive down, kicking out. Under the surface, a vice of icy water clamps around my skull. I surface, gasping, then plunge down again, reaching out. Nothing.

I come up for another lungful, then flip and dive steeply, deeper than I feel I should, until my own chest is alight, the air bubbling from my lips. My thoughts are screaming.

Three minutes. Three minutes.

And still nothing until – something soft. A hand? Clothes? I grasp the fabric, yank and pull, flicking my body upwards, tugging something to the surface – heavy, like some sea creature dragged up from the deep.

God, oh, God. He's dead and I'm too late.

The bone-breaking cold of the water squeezes me as I slap him across the face. Again and again I shout at him, some wordless cry. This will be what the islanders talk of later – this moment when I pulled a drowned foreigner from the water and screamed life back into him.

They will agree that it was unnatural I'd dived for him, uncanny that I'd saved him. And that shriek I'd given — *Good Lord, but did you hear it? Echoed off the cliffs, it did, as if it was some beast screaming, not a woman.*

But that is all later.

Now, the man in my arms coughs and heaves and splutters. I turn him in the water and strike his back, keeping his head out of the sea with my other hand.

When he has stopped choking, I pull his face close to mine and put my hand under his chin. His skin is chill, but I can feel the rasp of his stubble, can feel the heave of air in his throat and down into his chest. His hair brushes my cheek. I rest for a moment, panting, counting the hammering beat of blood under his skin.

I swim slowly, turning my face from the waves that keep filling my nose and mouth. A heaviness creeps into my limbs and I am suddenly aware of the yawn of water beneath me, the way my body is slowing, pulling me downward, as if towards some invisible rope attached to the sea bed.

I am so tired. Saltwater fills my mouth.

I could let him go, this man, this foreigner. I could let him sink and I could swim to the ledge. I could rest.

No! I keep my eyes fixed on Con's face; she is waiting for me near the gangplank, her hands outstretched. I kick my legs, my muscles screaming as I reach out and clutch the ledge. The guards shout. Hands reach down and grab the man around the arms, lifting him from the water and dumping him on the ground.

A wave buffets me, water filling my nose and mouth. Everything is dark and indistinct. I flail, trying to swim, to surface – but which way is up? Again, that heaviness in my limbs, that downward tug towards the sea floor.

Suddenly, hands are on mine in the water, and then I'm dragged upwards towards light and air. I splutter as Con, in the water next to me, heaves me out of the sea.

We both lie panting on the ledge, then Con puts her arm across my chest.

I grip it.

Heat. Life. Home.

Dimly, I am aware of the guards calling to us, and the Italians muttering, but all of it is a blur of sound.

'You stupid fool! You could have died,' she gasps.

'But I didn't.' I smile shakily. 'You saved me.'

'I could have died too.' She pulls away. A finger width of chill between us.

The prisoner is being half lifted, half carried by the guards as they walk up the hill towards the camp. He is still coughing and unsteady on his feet.

As he approaches the barbed-wire fence of the camp, the wind yanks a damp piece of card from his hand. It flutters through the air.

I run forward to pick it up. It is a tiny picture of

Mary and Jesus and a blood-red heart. Crumpled and grubby, and now sea-soaked, but clearly much-loved.

I can feel eyes upon me, can feel warmth travelling through my chest, into my cheeks. He is staring at me, the prisoner. His hair is wet and his eyes wide.

You'd be dead, I think, *if it wasn't for me.* It is a strange thought – it makes him seem more present and more real than any other person there. More, even, than Con.

The prisoner nods at the card. 'For luck,' he says.

I hadn't expected any of the prisoners to speak English. His voice is lilting – there is music in the words and I'm suddenly dry-mouthed, wanting him to speak again.

And he does. 'For luck,' he repeats. And then his face breaks into a smile, and he inclines his head towards the sea and shivers; his dark hair falls over his eyes and he pushes it back. I think of how close we had both come to drowning and I grin too, heat travelling through my limbs, a pulse beating in my chest, in my stomach, on the surface of my skin.

The sensation is almost as though I know him already, this man – as if something in my body recognizes him. It is something in the span of his shoulders, but it is mostly in his eyes, in his smile.

He watches me, with the card in my hand, and his head tilted slightly to one side. His shoulders are broad, although he is thin; his stance is upright and proud, even though he is shivering. I am used to people looking at me and Con together, as one, their gaze shifting between us, but this man looks only at me. And, as I gaze back at him, I feel again there is something in this stranger that I understand, or that he understands or knows something of me – impossible as that is, ridiculous as it is. Foolish.

I hold out the card – my hand is steady, even as I feel I should be trembling. Without looking away from my face, he takes the card and puts it back into his pocket.

'Thank you,' he says.

My pulse skips and the heat spreads even further, a steady pulsing flame licking over my skin, down to my fingertips. I want to say something to him, but I can't think of a single word, so I watch him walk away, until he disappears behind the gates of the camp, until his brown uniform blends with all the other men's.

Con's eyes are on me. There is stillness between us. A gull caws.

'Thank you for diving in for me,' I say.

'Let's go back to the bothy,' she says, and turns her back. My skirts slap against my legs and each step feels colder than the last.

That night, the air is raw and the wind whips through the hole in the bothy roof. Next to me, Con's breathing is steady, regular, peaceful. I ease myself from the bed and slip out of the door, like a ghost. The grass crisps beneath my bare feet and the chill is instant, numbing: I won't be able to stand here for long.

On the breast of the opposite hill, the huts cast cut-out shadows against the night sky. Dimly, I can make out a faint orange glow from the fires inside. It looks almost cosy from here, like something in a fairytale. All such folktales end in death, but I can't imagine how this particular story might finish. It feels new, something that has never been told so far north: the hundreds of men brought as prisoners to an ill-fated island during wartime. And somewhere, in one of those huts, the broad-shouldered man with the card.

I remember the weight of his body in the water. I remember the heat of his cheek against mine as I swam.

The next morning, Con and I take the rods down to catch mackerel.

Our feet lead us in the direction of the camp, even though we haven't discussed it. What will the men be doing today? When will they start work on the barriers – and how? We know ships will be bringing in some of the supplies, but the men will need to dig the rock from the islands, somehow.

At the town-hall meeting, someone had mentioned explosives. A quarry.

The barbed wire around the camp glitters in the early-morning sun. A whistle rings out, then the sound of boots thudding. A shout, quickly smothered. My heart hammers in my chest. So close to the camp, the sounds seem spiked with violence.

I stop, unable to make myself go any closer to the wire.

Con stops, too, and we sit in the long grasses near the huts. It's possible to remain unseen, if you're still enough. Some of the prisoners walk to the square of dirt in the centre of the yard, where one of the guards shouts orders at them – the wind whips away his words, but the anger of his tone carries, and the Italian men stare down at their boots, their shoulders hunched.

'They must feel so far from home,' I say.

Con nods.

Another whistle sounds and the men flinch to attention, then turn to go into the large central hut. For food, I suppose.

What would have to happen to men so that they react to a whistle like that? Like weary dogs, wary of the constant threats of fist and boot.

There is another shout from further down the hill, on the shore. A dozen people, most of them dressed in civilian clothes, are pulling a boat up onto the beach.

'They must be from Kirkwall,' I say, waiting for

Con to protest against yet more men arriving on our island, but she says nothing and we watch the group walking up the hill – men and women both, I see now. Some are carrying baskets and boxes, and some of the men are dressed in the dark uniform of the guards. They are too far away for us to make out their faces or hear their conversation but, still, there is something fascinating and horrifying about seeing them moving towards the camp. It is like watching a show – the sort of performance that used to be played by travelling companies on the Kirkwall streets in the summer, where the actors put on plays by Shakespeare. We'd liked *The Tempest* best. Magic and secrets and the sea. The actors had their entrances and exits and some held weapons, and you knew that, at any moment, everything might change. As children, we'd cheered at love and death alike.

Over the coming days, we go back to the camp again and again to watch the men: their daily routine of walking down to dig gravel or rocks out of the new quarry on the shore. I search for his face among them. His eyes had been serious, but warm. He had smiled at me – or perhaps I had imagined that. Each time I try to picture him, his face blurs in my mind until I can't remember exactly how he'd looked. If I close my eyes, I can still feel the scratch of his stubble against my hand as I'd held him in the water.

The Italians unload equipment from the ship: a lorry, a digger, a drum for cement. Each noisy machine that rolls off the boat brings new sound and activity to the island. And even during the night, our peace is shattered. The light from the camp obliterates the stars, and the shouts of men – in pain, despair or joy, we never know – pull us awake.

And at night, while Con sleeps, I fiddle with the twisted radio aerial until I pick up stray words, fizzing through the darkness: *invasion . . . utmost violence . . . death toll.*

One morning, about a week after the Italians arrived, Con and I are sitting near a patch of gorse, close to the camp.

We are absolutely still when I see a flash of movement from the corner of my eye. A man is walking alongside the barbed wire, dressed in the dark green uniform of the prison guards. Too far away to see the face, but I can make out the blond hair and wide shoulders of Angus MacLeod. And he is staring at us.

I feel a wash of ice water running through me.

'Bastard,' I mutter, all thoughts of the Italians driven from my mind. 'Come on, Con. Back to the bothy.' There is still time: she hasn't seen him.

Con makes to protest.

'Come *on*,' I say, my chest tight, my mouth dry. *Please don't see him, please don't see him.*

It is too late: Angus is walking towards us. Grinning.

My heart drumming, I stand and try to keep my voice steady. 'What're you doing here?'

'What sort of a greeting is that now, Dot? I thought you'd be pleased to see me. *Con* is. Aren't you, Con?' Angus had usually been able to tell us apart, somehow, ever since we had been children together at school.

'You're a *guard* here?' Con's voice is tight. 'Who made you a guard?'

Angus turns around, spreading his arms wide, as if showing off his uniform. 'I hear you went for a swim in the sea last week, Dot.'

'Never you mind.'

'There's talk of it. Jumped off a cliff. Half drowned yourself. Much suspicion as to why you're so intent on rescuing foreign men from the sea. Some have said that you're feeling the lack of a man here.' He gives a lewd grin.

'You're best to stay away from this island, Angus.'

'Oh, I don't believe any of the rumours about this place. The pair of you seem safe enough here. And there's such a beautiful view.' MacLeod gestures towards us.

'Go back to Kirkwall,' I say, my jaw clenched.

'Now, Dot, you be careful, or you'll get the same vicious reputation as your sister. I'm just looking. No harm in admiring beauty, is there?'

Next to me, Con's breathing is loud, laboured. I put my arm across her shoulders and pull her towards me.

'Come on. Let's go home.'

We turn away from him.

'Oh, now, that's a shame,' Angus calls. 'Aren't you going to invite me for a bannock?'

I can feel his gaze following us, all the way to the bothy.

And even after I have shut the door, I still sense his eyes on us. I can't escape the feeling that, no matter how hard we try, we will never escape him.

We can never keep him out. The realization is a cold fist twisting inside my chest. Suddenly, it is hard to breathe.

I press the old piece of sailcloth more closely around the window, then wedge half an old plank across the window frame, piling stones around the base to secure it. Con uses a nail to tighten the screws in the door's hinges, and then we stand on the bed together, steadying each other as we rearrange the wood, plastic sheeting and sailcloth that covers the hole in the roof. There is still a small gap, revealing the darkening sky, but it will have to do.

Then, without a word, we get our father's gun from

the kitchen cabinet. I pass the bullets to Con, and she loads them into the barrel, one by one.

We keep the gun between us on the bed.

That night, there is a rattling at our door. A scrabbling noise, as if something is clawing at the wood, then at the metal handle. Silver moonlight splashes through the hole in the roof, shifting as the wind lifts the tattered piece of sailcloth.

There's a *scratch, scratch* of something at the door. A rat? A fox? But, no, there are no foxes here. My hands are clammy, my heart knocking against my ribs.

The bothy wall is hard against my back, and Con's breathing is loud. 'What is it?' she gasps.

I shake my head.

The lock on the door holds fast, and the board in the window doesn't move but, still, we sit with our backs hard against the wall, watching the door, waiting. The metal of the gun is cold; I clutch it so hard that my knuckles ache.

The scratching continues, then turns to a series of rattling thuds. And with every thud comes a cold, creeping terror and, a dank smell, like old soil.

In Kirkwall, they tell so many tales about lost lovers: drowned men and women – stories of adoration, stories of despair. For years, they've kept people away from this island, this *damned place*.

There is another tale told about a girl – a shepherd's daughter – who grew up poor on Selkie Holm and lived in this bothy. She fell in love with a rich Scottish man, though she had a lover already, to whom she was betrothed. But he was poor and she was tired of being cold, sick of Selkie Holm, sick of the taste of potatoes and the texture of dry bread. The rich man would never look twice at her, she knew, while she was engaged to this poor man. Quietly and without fuss, she cooked a stew of potatoes and hemlock for her lover. When he complained at the bitter taste, she wept, so that he ate every last drop, just to dry her tears. Then she rowed his body out to sea and married the rich man. But she was driven mad by guilt and couldn't rest, even in death. On some nights, the people in Kirkwall believe that her cold ghost and the ghost of her murdered beloved both walk the island on Selkie Holm, tormenting those who feel guilty. They are trying to return to the bothy, shivering. Searching for a body, hot with shame that might lend them warmth.

When Con first heard the story, she said that the girl should have buried the man, because you can never trust that the sea won't wash things up.

People only feel guilty if they're worried about being caught.

It's easy to believe the old tales in the middle of the night, as the wind buffets the door and the moonlight slews across the walls and the scratching, rattling thuds continue.

I imagine the door swinging open. I will raise the gun and steady it. I will aim for the heart or the head. My muscles ache. I count to one hundred, one thousand, ten thousand. I eye the hole in the roof, waiting for someone to climb through it. I watch the door, waiting for it to open. But the lock holds and the ragged rent of sky above remains a dark blank.

The wind drops, the scratching stops and, eventually, Con rests her head against my shoulder and I feel her body slump into sleep. Her breath whispers against my neck. I think of all I would do to protect her, everything I would sacrifice.

I try to imagine tomorrow and the days after with Angus MacLeod here and with the souls of a thousand men on the island. I imagine them all breathing into the darkness: the prisoners, the guards and the cooks and the people who will deliver letters and food. It is as if our lives have become a map, which is being folded ever smaller, as the world outside crushes everything together.

'We're not alone any more,' I whisper, to Con, to myself, to the noises in the darkness, to the buzzing of the words circling in my thoughts. 'We won't ever be alone again.'

PART TWO

It is the way you lean into me
and the way I lean into you, as if
we are each other's prevailing.

From 'Orkney / This Life', Andrew Greig

Mid-January 1942

Cesare

These are the things he finds hard in Orkney: the sky, the open space, the weather. The sea, a yawn of water that roars and growls and threatens a cold grave. The ice that gnaws at his bones, day and night. The eyes watching him – the guards watching him dig, or his fellow prisoners watching him sleep in the hut at night. Never alone but always lonely. The anger. He finds the anger hard because there is nothing to do with it, except clench it inside.

Home for Cesare was Moena, in northern Italy. Border country, surrounded by mountains, bursting with green life. It had been invaded time and time again over the years, and had a language unique to the area – Ladin – and flew a Turkish flag. They were outsiders, the people of Moena, but, like the people of Orkney, they were also insiders: they belonged wholly to each other, to themselves. None of this mattered to the small boy that Cesare had been – dark-haired, broad and muddy-cheeked from pressing his face against the ground to watch a procession of ants, or grubby-kneed from crouching to study a spider's web.

He went to the local school and was a sharp

student, but always wanted to be outside. Wild-haired and full of daydreams – his teachers despaired.

My God, Cesare, you must sit still! Late again, Cesare, and will you look at the state of your knees?

But they smiled fondly as they said it for, late as he always was, he often brought them gifts: a picture of a kingfisher's head, sketched in exquisite detail; a carving of a field mouse, with bright wooden eyes polished to a shine. They ruffled his hair, pinched his cheek. *You will be on time tomorrow, Cesare.*

He smiled and nodded. And the next day he was late.

At eighteen, much to the disappointment of his parents, who wanted him to work on the family farm, Cesare gained an apprenticeship in the local church, where he would perfect his skill in carving stone and wood, and shaping metal.

His master was severe, used to apprentices who cut corners in order to leave early and chase after women or wine. But Cesare worked hard, and although he was often late and arrived with eyes heavy from lack of sleep, he came clutching sketches, which he then painstakingly copied onto the church walls and ceiling: doves soared in flight; olive branches twisted behind the heavy stone columns. People began to visit the tiny church to marvel at the way the paintings made it hum with life.

Within four years, the master had retired, leaving

the maintenance of the church in Cesare's hands. He carved leaves into the altar legs, engraved little birds along the lectern. Under the pews, he shaped tiny creatures, so that a bored child, half asleep during a sermon, might find a frog or a mole under his wandering fingers and, for the rest of the service, would sit transfixed.

By 1937, Cesare was well-known and well-liked. At least four different women had decided they wanted to marry him and took it in turns to wait for him outside the church, then take him to their parents' houses for dinner, brushing the wood-shavings from his hair, reminding him of their father's job and what day of the week it was.

The parents eyed him with a mixture of admiration and suspicion. He had a fine set of shoulders, to be sure, and a strong jaw, and of course his paintings were beautiful. But, my God, what would he be like as a husband? As a father? No child was ever raised on a diet of paint. Besides, the man was far too skinny and, really, was that *sawdust* in his hair?

War crept in from the north and south. Men in uniform marching the streets, shouting, *Il Duce!* Some winds carry such a relentless momentum that they sweep everything along with them. Cesare didn't hold strong political beliefs, but he also didn't hold with the idea of being called a coward, so he was sent along to North Africa with the other men from his village.

Desert heat. Salt sting of sweat in his eyes. Hot gun in his damp hands as he inched forwards on his stomach, firing into sandstorms and hoping he wouldn't kill anyone, hoping that none of the returning bullets hit him. It helped if he pretended the sand itself was some sort of beast he was firing at – a desert jinn he had to defeat. If he imagined other men firing back at him, his finger froze on his trigger. At night, he traced pictures on the cold sand: mountains; the curve of a woman's hip; the church in Moena. Then he watched the wind scrub them out.

After two months, surrender; the nightmare heat behind the barbed wire of a desert camp. Then onto a boat and north. Into the wind, into the cold.

Onto an island where the sky arches above, like an open mouth, and guards yell and hit him.

It is best, Cesare decides, to keep his mouth shut and his head down.

He and the other men are herded past steel gates and into a square of bare earth, surrounded by metal huts, which are surrounded in turn by a barbed-wire fence. Everything is sharp and cold and grey; the men shiver as the uniformed guards line them up and count them. Each guard carries a long wooden baton and a gun. As a guard counts each Italian man, he taps him on the head with the baton – not hard enough to hurt, but hard enough to convey a message: *Your body belongs to us.*

Each prisoner is then given a plain brown uniform — trousers and a shirt, which are dumped into the dirt.

'Get changed, quickly,' the guard in front of Cesare snaps. He has a thin moustache and a nose red from the cold.

'What're you staring at?' he demands, then jabs at the uniform with his baton. 'Move!' Then he continues down the line.

Cesare glances left and right, where all the men are unbuttoning their old grey shirts and shivering. Next to him, he can hear Gino's teeth chattering, and, further down the line, there is a cry from Antonio as a guard prods him for hesitating.

'*Basta!*' Cesare calls to the guard. 'He speaks no English.'

The guard strides back, stops in front of Cesare, holding up the wooden baton. 'And you do?' the guard says.

'Some.' Cesare avoids the guard's gaze.

'So you'll understand when I say that if you question me again you'll regret it?'

Cesare eyes the baton, nods quickly, once.

'Then shut your mouth and get into that uniform. Now.'

The guard watches as Cesare fumbles with his buttons, shivering at the cold cut of wind on his skin, pulling on the brown uniform as quickly as his numb hands will allow. The material is rough and thin and offers little protection from the biting chill in the air.

He watches the guard's black boots move on. He exhales.

A whistle blows and Cesare stands straighter, craning his neck to see the figure of a tall, uniformed man climbing onto a platform in front of the lines of prisoners. Like the guards, this man has a gun and a baton. His moustache is grey, his face weathered. His coat glitters with medals, bristles with ribbons.

'Attention, men!' he calls. 'I am Major Bates, your commanding officer. I expect to run an orderly camp. I expect you to do as you are instructed, without fuss or protest. Never forget that you are here as prisoners. Your lives are in our hands.' He looks down at the men and Cesare sees something hard in his eyes. This man, he knows, would not hesitate to punish them.

Major Bates continues: 'Your task, while you are here, is to build barriers in the sea between these islands. You will work in groups in the quarry, mining rocks to build these barriers.'

There are murmurs from around him, from the Italians who can speak some English, and Cesare shifts uncomfortably: if they are to build barriers, they will be helping the enemy, the people who are killing their friends and bombing their families.

Major Bates blows the whistle again and the Italians fall silent.

'If you follow orders and work hard, there will be no problems while you are here.' He pauses, shifts the baton from one hand to the other. 'You will see, however, that on your uniforms, you have two red circles. One on the shoulder and one on the leg.'

Cesare glances down, touches the red patches of fabric. Around him, the other men are doing the same.

'These are targets,' the major says, his voice level. 'If you try to escape, the guards will aim for your arm. If you do not stop, they will aim for your thigh. If you continue to run, they will aim for a larger target.' He raises his hand to his head, briefly touches his grey hair.

The prisoners – even those who don't understand English – stand very still, as if the guards are, at this moment, pointing guns at their legs and their arms. As if they are aiming at their skulls.

Major Bates's smile holds no warmth. 'You will take your meals in the mess hut behind me. You will rise with the first whistle in the morning, be out for reveille and to be counted in the yard by the second whistle. You will obey orders, and by obeying, you will be safe. If you do not obey orders, you will be put in the Punishment Hut, and given only bread and water. If you do not work hard enough, you will be taken to the Punishment Hut. If you are late to be counted, you will be taken to the Punishment Hut.'

All the Italians, no matter how little English they

speak, are able to discern the threat in the repetition of these words: *orders, obey, punishment.*

Cesare's mouth is dry as he is led towards his hut, with fifty other men. They file into the dark building, which has wooden bunks around the edges, and a small stove in the centre.

Gino and Antonio are in the same hut, and take bunks near to Cesare's. The guard in charge – short, cheeks flaming with acne, barely more than a boy – gives them each a piece of soap, tells them they will be able to shower later, but that now they are to walk down to the quarry and begin.

No one moves, and the guard flushes brighter red. Before he can shout, before he can brandish his baton, before anyone can be taken to the Punishment Hut and whatever that might involve, Cesare calls to the other men, in Italian: 'Come on, we're going to the quarry. We need to line up now!'

The prisoners stand in line – slowly and reluctantly, with some of them shooting dirty looks at Cesare. Their expressions darken further when the guard nods gratefully at him.

'What's your name?'

'Cesare.'

'Well, Cesare lad, you'll be getting extra bread at dinner tonight.'

The other prisoners jostle past him, some of them still glaring.

'You are a dog for the English, then?' one man mutters.

But before Cesare can explain anything – before he can say that he was trying to help, that he wants to keep them safe, that these guards are dangerous, that the commander is willing to shoot them in the skull – the man has shoved Cesare so that he falls backwards and bangs his head on the hard wooden bunk.

'*Traditore!*' the man snarls. *Traitor!*

Gino and Antonio help him up. Cesare's hands are balled into fists, but the man who pushed him has already gone.

Gino's face is stern. 'It is best to stay quiet, Cesare. You know this.'

Cesare nods, remembering the months in the North African camp. The fat black flies that rose in clouds from the bodies of the men who'd protested, or drawn too much attention. The best way to survive is to be invisible – to imagine your body as part of a machine that does whatever is expected, without protest or hesitation.

'We must line up now.' Antonio claps him on the arm – his hand, for a moment, on the scrap of red fabric that would tell the guards where best to put a bullet – and then they follow the rest of the men out into the grinding cold and line up, ready to walk down to the quarry.

*

That first night in his hut, Cesare shuts his eyes and listens to the exhalations of fifty frightened men around him. It is dark, but there are no snores yet – impossible to sleep when your whole body is coiled like a spring, when your breath is tight in your chest and you're waiting for the sound of a baton on flesh.

He hears again the sound of the guard's shouts in the quarry, feels again the sensation of his shovel striking rock, the echo reverberating through his shuddering arms. The explosions that had rocked his bones and made his teeth ache. He'd lost count of how many wheelbarrows of rocks they'd filled. His hands had blistered and the blisters had burst, and still he hadn't stopped digging.

He moves his lips in prayer, closing his eyes, trying to remember the arched roof of the church in Moena. The painted branches, the illuminated birds, their wingtips touching as they soar upwards.

Just before he falls asleep, he traces the outline of the card, which has dried out and is tucked into his pocket still. He tries to see again the face of the girl who'd dragged him from the sea. He tries to picture her eyes and what he'd seen there: that warmth, that kindness, that sadness. The expression that had quickened his breath and set a repeated thrumming detonation in his chest.

Late January 1942

Orcadians

Frost has hardened the paths up to Kirkwall Town Hall as people gather for another meeting. There is a white rime on the leaves of the bushes, which glitter as bodies brush past, breath steaming from open mouths. It is past blackout, so they shuffle and huddle close together to avoid stumbling.

In the dim light of the hall, John O'Farrell is waiting, his jaw tense, his hands in fists on the table in front of him. There is a serrated, raw feeling in the air, like the metallic tang of a gathering storm, and no one has ever known John O'Farrell to flinch from a fight.

When this meeting about the newly arrived prisoners was called, there had been plans to stage a protest – as if a meeting would do any good! As if talking would make a difference! Some had even said that they should boycott the meeting, should deal with the problem themselves, quickly and finally. Someone else had pointed out that there could be nothing quick or final about getting rid of a thousand foreign men.

Now the people mutter to each other, waiting for

John O'Farrell to speak. The women rustle their skirts and the men clutch their caps. They know what they will do, if the meeting doesn't go their way.

O'Farrell gives a sigh, a tight smile. 'I'll get directly to the point,' he says. 'It's not escaped my attention that there's been some distress around the idea of our Italian guests.'

'It's not the *idea* of them,' a man calls. 'Ideas don't eat all our food and leave our children hungry.'

'Aye,' agrees O'Farrell. 'And *ideas* don't paint threats on the side of buildings, either, Robert MacRae. But I don't suppose you'd know anything about that, would you?'

Earlier that day, someone had noted the black letters on the town-hall door, reading, 'Fuck the Italians!' The words were three feet high and had taken hours of scrubbing to remove. A faint scent of turpentine still hangs in the air.

MacRae colours and shifts in his seat, and the men surrounding him, who had been grinning at his smart response, look down at the floor. The mood of the crowd warms towards O'Farrell – MacRae and his cronies are a bunch of thugs and have been the cause of various troubles over the years.

O'Farrell continues: 'While I'm not in approval of some of the protests and grumblings that have reached my ears, neither am I ignorant of the problem we have. I'll not stand and watch your children going hungry any more than you will. But the barriers must be built and the Italians are here to stay. We must play our part in the war, like everyone else –'

There are grumbles at that. Some telegrams and letters from the brothers and sons who are fighting have found their way home, but some have not.

We're shedding blood in this war. Orcadians are laying down their lives. Isn't that enough?

As if he can hear their thoughts, O'Farrell raises his hands. 'You'll all have got wind of the rumours about the horrors happening in France and Belgium, of Russia being invaded, of England being bombed.'

Nods and grumbling from around the room.

'Folk say there's nothing left of some parts of London,' someone mutters.

'Exactly,' O'Farrell says. 'And there's no purpose in panicking, but what we must remember is that we've a chance to do our bit here –'

'By feeding Fascist soldiers?' one of MacRae's cronies calls.

'By fortifying these islands. Stopping ships and submarines striking us from the north and going down through Scapa Flow to the rest of Britain. Or have you forgotten the submarine attack? Eh? That sinking ship slipped your memory already, has it? Or maybe it's your geography that's off, Matthew MacIntyre? Perhaps you should have stayed longer in school, rather than running about on the streets and giving yourself flat feet so you can't go off and fight.'

Laughter then, and MacIntyre hunches lower in his seat.

'As I was saying,' O'Farrell goes on, 'we've all to do our bit. But there's the problem of feeding these men, while making sure there's enough to go around for the rest of us. So, to that end, I've spoken to Major Bates, and he's willing to let some of the men come across to Kirkwall and help with the farm work and so on –'

'Are you mad?' a voice calls. 'I'll not have foreign men working my land –'

'And no one will force you to, George,' O'Farrell cuts in. 'But you've a fence that needs mending and a field that'll go unplanted this year without your lads here.'

George scowls but has no reply.

And by the time the meeting ends, half an hour later, John O'Farrell has a list of tasks for the Italian men, which he will take across to Major Bates the next morning. The feeling of unease in the room has shifted: no one will reject the offers of help – they're not fools, after all. But, still, it's important that people prepare themselves. It's crucial that no one falls into the trap of trusting these soldiers, these foreigners who will be working their land.

Back in their homes that night, the women will

press kisses into the cheeks of their sleeping children and promise to protect them. The men – old, thin, weak-chested – will fetch out the knives they use to gut fish and trim hoofs. The darkness will be full of the scrape of metal being sharpened on stone.

Late January 1942

Cesare

The quarry has been hollowed out from the rock face using explosives. Time and again, the guards shout at the men to stand clear, to run, to get *down*, for Christ's sake, you fucking Eyeties.

It's not a word Cesare has heard before, *Eyetie*, but he has come to realize that it is the word the guards use for *italiano*, only it means more than that. It means foreigner. It means idiot. It means animal.

Cesare crouches alongside Gino, hands over his ears, and counts. He has grown used to the tremble of the ground, the blast of the air, the sound that moves through his body, shaking everything inside him for ages afterwards, so that, even hours later, as he digs, as he eats, as he sleeps, he feels as though his heart and lungs have been thrown out of rhythm.

Everything has fallen out of time: each morning is grey and cold when they jump out of their bunks to be counted. Dark. It is always dark, it seems. As they line up in the yard, in what feels like the middle of the night, swaying with sleep and waiting for the guards to tap their heads with the baton, Cesare is gripped by a fear that this darkness will last for ever. The sun will never rise again and all of them will be trapped in this cold place until they die, or the world forgets them.

Marooned as they are on the island, he worries that they might simply drop off the end of the earth.

When the sun finally casts pale fingers of light over the horizon, the prisoners cheer sometimes, or they hum the threshing songs that the girls used to sing back home. They pause in their digging, and turn their faces to the light, until a guard shouts at them to *Dig, damn it!*

At night, they kneel together in their huts and they pray. Cesare moves his lips along with the others. He has never doubted before, but it is hard, in this place, to know where God might be found.

In the day, he digs stones and heaves them into a wheelbarrow, which Gino then loads into a lorry. When Cesare grows tired, they swap roles. The guards shout orders and the men slowly obey – those who speak no English copy the others. If they move too slowly, the guards brandish their batons.

One morning in late January, when they have been on the island two weeks, Cesare is trying to dig out a stubborn piece of rock. It is too heavy for him, really, and sharp besides – it teeters on his shovel. As his arms shake, it occurs to him that if he lets it fall on his foot he won't have to dig any more. In the mornings, at reveille, he's caught a glimpse of the rows of beds in the camp infirmary, felt the warmth from the two stoves as he walked past.

He looks at the rock, watches it wobble, imagines it falling, imagines the thud and crush of it on his foot. The pain. The warmth. The rest.

As he tips the shovel to one side and the rock slides off, there is a shout and Gino is suddenly there, grabbing his hand. The stone falls, glances off Cesare's toes and rolls onto Gino's foot.

A beat, half a breath. The pain is exquisite. Cesare can hear howling – his own, and Gino's, then the shout of the guard and hands pulling him upright, though he hadn't been aware of falling to the ground. And the guard's face is close to his, shouting words that Cesare cannot, for a moment, understand.

'Let go! Let me see.' The guard is pulling Cesare's hands away from his foot and Cesare doesn't want to let go, wants to hold onto the pain somehow, keep it trapped beneath his fingers. Someone yanks his hand away and the guard looks at his battered boot, curses, then turns to Gino, who is still doubled up on the ground.

'Shit!' the guard says, after seeing Gino's foot, which, from the state of his boot, looks crushed. 'Take them up to the infirmary.'

And then there are arms supporting him: Antonio is on one side and on his other is Marco, the man from Cesare's hut who had called him a traitor when he'd translated the guard's orders. In the weeks since, Marco has occasionally glared at Cesare, but hasn't pushed or threatened him – they have dug together, shivered together, torn through dry bread and thin soup together. On occasions, when Marco has wheeled the barrow towards Cesare, they have locked eyes and there has been a moment of understanding.

Now his arm is slung across Marco's shoulder and he can smell the other man's sweat.

Cesare's foot throbs. Next to him, Gino moans. His boot is misshapen and blackening with blood. Cesare looks away. '*Mi dispiace*,' he says to Gino. '*Scusi.*'

But Gino waves away his apologies.

When they reach the infirmary, warmth and light enclose them. Most of the twenty bunks are free. Antonio and Marco sit them down on beds near the door, then collapse onto beds themselves, panting.

The nurse taps rapidly towards them, her footsteps sounding irritated. She introduces herself as Nurse Croy: young, neat and blonde-haired, with the strong accent of these parts. They try to explain what happened. She waves Antonio and Marco away, tight-lipped, pointing them towards the door, her eyes never leaving the bright red targets on their uniforms.

After they have left – not without protest – she turns back to the two injured men. Gino has gone very pale and is lying on the bed.

She claps her hands at him. 'No, you don't! No lying down in that dirty uniform.'

She waits, hands on her hips. Then, when Gino doesn't move, she leans forward and pokes him.

'He is hurt,' says Cesare, through gritted teeth, his own foot throbbing. 'A rock falls onto his foot. My foot also.'

'You speak English.' Nurse Croy frowns at Cesare. Her eyes flick again towards those red targets, then away.

He attempts to smile. 'Some. A little.' When her expression doesn't soften, he says, 'I learn in church.'

'Well, you must tell your friend that he can't lie down. The doctor will be across from Kirkwall later today, but your friend must put these pyjamas on if he wants to lie down. Otherwise, he needs to get off my clean sheets.'

She throws a pair of pyjamas at each of them. The material is soft and slightly warm; Cesare has to stop himself pressing them to his face, stroking the fabric across his cheek and inhaling.

His foot throbs. He heaves himself upright, then rouses Gino enough for him to stand and for them to hobble together behind the curtain where the nurse had indicated they should get changed. They nearly fall on two occasions, but Cesare manages to lean Gino against the wall and a filing cabinet, then encourages him to step into the trousers. He daren't take their boots off, daren't look at the damage.

His throat is dry with guilt. It is hard to swallow,

hard to know what to say to Gino, whose face is pale and gleams with sweat. Cesare whispers apologies with every breath.

He doesn't know where to put their uniforms, but is ashamed to leave the muddy clothing on the floor for the young, harried-looking nurse to pick up, so he hangs them over the back of a chair, half folding them so that the red targets are hidden.

They limp back through and Cesare helps Gino onto a bed, to lie diagonally so that his boots don't touch the mattress, before he himself sinks onto the crisp white sheets.

When Nurse Croy marches back through the ward, she eyes their pyjamas, glances at their boots and nods.

'That's better. The doctor will be across soon.' Her voice is softer now and, as Cesare watches her giving water to the other three prisoners in the infirmary – all of whom have a hacking cough – her hands are gentle.

'Thank you,' he says, when she brings him the water. 'You are nurse for a long time?'

'No,' she says. 'I've three younger sisters and two little brothers, so we need the extra food and the money. I didn't want to work with the prisoners, but now you're all coming across to Kirkwall anyway.' She shrugs.

'Italians in . . . Kirkwall?' He forms the unfamiliar word. 'Where is this?'

'The Orkney mainland.' She gestures. 'Just across the water.'

He's heard nothing of it: the men are put into their groups in the morning in the camps and who knows where they go?

'Who is going to this Kirkwall?' he asks.

'Oh, no one yet,' she says. 'They decided it just two days ago. Some of you will be coming across to help with the farm work, so we all have more food. No one's happy about it. But my mother said that if we were having prisoners among us anyway I should try to earn some extra food for the family.' She is staring at the glass of water in her hand, and seems to have forgotten Cesare's presence altogether. He waits, his mind whirring, his toes throbbing.

She continues: 'It means me coming across to this island, of course, but then there's no truth in the stories, at least that's what my mother said. Although she did give me this sprig of white heather for protection. It's usually above our door.' She brings out a bunch of dried-out leaves – brownish, not white, then nods, half smiling. 'And those twins have been safe enough, living here.'

'Twins?' Cesare is suddenly alert: he can't help himself. But then he wishes he hadn't spoken, because the girl's eyes focus on him again and her smile fades. She straightens her skirts.

'I don't have time to be talking to you. I must write my notes for the doctor.'

She taps away, tutting.

Gino is sleeping. The square of light from the window creeps down the wall. Cesare counts the beat of his pulse in his foot.

He is beginning to think that the doctor might not come after all, when he hears footsteps again, two pairs, and Nurse Croy is back with a tall man – elderly but straight-backed and sharp-eyed.

'Let's get this over with,' he says, bending to take off Cesare's boot. The pain ricochets up through his leg and he clenches his jaw to stop himself crying out. The doctor prods his swollen, blackened toes firmly and instructs Cesare to bend them, which he does with difficulty and a groan through gritted teeth.

'Possibly broken, or badly bruised if you're lucky.' The doctor speaks slowly and clearly. 'I'll bandage them. Rest. Two days, then we'll see.' He mimes bandaging and holds up two fingers.

'Thank you,' Cesare says. 'My friend, I think, is worse. There is some bleeding and he cannot walk without help.'

'Your English is very good,' the doctor says, eyeing Cesare. 'Can you write?'

Cesare nods.

'You have good relationships with the other prisoners?'

Cesare pauses, thinks of Marco, and nods again.

The doctor taps his pen on his paper. 'Major Bates

will come and see you later today, I should imagine. If you want to avoid breaking more toes in the quarry, I'd suggest best behaviour.'

And with this mysterious instruction, the doctor moves on to examine Gino, who has indeed broken his big toe, the doctor is almost certain, and has *significant trauma* besides. The nurse frowns as she writes this down, and Cesare rolls the words around his tongue – such beautiful words to describe something so damaged.

Significant trauma.

And as he tries to ignore the pain and drifts off to sleep, the words blur with those of the nurse earlier.

Protection. Those girls have been safe enough. Significant trauma.

And he remembers, again, the red-haired woman. The sensation of her fingers gripping his shirt, pulling him upwards towards air and life. He remembers her hand under his chin, her breath loud in his ear as she'd whispered, *Please, please, please.*

Early the next morning he is woken in the darkness by the whistle in the yard and the sound of the men stumbling from their huts into the cold to be counted.

Gino is awake too, his face tight with pain in the dim lamplight.

Cesare reaches across to him.

'I'm sorry,' he says again, in Italian.

Gino gestures at the warm room, the beds, the clean sheets. 'I'm not.'

They both laugh softly and Cesare sleeps again.

When he next wakes, a tall uniformed man is standing next to his bed, scowling at him.

Major Bates.

Out of habit, Cesare tries to stand, then cries out at the pain in his foot.

'Not too clever, putting all your weight on an injured foot,' the major half smiles, but not unkindly. 'Lie down, at ease.'

Cesare nods, sucks in air, and waits for the nausea to subside.

'Now,' the major says, 'Dr Tulloch tells me you speak English.' He indicates the nurse. 'And young Bess here says you've nice manners – for a foreign chap. Would you say that's fair?'

'I . . . I speak English, a little, and . . .'

'You're modest, good. I like that. You'd be able to translate for your fellow prisoners? Talk to them about their skills and so on, and give them my orders?'

He doesn't understand what he's truly being asked, but still Cesare nods. It is unthinkable to do anything else, when he is faced with those medals and dressed in pyjamas, in this warm bed, and all the while, from somewhere in the back of his skull, he feels the reverberating *thunk*, *thunk*, *thunk* of spades on rock. As if the endless act of digging, and the danger and the fear, have sunk into his bloodstream, into his bones.

'Very well, then,' the major says. 'You'll be sitting at a desk and you've not far to hobble to get to my office, so what say you start this afternoon? Nurse Croy here will help you across the compound. After lunch should do nicely.'

Nurse Croy bobs smartly and both of them turn to Cesare.

'Yes, sir,' he says, finally. 'Thank you.'

After they have gone, Gino turns to Cesare. 'What were they saying?'

Cesare shakes his head, not daring to hope. 'I think I've found a way to survive.'

Later, Nurse Croy holds his arm as he walks across the yard to the major's hut. Cesare has dressed in his uniform, which has been washed, and Nurse Croy speaks more tersely than before, taking care to touch him as little as possible.

'Now, the major has a short temper, they say, but he's not unkind.'

'Thank you,' Cesare says. 'You will look after my friend, Gino?'

She nods, helps him up the step and opens the door for him. It bounces off a heap of letters and dislodges some envelopes, which flurry into the air and come to rest on the floor, along with the piles of paper, files and boxes that already crowd the room.

The major sits behind a small wooden desk, which is loaded with yet more papers. A single lamp gives off a dim light and the hut is as draughty as the one Cesare sleeps in. Major Bates's eyes are red-rimmed and he blinks at Cesare for a moment, before standing.

'Ah, yes. There's a small table for you in the corner. Thank you, Nurse Croy, you can return to your patients. And you . . .' He looks at Cesare. 'I don't suppose you can help much with this just yet.' He bends and picks up a sheaf of papers and passes them to Cesare. 'But if you can try to get at least some of the floor clear. The islanders are sending a man over with a list of jobs and then we can get started. Ah! This'll be him.'

Cesare turns as the door opens, hoping that this local man will be able to explain something of what he is supposed to do, will be able to tell him how to make sure that he can do what is asked of him – whatever it is – so that he can stay in this draughty office, with its snow of paper and Major Bates, who seems such a different man from the one who had shouted threats and commands when they first arrived here. He needs to know how to do his job well, to be useful, to stay out of trouble.

In the flare of bright light from the open door, it takes him a moment to register that the figure is not a man at all. It is a woman, in a long, full skirt and a heavy fisherman's jumper. She walks into the hut. The lamplight falls on her face.

His heart leaps. His breath catches. There she is, just as he'd remembered her.

The red hair, the pale skin, the firm mouth, the delicate hands. And those blue eyes. The eyes that meet his, then widen slightly as she stops and stares at him.

'*You!*' she says.

Dorothy

'*You!*' I say, before I can stop myself, and the man stands in the shaft of golden light from the open doorway, squinting at me. It is as if, by thinking about him daily, I have summoned him. The hairs on my arms rise and I think about the stories they tell of this island, the stories I've tried not to believe, of selkies and curses and people who appear and vanish in the swirling mists.

The English commander steps forward, blocking my view of the office and the Italian man.

'I think you are in the wrong place, young lady,' he says sternly. 'How did you get into the camp? I'll be having words with the guard on the gate.'

'Don't!' I say. 'It's not his fault. I told him I had a message for you.'

'You can make an appointment to see me –'

'It's urgent.' My mouth is dry, my blood thrumming. 'Please, I . . . I've an important request.'

'Ah.' The commander folds his arms. 'So you've a message from Kirkwall? I thought they were sending a man across. John O'Farrell.'

'I . . .' I can feel the Italian man's eyes on me, like a touch. 'I don't live in Kirkwall –'

'Well, then, you'll have to go –'

'Please,' I say. 'I live here, on the island, in a bothy – a shepherd's hut. The roof is falling in and the weather has made it worse and I'd heard some of your men – they said, in Kirkwall – that some of the prisoners were going to help with jobs there. Repairing fences, and so on. I thought . . .' I swallow.

Behind the commander, the Italian man is still watching me. It is searching, his stare, as if I am standing in the dark and he is holding a lamp close to my skin. I can feel the heat of it and my skin warms. Something in me wants to turn away, but the commander is watching me, too, frowning, and I can tell that he is going to refuse me, and he must not. He must say yes, because back in the bothy, the hole in the roof is growing with each passing day of wind and rain, and now Con has a cough that wakes us both at night. The sight of the tendons in her neck straining as she tries to breathe is terrifying.

'Please,' I say again to the commander, before he can speak.

He shakes his head. 'You can't simply barge in here asking for help. We're only releasing prisoners for agricultural work, or related matters – lots of mouths to feed here, so our men will help to grow their own food. I'm sure there's someone from Kirkwall who could mend your roof.'

'No. They don't like the island and they won't come to the bothy. You must be paying well to persuade anyone to work here.'

'I . . . Yes, well . . . I'm sorry I can't help you.' And he does look sorry, suddenly, this commander, in a uniform clustered with medals that he must have won for killing a man – or perhaps saving a man. Or both.

I nod, glance at the Italian, with his dark hair and his warm eyes, and I open the door to the frost-rimed yard. I'm suddenly desperate to get away. Away from the pitying expression on the commander's face, away from the searching gaze of the Italian man.

The yard is cold and I hunch my shoulders, trying to ignore the hollow disappointment inside me, and the heat in my cheeks, which feel as though I've been slapped.

A shout from behind me.

I stop, turn.

There is the Italian – again, as if I have conjured him with my thoughts. He limps across the frozen compound and stops three paces away, resting his weight on one leg. He looks thinner than when I saw him last, his face sharper. On his cheekbone, the faint shadow of a fading bruise — something has struck him, hard.

'You are injured,' I say.

'A rock falls on my foot. It is not bad — not broken. Your roof is broken.'

'Yes,' I say, still wondering about that bruise on his cheek.

'You are cold. And is dangerous for you.'

'A little, yes, but —'

'I will like to mend.' He gestures with his hands, lacing his fingers together. His hands are strong and broad, marked with cuts and bruises.

'I . . . How?' I ask, raising my chin. I don't say, *Why?*

He nods towards the commander's hut. 'Major Bates gives me new job. I tell him which Italians can help on island. I can help you.'

'Thank you, but I don't think you'll be able to.' I turn away.

He reaches out, catches my sleeve. I stop, frozen.

'I try,' he says, then releases me.

As I walk away, he calls after me. 'Your name? You have not tell me.'

I turn back to face him. The wind snaps my hair into my eyes, so he is framed, for a moment, in a twisting roil of red.

'Dot,' I call. Then, 'Dorothy.'

'Dorotea.' He smiles. 'I am Cesare.'

My name on his lips sounds like music, like bells, like something beautiful, like something I've never imagined for myself. *Door-oh-tee-ah*.

And the lilt in his name, which I find myself repeating with each step as I walk back to the bothy. *Che-sa-ray. Che-sa-ray.*

Cesare

Before he hobbles back into the office, Cesare takes the card out of his pocket – he'd pretended to lose it so that he could limp after the woman.

He holds it up to the major as he opens the door. 'Thank you. It falls from my pocket when I come here.' He gabbles the lie anxiously.

Major Bates is hunched over some papers and barely looks up. 'I need you to read through this list of names the guards have given me – they've indicated those prisoners they feel are responsible enough to work in Kirkwall and those they can spare from the quarry and other work. You must cross out the name of any man you don't think will be trustworthy, and underline any man you think will do a good job.' He hands Cesare a pencil.

'And if I do not know the man?' Cesare says.

'Well, then, make it your business to know him.

The men's hut numbers are next to the names. You've time to talk to them – in the mess hut, for instance, or I can give you dispensation to go between the huts in the evenings, before lights out.'

Cesare nods, dizzy at the prospect of sudden freedom.

Major Bates raises an eyebrow and, as if he's read Cesare's mind, says, 'It's hardly a risk that you'll try to run, given the state of your foot.'

Cesare shakes his head. 'I will not –'

'Ha! I'm jesting, man.' Major Bates reaches out to clap him on the arm, recoiling at the last moment from the circle of material that is the colour of blood, wiping his hands on his own trousers.

He turns back to his desk. 'Best get on with it, then. You can talk to the first group of men tonight in the mess.'

The mess hut is crowded and filled with the smell of old cabbage and something metallic and meaty, but it is warm, at least. Cesare limps past the tables of men, who are tearing into bread and dipping it into stew that looks like dishwater. All of them are visibly thinner than when they arrived – Cesare's hip bones grate against the flimsy mattress when he lies down at night – and the food, grey and tasteless as it is, is usually devoured before the men talk to each other. The major has told him that they are expecting a shipment of more food and supplies any day.

Cesare's stomach clenches and he tries to hold his shoulders back and his head high, but doesn't attempt to conceal his limp. If he walks too confidently, the men may accuse him of shirking his work, but if he seems weakened by his injury, some may see him as easy prey – prisoners and guards alike. Many won't know how he was hurt; several will assume a guard has beaten him. He tries to lock eyes with one of the taller guards, Sergeant Hunter – an Englishman who has a reputation as a bully. He has to hope that will be enough.

He picks up a tray of bread and stew, finds the table with the other men from his hut and slides along the bench.

'How is Gino?' Antonio asks. He is holding his spoon awkwardly and it is clear, as he eats, that his arm pains him. Some other injury from a guard.

'He is enjoying the rest,' Cesare says.

'And you?' Marco says, from across the table. 'Are you *resting*? You haven't been back to the quarry. Maybe we should all drop rocks on our feet. Leave others to do the work.' His voice is hard.

'I am not resting,' Cesare says. 'I am working in the office.' And he unfolds the piece of paper the major had given him. It is covered with names, some typed, some scrawled.

The men lean forward.

'What's that?'

'Why's my name there?'

'Why do you have our names?'

Marco snatches the piece of paper. 'What is this?' he demands. 'You're giving our names to Major Bates?'

'No, no!' Cesare grabs the piece of paper, smooths it. 'These are for other jobs. Not in the quarry. These are the names of men who will be helping in Kirkwall, on the big island across the water. They need men who have experience of farming. Animals, fencing, planting.'

The men are leaning forward now. Marco has pushed his plate to one side. Antonio wears an uncertain smile. 'You mean,' he says, 'we can get out of that quarry?'

Cesare nods. 'If you behave well with the guards, don't get into trouble. Now,' Cesare grins, 'who has farming experience?'

The men's faces light up and they begin to laugh, quietly at first, then louder as, one by one, they raise their hands.

'Me!'

'I grew up on a farm.'

'I built all our fences.'

Cesare chuckles and begins underlining names.

'Hey,' a voice shouts. It's one of the other guards – a

mean-looking man called MacLeod, who's already renowned for being free with his baton and, occasionally, his boots. There are rumours that he broke a prisoner's ribs. 'Hey, what's that?'

He strides over and wrenches the piece of paper from Cesare's hand, so that the corner rips. The men's laughter stops.

Everyone in the mess hut turns to stare.

'What is this?' MacLeod demands again, glaring at Cesare.

'It is a paper for Major Bates,' Cesare says. 'Names of prisoners for Kirkwall jobs.'

'I can see that – do you think I can't read? But why do *you* have it?'

'I am . . . I begin working in his office. I give him names, translate.'

'Are you now? Well, I'm not sure I trust someone who's going between sides.'

Then Sergeant Hunter is there, heavy-shouldered, grim, weary-looking.

'Give it back, MacLeod.' He takes the piece of paper and puts it on the table in front of Cesare. 'And stop throwing your weight around.'

'But –'

'Don't you question me, lad. You're not even in the army, or you'd be fighting somewhere, not traipsing your flat feet around here. Or is it a weak chest you've got?'

MacLeod scowls, but mutters, 'I'm a conscientious objector.'

'Oh, are you now?'

Cesare doesn't know what that means, but Sergeant Hunter's lip curls in contempt.

As both men turn to go, the Italians wink at Cesare, and even Marco gives him a smile.

Occasionally he sees her – a flare of red from the corner of his vision which makes him turn. Sometimes it is simply the target on another man's arm or thigh. Sometimes it is his imagination: he looks and finds nothing but brown uniforms, and the hopeless faces of his countrymen, who all look like strangers at such moments.

But sometimes it is her. Standing on the edge of the camp, looking in. Her face pale, her arms wrapped around her body. She must be cold. He shivers in sympathy and imagines how, if he could find a blank piece of paper, he might trace the curve of her cheek, the angle of her jaw, the shape of her mouth. He sketches in the margins, alongside the men's names, but all his drawings are empty. Lifeless lines scribbled on dead trees. He scratches them out.

He hasn't found a way to ask Major Bates about repairing the roof – what if he asks and is refused? He is waiting for the perfect moment. When he sees her standing at the edge of the camp – Dorotea, that name that reminds him of the word *adorare* – he raises his hands to her, shrugs his shoulders, meaning, *Not yet, but I'm trying.*

He watches her walk away.

And what if, he suddenly panics, what if his shrug means something different to her? What if she thinks he is saying, *I don't know how to solve your problem?* Or, worse, *I don't care.*

It has been a week since she visited the major, and each day Cesare watches a boatload of prisoners being rowed towards Kirkwall. They return after dark, laughing, exuberant, their voices carrying through the night. He tries to picture Dorotea in her hut, with the hole in the roof. Can she hear their voices, too, in the darkness? Does their laughter reach her, where she waits with her sister, staring up at the stars, shivering?

Early one morning, he makes a decision: he sneaks out of bed in the dark and waits for the major in his office.

Cesare has cleared the floor. Every piece of paper has been tidied and filed.

The list of Italians going across to Kirkwall is complete, along with a new list of jobs.

Major Bates comes into the office quietly, jumping

when he sees Cesare waiting. 'Ah, you're early. You shouldn't really be in here without me. But . . . Have you filed *all* those papers? Good Lord! You must have been here half the night. I suppose I can forgive you, then. How's the foot doing?'

'Some pain but is better. Thank you.'

'Good, good. Bloody cold out there – bet you're glad not to be in the quarry.'

Cesare returns the major's smile, although he feels, in truth, very guilty. Some of the other men have begun to make snide remarks about his easy office life, and Marco has again taken to glaring and shoving past him in the mess hut. At night, Cesare is able to sleep only once he is certain that Marco is snoring.

Now, Cesare picks up the piece of paper he'd placed on the major's desk early this morning. 'There is a ship from England yesterday and they send more food. And some other things. Too much, I think.'

The major scans the piece of paper. 'What the devil are they doing sending us so much wood? We can't use all of this in the quarry. Send it back.'

'The ship is gone.'

'I suppose we'll use it eventually. Bloody waste, though.'

'I think . . .' Cesare swallows, inhales. He pictures her face: her disappointed expression as she'd turned from him after he shrugged; the way she'd held her arms tight around her body. Trembling.

Hailstones patter against the window.

'We can use this wood. For the lady's roof.'

Major Bates looks up from his paper. Cesare can feel his neck growing hot.

'It is cold and I do not like thinking . . .' Cesare nods towards the window, the wind-whipped hail, the ice riming the glass.

'I agree it's bitter. But we've no men to spare –'

'I . . . I can go?'

'You? But I need you here. And your foot –'

'My foot is not hurt now. And . . . I am doing all this work.' Cesare gestures at the tidy office, the stacks of files.

The major looks around, sighs, scratches his head.

'It is so cold,' Cesare says. 'Please.'

February 1942

Dorothy

Con has kept me awake with her coughing. When she'd first begun to wheeze and pick at her food, I'd wondered if she might be exaggerating to get attention – she'd often done this when we were younger; our mother had scolded her for it, and teased her. *The wee bampot wants every eye on her*, Mammy and Daddy had said, laughing as Con had scowled at them.

A week ago, when Con's coughing worsened, I'd thought maybe it was in her head – she hadn't been right since the sinking of the *Royal Elm*, since the man who'd died in our boat when we'd held a coat over his face. But then she'd developed a fever and chills.

Now her eyes are glassy and I can feel the burn of the sickness in my own skin. I have a constant roiling in my gut, as though the illness is creeping from Con's body to mine.

There is an old belief on these islands that our souls can be tethered to another's before birth, and that the moment you meet your soul's twin, you recognize them. Our mother had told us that you couldn't bind your soul to a stranger: we were each other's soul twins because we had known each other always, she said. Anything else was ridiculous, a fairytale, something to be woven into a story, along with family feuds and shipwrecks.

'And you must look after one another,' Mammy had said sternly. 'I'll know if you don't.'

It has been a year since our parents disappeared.

And now Con is ill – really ill – and I know I must do something. I feel itchy with anxiety, untethered. A week of her coughing through the nights, wheezing on each breath. I sit on the bed beside her, wiping a cloth across her sweat-sheened forehead, over the growing shadows above her collarbones. When I gather her in my arms, the rungs of her ribs feel fragile, as if she is shrinking.

'I need to take you to Kirkwall,' I murmur. 'The hospital –'

'No,' Con gasps. Her eyes are glassy with fever.

Above my head, through the hole in the roof, I see clouds, then blue sky, then stars. Time blurs and I begin to count the days by listening for the whistles from the camp, the shouts that carry on the wind, the explosions from the quarry that ripple through the ground, like seizures.

I imagine him walking down to the quarry. I remember his promise. *I can help you. I try.*

The wind blasts through the bothy. In the mornings

the sailcloth over the window is crisp with ice. He isn't coming – how could he?

The shrill of the whistle wakes me. Con is worse, her lips pale, her skin translucent. I count to five and then I force myself to stand, to pull on my dress, to open the door and feed the chickens, to boil water for porridge that Con will not eat.

I will row across to Kirkwall myself, I decide. The hospital will have medicine and, if I explain, they will surely give me something. Or the doctor may come to see her – I will use some of the money we have saved from selling the house in Kirkwall at the end of last year, when we decided that, no matter what, we wouldn't be leaving Selkie Holm.

I take the porridge off the stove and put it on the table to cool. I will leave Con to sleep a while longer, then tell her I am going.

There is a metallic rattling outside, then a knock at the door. I jump. Con doesn't stir.

I open the door, ready to tell Angus to leave us alone. And there he is.

Che-sa-ray.

'Dorotea,' he says.

The expression on his face is serious, uncertain, and, for a lurching moment, I think he must have escaped from the camp somehow, that he has come here expecting to hide. Or that he has died and this is his ghost. That the curse on this haunted island is exactly as they describe it in Kirkwall.

I begin to shut the door.

'Wait!' He puts the toe of his boot in the gap. The door stops. No ghost, then. 'Do not be frightened,' he says.

'Why are you here? *How* are you here?'

'The major says I can come. For your roof.' He cranes his neck and gestures at the hole, which shows a cloud-scudded patch of sky.

I open the door and peer outside. Behind him, a large wheelbarrow, full of wood and some pieces of slate.

'I make a promise to you,' he says.

'Oh.' I can find nothing else to say.

I follow him outside into the weak winter sunlight, flinching at the scouring wind. Cesare begins to unload the wood from the wheelbarrow. His shoulders are broad and he lifts the wood with ease at first, but he looks thin and he has to pause at one point to catch his breath.

'In Italy I am strong,' he says, as if reading my thoughts. 'But here . . .' He indicates the sky, hunches his shoulders at the wind and shrugs. 'Hard to be strong.' He stops, looks at me. 'You are here alone? It is dangerous. Cold.'

'I live with my sister. We like it here.'

He nods. His eyes are dark, warm, unreadable. 'Very beautiful here.'

I can feel the heat in my cheeks. I look away. 'My sister is ill. She's sleeping now. I . . .' To my horror, I feel tears burning my eyes, an ache in my throat. I blink rapidly, until the feeling passes.

Cesare reaches out, as if to touch my arm, and stops. 'I will make your roof good,' he says. 'Your sister will be better. She will be warm.'

I swallow. 'Thank you.'

He looks up at the roof and picks up pieces of wood, measuring them with his eye before selecting one. 'I must climb up.'

'I don't have a ladder, but here . . .' He follows me to the side of the bothy, where our three chickens peck and scratch in their wooden coop. 'Will this frame be strong enough?'

He eyes it, pressing down hard on one of the wooden struts. 'Maybe strong. Maybe break.' He grins, apparently unconcerned at the idea of fracturing his leg or neck.

He lifts it; the chickens, suddenly homeless, cluck in disapproval and rush towards their nesting box. Cesare scoops up one bird and holds her for a moment against his chest. She squawks indignantly but doesn't struggle.

'Is warm,' he says.

'She's called Henrietta.'

'*En-ree-ayt-ah*,' he echoes, and again, it is music. 'You are living only from eggs?' He releases Henrietta, who stalks off, clucking.

'No. My parents had a house in Kirkwall. We sold it and moved here after they . . .' *Left. Disappeared. Vanished.* 'Well, some time after.' We had been in the Kirkwall house for three months before we had had to leave and it had taken us longer to sell it. I take a breath. 'And I sometimes work at the hospital in Kirkwall.' *When I can leave Con.*

'You are doctor?' His expression is serious, not a hint of mockery.

'Perhaps one day. But now we are here. So I am a nurse. Sometimes.'

'And your sister is ill,' he says. 'And your roof is bad.'

He doesn't ask again why we are on this isolated island, doesn't question me about why we haven't gone to the hospital, and I'm filled with gratitude for the way he simply places the chicken coop next to the wall and begins to climb.

It wobbles. I grab the wood and try to hold it steady. He flashes a quick grin at me, then pulls himself up onto the roof, lying flat along the solid section and working his upper body up to the broken part.

'Careful,' I call.

He nods, then eases himself further up. I watch

him inspecting the hole, using his arms to measure the gap. He cranes his neck and looks into the bothy.

He will be able to see Con in the single room below, lying in the double bed pushed into the corner. He will be able to see the small stove, the battered table, how the damp has stained the walls and swollen the wooden floorboards so that they bow and buckle.

I shift my weight from foot to foot, wanting to call that he should come away, that he shouldn't look at other people's things, at *our* things.

He pushes himself back down to the edge of the roof. His expression is grave. 'She is sleeping,' he whispers.

'Yes.'

'She is thin.'

'Yes.' Again, that pain in my throat.

'You can lift the wood for me? Is heavy.'

I nod, hoist each piece of wood upright and pass it towards him. My arms shake a little but I hold each piece steady while he reaches for it. He moves around the roof easily and seems to feel no fear, while I constantly imagine him falling, the smash of his body hitting the earth.

He uses the wood to hold down the piece of sail-cloth that has flapped uselessly in the wind throughout the winter. I watch him lay each piece gently, as quietly as he can. Sometimes he cranes his neck to look down at Con, then glances at me and nods. She must still be sleeping.

He is just laying the last piece of wood when I hear him give a cry, as if something has startled him.

From inside the bothy, screaming.

On the roof, Cesare scrambles to get down. I watch, as his boot slips, as his hands slide off the slates. I watch as he rolls towards the edge of the roof, his body gathering momentum. His hand clutches for a slate, misses.

For a moment, he is suspended in the air.

Then his body falls from the roof.

He lands at my feet with a sickening thud.

Cesare

The shock of the impact travels through his body, jolting his organs. For a moment he feels no pain. Then, when he tries to straighten, there is a searing bolt of agony in his skull.

Dorotea is there immediately, her hands on his arm as she helps him sit up.

'Can you hear me? Where does it hurt?'

He nods, puts his hand to his forehead. Wet. And his hand is covered with blood.

From somewhere, there is screaming and, for a moment, his mind lurches, because a woman with red hair is standing in the doorway of the bothy, hands clapped over her mouth. And he cannot understand how Dorotea can be holding his arm and also watching him, crying out in terror. He worries that the blow to his head must have dislodged something inside his skull, and now he is seeing double.

'Enough, Con!' Dorotea snaps, and the other woman stops screaming.

And then he remembers. Of course: her sister, ill in bed.

She is still staring at him with dread, and he holds up his hands, palms outwards, to show that he means her no harm, but she jerks away and he is aware of the blood on his palm and, *mio Dio*, there is a whooshing inside his skull, as if someone is blowing a bellows somewhere in his brain.

'*Scusi*,' he says, because he cannot summon the English word. '*Scusi*.'

'Can you stand?' Dorotea asks, and he manages to nod, to follow her into the little bothy, which is barely warmer than it is outside, despite the small fire burning in the grate.

He tries to protest, tries to tell them both that he is well, really, that he doesn't want to cause any trouble, that he will go back to the camp.

But Dorotea gets a cloth and a jug of water and sponges his forehead.

He grits his teeth so he won't wince and Dorotea dabs carefully with the cloth. Her face is fixed in total concentration, her focus absolute. With her face so close to his, he can see the delicate skin of her eyelids, which makes him think of white rose petals in water. He can feel the stir of her breath on his cheek. The smell of her is sweet. He thinks of the pear trees outside his house in Moena.

He swallows.

'*Grazie*,' he murmurs, then finds the English words. 'Thank you.'

'What is he doing here?' asks Con. 'He was staring at me through the roof.'

'He was *mending* the roof,' Dorotea says, without looking at her sister. To Cesare, she says, 'It is not as bad as I thought. Forehead wounds often bleed a great deal. Here, hold this cloth against it. Are you hurt anywhere else? You can move your fingers, your toes?'

She is brisk, her movements certain but gentle. Under her instruction, he wiggles his fingers and toes, bends his arms and legs, stands and stretches – this sends a shooting pain through his side.

He groans, puts his hand to his ribs.

Dorotea says, 'May I look?'

He nods.

She reaches out and slowly lifts his shirt. He stands very still while she grazes cool fingers over his side. Under her touch, his skin stipples. She watches his face, pressing each rib in turn.

'There are some old marks here. Some old bruises?'

He nods, remembering the quarry. The jab of a guard's fist into his chest. The thud of a rifle butt into his side. The smack of the baton on his back.

'Do they hurt?' she asks, brushing her fingers over the bruises.

He shakes his head. His face and neck are hot. He watches her mouth, the way she bites her lip as she concentrates, pressing on the darkness of the newest bruise. It is painful. He stands very still, not wanting her to stop.

'Badly bruised, I think,' she murmurs, then clears her throat and says, more loudly, 'Nothing broken. And your head is bleeding less.' She lifts the cloth and nods to herself.

On the bed, Con is still watching. Her expression is unreadable, but there is a sheen of sweat on her forehead and bright spots of colour on each cheek. She coughs.

'You have medicine?' Cesare asks.

Con looks at him warily, then shakes her head.

Dorotea sighs. 'I was going to Kirkwall, to the hospital, but –'

Cesare nods. 'Kirkwall is far,' he says. He turns to Dorotea. 'Do not go to Kirkwall. There is a hospital here –'

'For the prisoners,' says Con.

He spreads his hands outward. 'I am a prisoner. I can get medicine.'

And, as he watches, a smile spreads over Con's face, and over Dorotea's too and, for the first time since meeting them, he can see how people might think them identical.

'Thank you,' they say, at exactly the same time.

And Dorotea skims his sleeve with her fingers. 'Thank you,' she whispers, just loud enough for him to hear.

He nods, forgetting, for a moment, the throbbing in his skull and the pain in his side. Forgetting the cold and the uniform he wears. He could be any-where, with this woman smiling at him, with the feeling of her hand on his sleeve still.

As he walks back down to the camp, he barely sees the barbed wire, barely notes the glare of steel and the lifeless blank of the dusty yard. Again and again, he remembers the brush of her breath on his face, the curve of her mouth as she smiled at him, the slight pressure on his arm as she mouthed, *Thank you.*

So he isn't prepared when, just as he walks through the gates, a guard steps out in front of him, scowling.

'Where have you been? Who gave you permission to wander off?'

'I . . . Major Bates, he say I can help to mend roof for the ladies.'

'Which *ladies*?' He is holding his baton in one hand, and Cesare is suddenly aware that there is no one else in the yard. There will be no one to see whatever this guard does to him.

MacLeod. The name comes back to him, the memory of his anger in the mess hut when he'd ripped the list of names from Cesare's hands.

Cesare stares at the ground. 'The ladies on the hill. The house is old. The roof has a hole. Major Bates say I can go –'

'Major Bates said? Perhaps Major Bates doesn't know that I'll be needing you in the quarry then. I must tell him.' MacLeod frowns. 'What have you done to your head?'

'I fall,' Cesare says. 'But . . . I must mend the roof and –'

'You must do as I say. I'll expect you in the quarry after lunch.'

'But –'

'But what?' MacLeod brings his face in close to Cesare's and, though he can't see it, Cesare is aware of the baton in the guard's hand, is aware of the way that the guard's whole body is tensed, like that of a dog when it sights a rabbit.

Cesare stays very still. 'The lady – she is called Con? She is sick. I . . . promise her medicine.'

The guard raises his eyebrows. 'Con is sick? Then I will get medicine. I will take it to her.'

The guard's slow-creeping smile has no warmth in it. Cesare thinks of the clang of metal on rock in the quarry, the curses and insults that the guards shout at them. It makes him think of the way that, after the thud of the baton, there is a moment of silence, when you know the pain is coming but there is no way of telling how much it will hurt.

With the guard still watching him, Cesare turns and walks towards the mess hut, his shoulders stooped and, in his stomach, a cold twist of anger.

Dorothy

I scrape the spoon along the bottom of the pot, where the porridge has burned, and over the sound of Con talking, I strain for the noise of footsteps, for a knock at the door that will tell me Cesare has returned, that Con will be safe, that I need not leave her alone while I go to Kirkwall.

I've never seen her so weak before. She was always the strong one, the certain one, the one who made decisions. I remember her deciding we should come to this island. I remember her rowing the injured sailors from the *Royal Elm* over to the little bay, where no one from Kirkwall would see us. I remember the horror in her eyes as she pressed the coat over the man's face. I remember her silence and fear in the days afterwards, as if she couldn't believe what she'd done.

And now she coughs and wheezes and struggles to

stand. I look out of the window again and again, searching for Cesare.

But it has been hours. The sun has sunk almost below the horizon, and he has not come.

'I told you,' Con says. 'I *told* you it was too much to hope for. I shall be well without medicine. There's no need for you to go to Kirkwall.' She coughs again.

The oats are a blackened mess on the base of the pan. I throw it into the sink with a growl of frustration. Con jumps and wheezes.

'Sorry,' I say. I go to her and rub her back, then sponge her forehead.

When she stops coughing, I move to the window, push the sailcloth to one side and peer out. The lights in the camp are bright still, and there are shadows of men moving around, but they will have to dim the lights soon for blackout. Then it will be another night of darkness, of counting the rattle of Con's breaths, of holding her hand while she coughs, of smoothing her hair back from her forehead until she drifts off.

An hour later, there is a light tapping on the door – tentative, as if Cesare is worried he might wake us.

Thank God! I run to the door and fling it wide.

And there is Angus MacLeod.

'Hello, Dot.' He smiles and holds out a small brown bottle. 'I hear Con isn't well.'

'What are you doing here?' I step out into the cold, half closing the door behind me. 'How did you . . . ?'

'I told you,' he says, his smile unwavering, as if he hasn't noticed my anger. 'I've brought medicine for Con. Can I come in?'

'No, you cannot,' I snap, shutting the door further. The wind picks up and I hope it is loud enough to cover the sound of his voice.

'Ach, that's a shame. You're not wanting the medicine, then?' He drops the bottle back into the pocket of his guard's uniform. A black baton hangs from his belt. And a gun, glinting in the dim lights from the camp.

'I . . .' My thoughts scrabble. 'Con needs the medicine.'

He nods. 'You'll not object to me giving it to her?' He moves to take a step past me, to go into the bothy.

I position myself in front of the door handle, praying that Con cannot hear us. 'Ah, it's . . . kind of you, Angus. But she's sleeping, you see.'

He stares at me for a moment, then nods slowly. 'Well. She must rest.'

I hold out my hand for the medicine. 'Thank you, Angus.'

He pauses, then places the little brown bottle in my hand. 'Sulfa tablets, the nurse said.'

I hesitate. Sulfonamide will cure Con's infection — it's what they'd give her in Kirkwall. But I sense these will come at a price.

I force a smile and nod again. 'Thank you. How many should she take?'

'There are four in there. One every six hours.'

'But . . . won't she need more than four?' Sulfa tablets only work if they're given over a number of days. I can see, from his raised eyebrows and expectant expression, that Angus knows this.

'I'll bring more tomorrow,' he says. 'Maybe I can see her then.'

My mouth is dry. I want to push the bottle back into his hand, to turn away, to slam the door and lock it.

'And,' he says, 'I hear you've a hole in your roof that needs fixing. I can do that tomorrow.'

'But . . . one of the prisoners is already repairing it.'

'Him? Oh, no. He's not the sort you want around. A troublemaker, you see. No, I've sent him back to the quarry to work.' Angus smiles.

'I thought . . . Wasn't he working in the commander's office?'

'He was, but I spoke to Major Bates, told him I needed the man back in the quarry. I said it wasn't a good idea to have a prisoner up here with two women, all alone.'

He looks genuinely concerned as he says this. That's the problem with Angus: he's always been convincing, even when you know everything he says is fiction. I truly think he believes his own lies.

'Said I thought you'd feel vulnerable, the pair of you,' Angus says, his face sincere.

I nod mechanically, thinking of the yellowing bruises on Cesare's ribs and chest. Imagining Angus climbing onto the roof, staring down at Con while she sleeps.

'So, I will come back in the morning, after the men have started in the quarry. I'll repair your roof and I'll bring more sulfa pills for Con. I'll look after you, don't worry,' says Angus.

He is watching me, his face earnest. He takes my hand in his and curls my fingers around the bottle. 'Thank you?' he says, raising his eyebrows.

I draw a shuddering breath. 'Thank you,' I whisper.

And then I go inside, and I shut the door and I lock it and I lean my back against it.

Con is dozing on the bed; she stirs and sits up.

'What's wrong?' she croaks. 'You look like you've seen a ghost.'

'Nothing,' I say, opening my hand and looking at the little bottle, tipping it so the four pills inside it rattle. 'Nothing's wrong. I'll get you some water.'

'What happened?' she rasps. 'Did Cesare hurt you?'

'Nothing's wrong,' I say again, brightly. 'Everything will be fine.'

I smooth my hand over her hair while she swallows

the water, watching the bulge in her throat, keeping my eyes averted from hers, hoping she won't look at me, hoping she won't see the lie – the first real lie I've ever told her – written on my face.

The night is long, the darkness silty. Con coughs and twists and turns next to me, her body giving off such a heat that I almost don't mind the breeze from the open patch of sky in the corner of the room.

In the morning, she seems no better, but also no worse. I watch her swallow another pill and then I pull the sailcloth to one side and look out of the window.

The light is filtering thinly through low clouds, and the camp is still shrouded in gloom and silence – the whistle hasn't yet blown.

Angus will take the men down to the quarry, he'd said, and then he will come back up here.

I'll look after both of you.

And suddenly I can't do it – I can't watch while Angus talks to Con. Can't watch his feigned *concern* and her terror. Can't stand to one side while my sister shakes in fear and Angus jovially repairs our roof, making conversation as if he can't see her trembling, as if he can't sense my rage.

'Can you walk as far as the camp?' I ask.

Con puts down her water. 'What?'

'Can you walk to the hospital in the camp?'

She shakes her head. 'I don't want to. I want to stay here.'

'You can't. You need medicine and warmth and –'

'I have medicine. That prisoner, Cesare, he –'

'There's not enough.' I take her hand. 'The hospital will have more.'

'But . . . he said he would bring more.'

'He did –'

'Well, then, I'm not going. I'm not, Dot. Cesare will bring more, and –'

I press my fingers over my eyes. 'He didn't bring it. Cesare didn't bring it.'

'What?'

'Angus brought it.'

'Angus?' She freezes, as if he's with her in the room, as if he's spoken her name, as if he's reached out to touch her.

I squeeze her hand again, to bring her back to me. 'He's coming again later. He says he's going to mend the roof.'

The colour drains from her cheeks and the breath wheezes out of her. When I put my arms around her, her whole body is rigid.

'I'm sorry,' I whisper into her hair. 'But if we go to the camp, other people will be there – all the time. He can't hurt you in the infirmary. There will be soldiers and nurses –'

'I can't go there. You can't leave me there.'

'Hush, I won't leave you. I've thought about it – I can be there, as a nurse too.'

'Will they let you?'

'I think so,' I say. *I hope so.*

'But Angus –'

'I won't let him anywhere near you.'

She shudders, then nods. 'You won't leave me?'

I kiss her hot cheek. 'I promise. I won't leave you.'

We wait until the whistle sounds in the camp, watching the troops of men marching down towards the quarry. They move like shadows through the mist, over the hill and out of sight. At this distance, it is impossible to tell one man from another: any of those grey spectres could be Angus, with the baton and gun tucked into his belt. And any of them could be Cesare. They all look insubstantial in the morning gloom – like the rumours of ghosts that have always haunted these islands, like the tales of the curses, brought to life.

As soon as they are over the breast of the hill, we begin walking down to the camp, my arm across Con's shoulders, supporting her as we move, holding her close, feeling the wrench of her coughing echoing through her body and into mine.

When we pass through the gates of the camp, the guard takes one look at us and stands aside. I suppose, emerging from the mist, we must have spooked him. Or perhaps he's heard stories from the islanders.

I knock lightly on the door of Major Bates's hut, then knock again, the wood bruising my knuckles. When the door doesn't budge, I kick it open, bundling Con inside.

Major Bates looks up sharply from his desk. 'What the devil –?'

'She's ill,' I say.

'Well, why are you bringing her to me? Take her to the hospital in Kirkwall, for Heaven's sake.'

'I can't. We . . . She's too weak for the boat journey,' I say, and the lie sounds convincing. 'So I thought she could stay in the hospital here.'

'With the men? Are you mad? This is a prisoner-of-war camp, not a public infirmary.'

'Oh, but . . .' How can I convince this man? His face is closed. He has already dismissed us, is desperate to return to the papers piled up on his desk.

'Please,' I say. 'I can stay with her –'

'Two of you staying in the camp now? Did you not hear what I said? No, it's Kirkwall for you.' He picks up his pen, frowns, looks down at the scribbled figures in front of him.

'I'm a nurse,' I say. 'At least I was, for a time, in Kirkwall. And I can help here. I know you've a need of nurses.'

'We have a girl who comes across from Kirkwall –'

'Bess Croy. I've seen her. That is, I've noticed her walking to the camp. But she can't work here all the time, and you'll not be able to get many other young women from Kirkwall to come to this island. And it's a large camp – if the men grow ill. I could . . .' He is scowling, but I carry on: 'I could stay in the camp, as a nurse, until Con recovers and then I . . . or we could both help in the infirmary.'

He puts down his pen. 'You're both nurses?'

I nod. It isn't true, but Con is a fast learner. All I need is for her to stay quiet now, not to contradict me. I squeeze her hand, hard, until she nods. Her cheeks burn; her eyes are bright with fever.

'She'll have to be kept curtained off from the men while she's ill. We don't want an outbreak and . . . well, for modesty's sake. And you'll have to work hard. We've a fair number of injuries from the quarry.'

I nod. 'Thank you.'

He's already looking back at his papers. 'Go on with you, then. Nurse Croy will set you up.'

Bess Croy's eyes widen at the sight of us, and although she sets up a bed behind a curtain for Con, and fetches the sulfa tablets, her movements are skittish, as though she expects one of us to lash out. When we are changing the sheets, her hand accidentally brushes against mine; she recoils.

'Sorry, sorry,' she gasps, rubbing her skin, as if I've burned her.

After Con is asleep, I help Bess to empty the

prisoners' bedpans, fetch them glasses of water, re-bandage a sprained wrist and change a dressing on a crushed foot. Gradually, she grows less jumpy, and at lunchtime, she fetches two bowls of soup from the mess hut and wordlessly passes me one. She eats quickly, watching me, like a nervous bird.

'Thank you,' I say, after I've soaked up the last drops of soup with the bread. Then I continue rolling bandages. It is satisfying to start with a snarled mess of fabric and finish with neat white rolls.

'It's nice to have company,' she says, although she still looks wary and skittish. She picks up the bowls and turns away, then stops. Without looking at me, she says, 'How do you live here?'

'Pardon?'

She still has her back to me. 'On this island. It's so . . . It frightens me. All the stories. But you live here. How?'

'Oh . . . they're just stories and –' I almost give her a sarcastic answer, the sort of thing Con might say in response to this question. *Easy enough to live on a cursed island when you're cursed yourself.*

But Bess turns to me, and her face is so young, so guileless. And she is still holding my soup bowl. And her hands were gentle before, when she changed the men's bandages. She deserves honesty.

'We were frightened,' I say, 'at first. But the island isn't a bad place. And Kirkwall . . .' I spread my hands, then smooth the bandage I've just rolled, add it to the pile. 'After everything that happened and –'

'I understand why you wanted to leave, after everything . . .' she says. 'I never believed him, you know. Some people did, but I never trusted him.'

My breath feels tight in my chest. I want her to stop talking, in case Con is listening. I want her to stop talking, so that I can push away the sudden memory of the dark bruises on Con's neck. The sand scrapes on her back. The way that, for weeks afterwards, whenever she'd reached for anything – a glass of water, a blanket or my hand – her fingers had trembled.

But Bess isn't looking at my face. She's staring at her soup bowl as she continues: 'So I understand why you wanted to leave, especially after . . . your parents.'

Stop it! I think. *Stop it, stop it!* My mind fills with the sound of the scouring wind, with the empty sea which echoed our cries back to us.

'But why come here?' Bess asks.

I swallow, collect my thoughts. I make my voice steady. 'Would *you* leave Orkney?' I ask quietly.

She shakes her head. 'Never.'

'Even if your family had disappeared? All of them?'

Her eyes are round, and I see how this could sound like a threat or a curse, even though I meant nothing of the sort.

'Especially not then,' she whispers.

I set down the bandages and smooth an imaginary crumb from my skirt, then look down at the floor, counting my breaths until I can trust my voice.

'Well, there, you see. We couldn't leave. I thought about going south after the war started. And again, after our parents . . . went. I wanted to join the Wrens. But . . . Con wanted to stay. She blamed herself. Because . . .' I close my eyes, remembering our parents pushing their boat out, away from Con on the shore, remembering her pacing, waiting for them to come back; remembering the dark weeks that followed, when I hardly saw Con because she felt too guilty to look at me; remembering the night when she stayed out so late that I fell asleep waiting for her; remembering the bruises on her neck, remembering the way she'd seemed terrified of every man; remembering how everyone had stared at her, the whispers, that she'd wanted to hide herself from everyone – she'd begged me to live somewhere alone, just the two of us. And I'd known she'd meant *away from men* and, particularly, *away from him*.

When I open my eyes, Bess is blurred. She passes me a handkerchief and I wipe my cheeks. I watch the movement in her throat as she swallows.

'And now it's all followed us. All the trouble has followed us here, and more besides. Perhaps we are cursed after all.' I give a quick laugh. 'Or this place is.' It doesn't sound as light as I'd intended it to. I give a tight smile, which she returns. And I notice her looking at my hands. I clench them into fists to hide the tremor.

'Are you frightened?' I ask.

'Yes,' she whispers.

'Me too,' I say.

And behind us, behind the curtain, Con sleeps, her breath bubbling on each exhalation.

Bess nods towards the sound. 'You can go and sit with her, if you want. You look tired. When did you last sleep properly?'

'I honestly can't remember.'

'I'll finish rolling those bandages.'

I pause, blinking back the sudden heat behind my eyes at this kindness.

'Thank you,' I say.

In my dream I'm swimming with Con and our parents – even though my father could never swim very well. My arms cut through the water; my body is borne upwards as I float and call to our mother.

'There's something I want to tell you,' I shout.

She turns and smiles at me – her face an older version of mine, of Con's. She is warmth and safety and I know I must reach her, must catch her before she swims away. But she turns and, like a seal diving, she disappears into the dark undertow. When I reach out, my fingers grasp her hair. I pull, although I know I must be hurting her. I tug her hair free of the water, filled with a fierce longing to touch her face, to tell her everything that has happened.

I lift my hands into the light and see only a mass of seaweed, which dissolves. A wordless cry echoes in my ears and I know that the voice is my mother's and that somewhere she is in pain. Somewhere she is screaming.

I wake with a sob and it takes me a moment to locate myself. I'm not in the bothy – the room is too warm, the bed too small. Then I remember: *The infirmary.*

I've fallen asleep curled up next to Con, both of us crammed into her single bed. And the noise that has dragged me from my dream is Angus MacLeod's shouting. I'd know his voice anywhere.

'Where are they? Are they here?'

I'm instantly wide awake, my muscles tensed. The curtain is pulled around the bed, so he won't be able to see us from the door, but he could easily pull it back.

I hear Bess's voice. 'I don't know who you mean.'

'Those girls, the twins. Have they been here?'

A pause. 'I'm sure I haven't seen them. It's just injured men in here,' Bess says, and her voice is smooth as she lies.

I wait, my breath held, my body wrapped tightly

around Con's. She stirs in her sleep but doesn't wake. Her skin is still hot, but perhaps cooler than earlier.

I hear Angus say, 'I hope you're not fibbing to me, miss.'

'And I hope you're not threatening me. Or Major Bates will be hearing about it. I'll be telling him that you're coming in here, disturbing the men who are trying to sleep and recover. Now,' her voice wobbles, 'I've work to do, if you don't mind.'

And I hear her footsteps tapping towards the door, followed by his slower, heavier tread, then the sound of the door opening, and her saying, 'Don't be disturbing us again.'

The door shuts behind Angus and I wait.

Bess's tense face appears around the curtain. I smile at her. 'Thank you,' I whisper. 'Thank you.'

She gives a curt nod and taps away.

I lay my cheek on Con's hot chest and listen to her steady breath, where the wheeze, it seems, has faded. And I put my hand on my own chest and pray for the rhythm of her heart to fall into time with mine.

Over the next weeks, Con improves, and life descends into a steady pattern, with few alterations. The nurses rise in the morning with the whistle and don't go to bed until nearly midnight. All tasks outside the camp, such as feeding the chickens, or Bess's visits to her family in Kirkwall, have to fit around the demands of the infirmary. The work is unrelenting: washing wounds and changing sheets; fetching food and water; administering pills and powders. We are all exhausted – Bess and I, along with another young nurse from Kirkwall, Anne, who says very little and sometimes cries because she is scared of rumours she has heard: that the prisoners may try to hurt her, or that the Germans will be trying to invade, or that everyone who lives on this island will go to an early grave through some misadventure. Anne's terrors are endless, it seems, but her fear makes Bess braver with me and more conversational, I think.

For six days, Bess manages to keep Angus MacLeod from knowing that Con and I are there, and then, when he discovers the truth, she is as good as her word, and tells Major Bates that he is a menace and must be kept away from the infirmary.

'The prisoners say he beats them,' she whispers to me.

I nod, remembering Cesare's bruises. I wonder where he is now. I like to imagine him in Major Bates's office, still, surrounded by paperwork. Warm and safe.

Sometimes I look out of the infirmary window at the morning reveille, the men standing to be counted, swaying, half asleep. I fold sheets as I stare out at the lines and lines of brown-uniformed prisoners, trying to see him. But through the grimy window, they all look like the same man: thin and stooped and broken. Hunger is ageing them, bowing their shoulders, making them shuffle and stumble. When they first arrived, Con and I used to hear snatches of songs that they would sing together, but now I hear only the shouts of the guards.

Con's fever fades and she begins to eat again. She is wary of Bess at first, but gradually, she thaws. She begins to return Bess's cautious smiles; she thanks her for the bread, the stew, the water.

And then, after two weeks, I hear laughter from behind the curtain and find Bess and Con rolling bandages. I watch them talking and try not to feel a stab of jealousy at their heads, close together, at their shared smiles over some story that I haven't heard.

Con looks up and sees me; her face is bright. I haven't seen her look so happy since before the *Royal Elm*. Or perhaps for longer. Perhaps I haven't seen her so happy since before we decided to leave Kirkwall.

'You look too thin, Dot,' she declares. 'It doesn't suit you.'

I perch on the side of her bed. 'You're one to talk.' I poke her collarbone.

'My nurse hasn't been feeding me properly.' She grins.

'My patient's been running me off my feet.' It feels good, this gentle barbing of each other. It feels like something from long ago.

After a pause, she says, 'I want to stay in the hospital. As a nurse.'

I put my arms around her, and I feel, beneath the thin skin and the prominent bones, some of the old strength in the Con I remember from before we came here, as if she's cast off that fragile, bitter armour and I can feel her returning to herself, opening up again, like an oyster revealing a pearl.

Cesare

Cesare thrusts his shovel into the rock of the quarry again and again, listening to the clang of spade on stone, but nothing quells his rage. It is three weeks since MacLeod made him return to the quarry, and although Cesare has been back into the office twice to help with some minor administrative tasks, Major Bates seems uncertain about allowing him to do paperwork. Cesare understands that MacLeod must have said something against him. When he asks about being allowed to go up to the bothy to finish the girls' roof, the major shakes his head.

'It's been repaired. One of the guards did it. Besides, they're not living there any more.'

'Where are they going? Where are they living?' The questions are out before he can stop himself.

Major Bates puts down his pen and frowns. 'And why would I tell you that?' His voice is hard, his face closed-off, and Cesare realizes that his reaction must somehow have confirmed one of the lies that MacLeod has told about him: that he is dangerous, perhaps, or unstable.

So Cesare presses his lips together and shrugs. This pretence of mute stupidity seems to reassure the major that he means no harm towards the girls, but Cesare is still sent to the quarry.

Day after day of exploding the rock face, digging out the stones, loading wheelbarrows of rubble, emptying them into a lorry. The vehicle, Cesare knows, will drive to the shore, where other Italians will tip the rubble into metal cages, which are then dropped, using a crane, into the sea. The water swallows them and the exercise starts once more. It is repeated, again and again, day after bitter day. The sea never changes, the barrier never emerges. It is like dropping coins into a well.

The men laugh, at first, that their task is a joke. They watch the rocks vanishing into the sea, and one – a scholar from Venice – talks about Sisyphus, who had to push a boulder up a hill, only to watch it roll back down again.

But after nearly two months of back-breaking work, unending hunger and exhaustion, there is nothing to laugh at. The men mutter to each other, just as when they'd arrived, that what they are being made to do is illegal: they shouldn't be building enemy fortifications. The scholar from Venice, whose name is Domingo, has told them it's against the Geneva Convention.

'We should lay down our shovels and refuse to

work for these pigs,' Domingo says, when the men compare bruises. 'They call us Fascist pigs, but they are the animals.'

In fact, very few of the men are Fascists, from what Cesare can tell. Some of them talk about Mussolini's plan to make Italy great and strong, to recapture its glorious past. But most, like Cesare, have found themselves swept up in a whirlwind where they have no choice but to defend their families; where they have no choice but to label a stranger *my enemy* simply because he speaks a different language or calls a different country home.

And now they are far from the land they love, from the families they want to protect – these peaceable sons of farmers and shopworkers, bakers and teachers – and they have found that they aren't treated as sons, brothers and young fathers. They are treated worse than horses or cattle or dogs. They are treated with less care than the machinery the men drive.

So, if the Geneva Convention says that the men's work means they are aiding the enemy, who are they to argue?

Rumours of a rebellion begin to brew.

'What would you do to him if you saw him in the street?' Gino nods towards MacLeod, who is patrolling the south edge of the quarry, shouting and swinging his baton.

'I don't know.' Cesare digs his spade into the ground, imagines the sound of metal on flesh. He pictures the bruise, the burst of blood. He shakes his head to dispel the image. 'Bring the wheelbarrow closer,' he says.

It is a cold day in late February, the wind blasting in from the north. Gino has been back working alongside Cesare for nearly a week, his presence steady and reassuring, but both of them move slowly in the chill air. A bone-weariness clenches around Cesare's body, making his arms shake and his chest ache; it is like nothing he has ever known. And the fear and rage that course through him when he thinks of MacLeod ... He jabs at the rock, watching his breath plume in front of him.

He imagines a man's cry, cut off. He imagines the rasp of breath being squeezed from a throat.

He shakes his head again. 'I don't know,' he repeats to Gino.

This morning, during the headcount, standing in the yard, Cesare had imagined he saw her hair. A flash of colour in the grey monotony that fills his days. But no. She must have returned to Kirkwall.

If he closes his eyes, he can picture her: the red hair, the white skin, the blue eyes. His hands ache for a brush and the colours he'd need to capture her. At night, in the dark, surrounded by the snores and coughs and grunts of the men, he traces her face in his mind, trying to create something beautiful.

Now he kicks at a stubborn rock and uses his boot to nudge it onto the spade. Gino pushes the wheelbarrow closer.

'I'm not coming too near,' Gino says, eyeing the rock. 'My foot still hurts.'

Laughter pains Cesare's lungs, or perhaps, he worries, it is the first sign of the infection that has begun making its way through the prisoners: sudden fever and a cough that racks their whole body.

As if reading his thoughts, Gino says, 'It would be worth it, almost, *sì*? I would catch that sickness, to be in the infirmary.'

Cesare shakes his head. 'You're scrawny enough, Gino. No more illness for you.'

Gino flashes a quick grin – his teeth shockingly white against his grubby skin. 'Ah, but those nurses . . .' he says dreamily. 'They are so beautiful.'

Cesare pictures Nurse Croy's serious face, her pursed lips, the worried crease in her brow. 'Not for me.'

Gino heaves the full wheelbarrow backwards, his face full of strain, but his eyes are still bright. 'Sometimes I dream of their red hair,' he says.

'Wait.' Cesare yanks the wheelbarrow back towards him, making Gino stumble. 'Who has red hair?'

'The nurses.' Gino rubs his palms against his trousers. 'Two of them. Twins. That hurt, *amico*.'

'There are twin nurses with red hair? In the infirmary?'

Gino nods, still rubbing at his hands, his gaze uncertain. And Cesare is aware, from Gino's expression, that this is unlike him, that he has hurt his friend's feelings as well as his hands.

'*Scusi*,' Cesare says, and then he tells Gino everything: about Dorotea – Gino remembers now that she is the one who dived into the sea – about their bothy; about Con screaming; about MacLeod sending Cesare back to the quarry.

'*Basta!*' Gino breathes.

'Yes. I must see her.'

A shout behind them, 'Get on with your work! Faster!'

It's MacLeod, pacing up and down the line, his baton in one hand. Gino rolls his eyes and pushes the wheelbarrow towards the lorry. When he returns, he is smiling.

'You know, Marco said that MacLeod has a woman's pocket mirror.'

Despite his anxiety about Dorotea, Cesare grins. 'No!'

Gino nods and beckons Marco over. He has lost even more weight than they have; his skin is sallow, his eyes dull. But his expression brightens when Gino mentions MacLeod, who, he confirms, carries a pocket mirror and a moustache comb.

'How can he comb it, though, a *coglione*? A bollock cannot be beautiful.'

Gino gives a shout of laughter and Cesare joins him, but then there is a sound, like a clap of thunder and he is lying on the ground, his face against the rock.

For a moment, he cannot understand what has happened.

He sees the black pair of guard's boots, and looks up to see MacLeod's blurred face, which is entirely expressionless, as if he is inspecting a rock.

Cesare blinks to clear his vision and tries to heave himself upright. As he does so, MacLeod hits him again, and he goes down.

'You lazy Eyetie.' MacLeod raises his baton and Cesare flinches, covers his head with his arms. But the blow never comes.

Marco grabs MacLeod's arm, wrenches the baton from his hand, and then throws it across the quarry. The whole group is frozen, waiting.

MacLeod stares at Marco for a moment, then pulls his gun from his holster and, as Cesare shouts, *No!* MacLeod smashes the gun barrel into Marco's face. The sickening crunch of metal on bone and Marco falls backwards, his head striking a rock.

He lies still.

Cesare doesn't even think, but hurls himself at MacLeod, fists flailing.

As a boy, Cesare had never liked violence, had drifted above it. No one had bothered to try to beat him up: he'd seemed too dreamy; but he'd often stepped between boys who were fighting. Sometimes he'd misjudged it and been punched himself. The trick was only to retaliate when you needed to. The trick was to read another man quickly: the tension in his face and muscles, the line of his mouth, the force of his fist. You don't have to be the strongest or the fastest to be able to dodge the blow, then elbow a man in the throat as he goes down.

But Cesare hasn't accounted for MacLeod's strength, for his own hunger-weakened muscles, for the lightness of his body after two months of digging in the cold.

MacLeod shoves him off and leaps to his feet. Cesare scrabbles for a rock, his spade, anything to defend himself, but MacLeod brings his boot down hard on Cesare's hand. Cesare howls in pain and tries to stand, but then stops, because MacLeod has raised his gun.

Cesare knows that he is a dead man.

A man's heart is the size and shape of his clenched fist. Cesare remembers studying the pictures of Da Vinci's dissections. He used to run his fingers over the tracery of veins in the drawings, then place his hand on his own chest. Now, his heart is thudding hard enough for him to feel it in his throat.

MacLeod points the gun at Cesare's chest. He can feel the other prisoners watching, can feel the tension in his muscles, the pull and push of the air in and out of his lungs.

A body holds about seven pints of blood. If a major vein is hit, a man might bleed to death in minutes. Or a bullet could lodge itself in an arm or leg and be removed. Or it might pass through a man's body, puncturing his liver, his lungs or his bowel.

In the desert in Africa, Cesare had held Alessandro for two hours after the bullet had gone into his chest. His final breath had sounded like the far-off rumble of a waterfall. There's an indescribable silence in a dead man's eyes. Cesare wonders what the last colour he sees will be. Red, he supposes, or black.

He hopes for blue. *The sky. Her eyes.*

MacLeod flicks the safety catch.

Someone cries out – Gino? One of the other men? Or maybe the shout is his own? It is hard to tell – everything is slow, dreamlike.

Cesare closes his eyes and counts. He pictures mountains and olive trees and the arch of a church roof overhead. He pictures a woman with red hair. He thinks of the shape her mouth makes when she says his name.

Another shout, a crash, a flurry of noise. Cesare's

eyes snap open, but he cannot see MacLeod, only a wall of brown uniforms, thin bodies, battered boots.

He realizes that the other prisoners have stood between him and MacLeod, that they are blocking the path of the bullet that the guard would have fired. The bullet that would have found his heart.

And, one by one, the prisoners are dropping their spades and clapping. It is a slow, rhythmic beat, like the marching of a far-off army, but as more of the men join in, the individual claps blur into an ocean of sound, a thunderous roar.

MacLeod is in the centre of the circle of men, his gun still cocked, but pointing at their feet as he spins around, shouting at them. His words are lost in the sea of noise and Cesare stands to join them, cradling his throbbing hand, which is dripping blood down his leg, but he doesn't care, he does not *care*, because, *mio Dio*, just look at the shock on that guard's face! And the prisoners, shouting and clapping – every one of them stands taller. Every one of them seems to have cast off some great weight, some grey cloak that has bowed his shoulders and made him flinch and cringe, but no more, not now.

And more guards are running over now – English guards, with their batons raised. But they freeze at the sight of the wall of prisoners, who are shouting and clapping still.

Cesare looks up to the top of the hill and sees other

groups of Italians stopping their work, throwing down their spades. And perhaps he is imagining it – perhaps he creates the idea later – but it seems that he hears the engines of the lorries cease; it seems that the cranes fall silent. It seems that the very sea holds its breath to listen to these men who have thrown down their spades and cried, *No, we will not dig for you. No, we will not help you fight our countrymen. No, we will not be your animals any longer. No!*

Major Bates marches up and down the line of prisoners shouting, but the men are deaf to the sound. Not one has picked up his spade.

Major Bates's face is puce – he has yelled at MacLeod too, called him a *fool boy* and an *imbecile*, and has sent him up to wait in his office, but still the Italian men won't work. There is an unspoken agreement between them: no matter how much Major Bates roars, no matter his threats, they will not dig.

The major's gaze falls on Cesare.

'You! Come here,' he calls. Then, loud enough for the other men to hear, he says, 'You know I'm a reasonable man. I don't want to threaten you. But you must work. I order it.'

Cesare is aware of all the eyes on him – all his countrymen, it seems. They have had so few letters from home, and those that have arrived have been battered or soaked or torn, or full of small domestic details that fill the men with a painful longing. In this moment it feels to Cesare as though these men *are* his home. They are his country, his safety, his belonging – these men who have been shot at and boiled and frozen along with him, and who all, as one, laid down their spades because it is the right thing to do.

'You must dig,' says Major Bates to Cesare, his voice loud and clear.

'We will not build enemy fortifications,' Cesare says, and as his eyes meet Domingo's, the other man gives a small nod of encouragement. 'It is against the Geneva Convention.'

Major Bates rakes his hands through his hair. His eyes are wide, slightly wild, his voice a little unsteady, when he orders the men to go back to the camp, to stay in their huts.

'There will be no food today, except bread and water. And tomorrow, if you do not work, you will have bread and water. And the day after, bread and water. And you will be confined to your huts until further notice.'

There is some muttering as they walk back to the camp, but all the men march upright, their shoulders thrown back. Cesare walks among them, marvelling: it is like watching them strolling towards the fields on their own land to bring in the harvest.

Cesare's own chest lifts; he breathes more deeply. He forgets entirely about the pain in his hand, about the blood on his trousers, about the heat he can feel, which is like the beginning of a fever and spreads an aching heaviness through his limbs.

So it takes him by surprise when one of the guards, who is holding Marco by the arm, also grabs Cesare and steers them both towards the infirmary.

Dorothy

I am bandaging a man's twisted ankle. Con is standing behind me holding the scissors and pins, passing me each item before I have even held out my hand for it.

'I will marry you after the war,' the prisoner says to Con, and she smiles. Even a week ago, she would have paled at his words and looked at the floor. I take the scissors from her and squeeze her hand briefly. Her colour is better too, her breathing normal, although she still has to rest often. Both of us are eating more, now that we spend most of our time in the camp. We return to the bothy occasionally, but it feels dark without the hole in the roof and, although neither of us says it, I know that Con thinks of Angus every time she looks at those new planks.

I pin the man's bandage.

'I will take you back to Florence,' the man says to

Con. 'I will bring you oranges and grapes every day. And the peaches! You will sit in the sun and eat peaches!'

She shakes her head, still smiling. 'I like the cold.'

He is about to answer when the door flies open. I turn and, for a moment, I think I must have misremembered his features, because Cesare's cheekbones are sharp under his skin and his face is paler than I remember.

But his eyes light when he looks at me. It takes me a moment to notice his hand, which is bloodied, his fingers bent.

'Oh!' I say. 'Oh, God! Come here! I'll get – Sit down!'

Dark patches of blood shine on his brown trousers. I steer him to sit on one of the beds, while Con and Bess take charge of the other man, who looks only half conscious, and is bleeding heavily from his forehead.

'What happened?' I touch each of Cesare's bloodied fingers in turn, bending them a little. He sucks in air through gritted teeth and shakes his head, eyeing the guard, who is watching them both carefully.

I nod to show I understand, and begin dabbing at the cuts on his hand. Some of them are deep and grit-filled and I wince as I wipe the cloth over his skin again and again.

'Sorry,' I whisper.

'Is no hurt,' he says, although his forehead glistens with sweat and his jaw is hard.

I put the back of my hand on his forehead. Burning. He turns his head to one side and coughs. I wince.

'You have the infection too.'

He coughs again, then shakes his head. 'It is nothing,' he murmurs. 'You are not sick? Your sister?'

'She is better.' I smile, nodding at where Con is helping to clean the other Italian's wounds.

'No talking to the prisoner,' the guard snaps. I am about to argue: this rule has never been enforced before. But then Cesare widens his eyes slightly, shakes his head.

There is a gust of air as the door opens again, and another guard appears. The stern-faced guard talks to him, briefly, then nods and comes back into the infirmary.

'You,' he says to Cesare. 'You're to be taken to the Punishment Hut. And you too.' He nods at the other prisoner, who is lolling forwards, barely conscious.

'No!' Con says. 'He needs proper care.' And although she won't meet the guard's eyes, although she's clearly terrified at challenging him, I can see a glimpse of the Con I remember and my heart lifts.

The guard considers for a moment, straightens the collar of his uniform, then turns to Cesare. 'You're still coming with me.'

'For what?' I demand. 'Why?'

I've only just finished bandaging Cesare's fingers, and he cradles his hand. I notice the slight tremor in his arm, the high colour in his cheeks, the sheen on his forehead.

'For inciting a riot and for striking a guard,' the uniformed man replies.

Cesare shakes his head, 'I did not —'

'Enough of that,' the guard says, pulling Cesare to his feet.

'But you can't take him!' I say. 'His hand . . . And I think he has the illness — he's feverish. Listen to his cough.'

The guard eyes Cesare with contempt and turns away. 'Looks like any other Eyetie to me,' he says.

'No!' I reach out to grab at the guard, but Con is there next to me, holding me back.

'Don't, Dot,' she says, her face tight with fear, just as it was in the days after the *Royal Elm* and the poor smothered man. I'd thought that her terror afterwards was for herself: disgust at what she had done. But now, looking at her wide eyes, her pleading expression, I realize that her fear is for me. She wants to protect me.

'Don't,' she pleads again.

'I have to!' I struggle, but she doesn't let go.

'You'll get hurt —'

I push her away. 'Get off me!' I snap.

'But —' She catches at my sleeve, and I feel a surge of frustration: why can't she understand that I'm not the one who needs protecting now? That it's Cesare who's at risk?

She pulls fiercely on my arm and I shove her away, slapping my hands against her shoulder hard – harder than I mean to, propelling her backwards.

She stumbles, her foot catching on the legs of one of the beds. She cries out, steadies herself and stands upright, staring at me. I can't look at her, can't watch her rubbing her shoulder where I'd shoved her. My palms sting.

I turn away from her; I watch Cesare being led from the infirmary, the guard twisting his arm behind his back.

When I look back at Con, she is absolutely still, holding one hand to her cheek as if I'd slapped her full across the face.

I feel a twist of guilt and, to cover it, I make my tone vicious: 'Don't look at me like that. You were grabbing at me and trying to make me do exactly as you wanted. You're always doing that. I'm tired of you hanging off me.' It isn't true, I think, but in that moment, with Cesare being dragged to the Punishment Hut, I don't care.

I walk away from Con, without looking back, to scrub the bloodied clamps and bowls in the sink. Steam from the hot water rises in a cloud around my face, so that I don't have to look at my sister, don't have to see the shock on her face.

I almost turn around to say it: *I'm sorry. I didn't mean to push you, to snap at you.*

But I don't. The water in the sink turns brownish red, then clear and clean. I rattle the metal implements to cover the sound of my breathing, the churning of my thoughts.

There is a gust of chill air and the door bangs, and when I turned around, Con has gone. I have no idea where.

I don't know where she is going. One of the tombs? One of the caves – the bothy? Where will she go?

I don't care, I think savagely.

The thought is strange – like the stomach-lurching moment of walking up a stairway and suddenly finding that one of the steps has crumbled away.

Bess has come back from the mess hut, bringing two sandwiches. She begins sweeping the floor; she avoids my gaze.

'What has happened with the prisoners?' I ask.

She keeps her eyes fixed on the brush. 'There was a riot,' she says quietly. 'They're refusing to work. They're all on rations of bread and water and confined to their huts.'

'But . . . you don't think that prisoner . . . ? They said he *hit* a guard.'

Bess shrugs, continues sweeping. A muscle twitches in her jaw and she won't look at me. 'Where's your sister gone? It's cold out. I think it might snow.'

I put my head out of the infirmary door, where the darkness is dropping, and call, but there is no reply. I sit on one of the beds and wait.

She doesn't return.

I boil a pan of water, stirring some honey into it, and I divide it between two small bottles. I close my eyes, trying to sense where she might be.

Nothing.

After another hour of waiting and pacing, I tuck the bottles of honey and hot water into my pockets and walk out into the clenched air.

A thousand cold stars are stamped into the frozen sky. I look to the north for a glimpse of the Merrie Dancers – those fine ribbons of light that pulse through the sky in winter to remind us that the world around us is a living thing. The night is dark, still, unbreathing.

'Con!' I call. 'Con!'

No answer. The prisoners' huts are all in darkness too. I imagine the men inside, shivering, listening to my voice echoing again and again. Perhaps they will think it's one of the spirits on this island. Perhaps the guards will imagine some transformed selkie, raising her voice to the wind, crying out for her lost mate.

I call again. Again.

No answer.

The door of the Punishment Hut is shut and a guard stands in front of it, his teeth chattering. From inside, I hear coughing.

Cesare.

The wind scrapes my cheeks and I huddle into my coat. When the guard sees me, a shadow moving in the darkness, his hand moves to the gun on his hip. I step into the light from his torch beam and take my handkerchief from my pocket, waving it in mock surrender. I do my best to smile.

He doesn't move his hand from his gun. I take a deep breath and walk towards him, still smiling, still waving the hanky.

'Cold night,' I say.

'You shouldn't be out here.' Close up, I can see how young he is – not much older than me. Perhaps his shivering isn't just from the cold.

'I didn't mean to frighten you,' I say.

'I'm not frightened.' His eyes are wide.

'Of course. I wondered if I could see the prisoner. I'm a nurse here. He's unwell.'

He shakes his head. 'Can't let you. That's a dangerous man in there.'

'He's ill. I want to give him something.'

He tightens his grip on his gun. 'I've got my orders.'

'Please.' I take a step towards him.

'What're you up to?' The guard's eyes flick over my face, and then away.

'Nothing at all,' I say. 'I only want to check on the prisoner.'

'I can't allow that. And you can't frighten me into it.'

'Frighten you? How could I?' I force my smile wider.

He licks his lips nervously.

'You do a fine job with the prisoners,' I say. 'You must be very brave.'

He stands a little taller. 'They don't try anything on. Not with me.'

'Of course not. It's an important job you have, to make all these decisions about what happens to the prisoners. A great deal of responsibility for you.'

He shifts his weight and swallows. 'Aye. Well.'

'I just want to see the prisoner,' I say. 'He's ill.'

'You're planning something.'

'What could I do? I'm only a wee girl. And you're here.'

He hesitates.

'Please,' I say. 'I'll be ever so grateful.'

He shakes his head.

'But he's not well,' I say. 'What if he dies? Because of you. What will you say?'

He sighs. 'Five minutes. No tricks. I've got my eye on you.'

It is pitch black inside. The guard goes in first and shouts, 'On your feet!'

There is a clinking from the back of the hut and then the guard shines his torch on Cesare, who cowers and shields his eyes against the sudden light.

His skin is pale, and when he coughs his breathing has a sea-stone rattle.

'Your cough!' I exclaim. 'Can I look at you?'

He spreads his hands; his chains clink. 'I am prisoner. You can do anything.'

'I must take your pulse, listen to your breathing,' I say. 'I have brought you some honey water. We used to have a hive, in Kirkwall, and I gathered the honey myself . . .' I can hear myself gabbling and am glad of the near-darkness to hide the heat in my cheeks.

I hold out a bottle. His hands are cold – the bandaged one is grubby – and they tremble as he takes the lid from the bottle and sips at the liquid. I put the other bottle on the ground next to him.

'For later.'

'Thank you.' In the dim light from the torch, his eyes are black.

'I need to take your pulse.'

'No tricks now!' the guard warns.

Cesare watches me while I hold his wrist, but the flutter of his pulse is too faint. I unbutton the top of his shirt, my fingers half numb with cold and fear. He stays absolutely still, barely breathing as I press my fingers into his neck. His skin is warm and rough; his pulse gallops under my fingertips. I count the rapid rise and fall of his breath.

He doesn't take his eyes from mine.

'I won't let them keep you in here,' I murmur.

He blinks, then coughs.

'Time's up,' the guard says, and ducks out into the night.

As I turn to follow, Cesare grasps my wrist and pulls me close. My stomach jolts.

Cesare whispers, his words hot and fast in my ear. 'I do not hurt MacLeod. There is no riot. But they say I lie. You must help me.'

Then Cesare releases me and I stand rubbing at my wrists, still feeling the warmth of his breath. He coughs again, his expression pleading.

I walk back to the infirmary with the feeling of his fingers on my wrist still, his words in my ear.

Help me.

I'd forgotten about Con, but there she is, waiting in the infirmary. She is sitting on one of the beds, her cheeks flushed from the cold.

'I'm sorry,' she says, and pulls me in close. 'I just want to keep you safe.'

I nod. I don't ask her where she went. I don't apologize.

Help me.

The infirmary lights are dimmed: all the men are sleeping. Con's hands are freezing. She leads me behind the curtain to our section of the room and, without speaking, we climb into the little bed. I turn my back on her. The sheets are cold and my head aches. I can hear her breathing in the darkness.

She bumps her hip against mine. 'You're taking up too much room.'

I pretend to smile.

She reaches for my hand. *'Take blood and breath and skin and bone.'*

'Take all between these seven stones.'

When we were children, we used to mourn for all the dead fishermen who disappeared in the storms. We'd sneak down onto the beach and say the old rhyme.

We had been warned never to lie down between the point of high and low tide: it was the place that was neither land nor sea, so it belonged to the devil. But we'd heard that you could lie on that piece of sand and place seven stones at seven points on your body and recite the words, and the sea would give back whatever it had stolen. In exchange, it would take part of your soul. It seemed a fair trade to us: our souls in return for all the lives that had been lost.

We had laid the stones on our head, heart, hands, feet and groin and we had chanted the rhyme together:

> *Take blood and breath and flesh and bone.*
> *Take all between these seven stones.*

Now, in the darkness of the infirmary, with those familiar words in my ears, I feel the hairs rise on my neck.

It's a strange question: what would you give up to save a life?

In the soft glow of the moonlight, I look at our hands – so alike that, with our fingers intertwined, even I can't tell whose hand is whose.

'I love you,' Con whispers.

'I love you too,' I say. And it is an odd thing: the words feel hollow, suddenly, but they are as easy to say as any others. As easy to say as, 'I didn't do it,' or 'I'm sorry,' or 'I'm keeping you safe.'

Orcadians

There's a whisper of snow in the air as people trudge up the path to Kirkwall Town Hall. It is late and dark, so most of the women and children are at home, where they have been told to stay because the meeting may be *upsetting*.

Marjorie Croy has come anyway. 'If my children's feet are hardy enough to stand worn-out shoes, then our ears can all cope with whatever's to be said.'

So, she sits in the hall, two children at her sides and one perched on her knees. Her cheeks are pink with cold, her hands folded across her lap. In her face, it's possible to see her daughter Bess's jawline – softened by age, but with the same pugnacious tilt to it.

She and her children sit quietly with the other Orcadians as John O'Farrell and Major Bates walk into the hall.

Everyone sits up: they've seen Major Bates on only

156

one occasion so far, when he came to the island to recruit for the camp, and the general thought, at first, was that he was an odd one: *severe*, they'd thought, and *a cold fish*, although there was increasing talk from some of the guards that he could be kindly too, at times.

Now, at the beginning of March, he looks thinner, older, greyer. Smaller, somehow.

John O'Farrell is thinner too. There's still more grey in his hair, people note.

He stands, looks at Major Bates, who nods encouragement.

John O'Farrell's voice is steady. 'I know there have been some new complaints about the prisoners —'

'It's not complaints *about* the prisoners,' Artair Flett says. 'It's a question of where the bloody hell they've got to —'

'Language!' someone shouts.

'Shit. Sorry.' Artair ducks his head in apology to Marjorie, whose children are wide-eyed and grinning at the expletives.

'I'm in a mither,' Artair says, 'and I'm not the only one. They're good workers, those men, and now I'm told they'll not be helping me? What am I supposed to do with my boundary wall? It's half finished.'

There are murmurs of agreement: Alasdair Neill has a ditch half dug, and Rabbie Firth needs help getting his sheep in.

John O'Farrell holds up his hands for quiet and, gradually, the muttering dies down. 'The prisoners,' he says gravely, 'are on strike.'

'On *strike*?' Rabbie says. 'Is it better wages they're wanting? Or a pension for when they retire?'

Muffled laughter, then Major Bates stands and silence falls.

'The prisoners are unhappy because they believe that their work contravenes the Geneva Convention, which stipulates that prisoners cannot be compelled to construct enemy fortifications.'

A sea of blank stares.

'So,' Major Bates says, 'we have been investigating the possibility that these . . . *boundaries* . . . are not barriers at all. Nothing to do with the war. They are,' he pauses, '*causeways*. Much-needed causeways to link the islands together. Civilian constructions, for use in peacetime. So that you and your families can travel easily between the islands. It's something you've long needed.'

'My arse it is,' someone mutters, and is quickly hushed.

'You need these causeways,' Major Bates says. 'This is a message that I would like to be unanimous.'

Silence.

At last, Rabbie Firth says, 'So . . . if we tell the prisoners they're building *causeways*, they'll come back and help with our work too?'

'Indeed.'

There's a general noise of approval as people rise to leave, but then Marjorie Croy calls, 'What about the treatment of the prisoners? Isn't that the real problem?'

Everyone stops, falls quiet, stares. Marjorie is still in her seat, her children around her, her baby still on her lap, and she repeats, 'What about the way they're kept? I've heard stories from my Bess.'

People sit down again.

'She's working in the infirmary,' Marjorie says, half turning so that everyone can hear her. 'And she says that those prisoners are being beaten. Horribly bruised, some of them. Fed on bread and water, she says. Locked up in the dark, she tells me. Left to starve.'

And as Major Bates tries to shout that this isn't the case, that it's all been blown out of proportion, his voice is drowned in the protests: people on these islands have brothers and sons who have been captured and imprisoned in Germany. Only last month, the radio told them, the Japanese invaded Singapore and took *sixty thousand* British prisoners of war.

'Are we treating these men like animals?' Marjorie calls. And her children, as if they have heard all this before, stare unblinking at the major, like the Fates sitting in judgement.

'Of course not,' he says, flushing. 'Of course not.'

And, as he sits down, John O'Farrell leans across and murmurs, 'News travels fast on these islands. They'll not be having this. These are a people who have their own separate land laws dating back to the thirteenth century and they're a close-knit community. They'll not be having men starved or beaten on one of their islands. It's against their sense of justice –'

'Their sense of justice be damned,' Major Bates says. 'They're not in charge of the camp or the men.'

'True,' John O'Farrell says, 'but we don't want a riot on the main island, as well as in the camp. The people here will only accept so much before they take the law into their own hands. It might be wise to listen to them now.'

PART THREE

How could it be? There was a stifling grove,
Yet here was the light; what wonder led
us to it?

From 'The Grove', Edwin Muir

February 1942

Constance

The day I first consider killing one of the guards is the day I nearly die.

Outside the infirmary it is cold, with darkness dropping like a stone, the sky sudden grey granite, fading to black. I search for the first star, but the bite of the wind makes me close my eyes. I have forgotten my coat but it is too late to go back. My ankle throbs where it caught on the bed and, as I walk, the memory of Dot's words beats out the timing of my steps: *I'm tired of you hanging off me.*

The first star glimmers. I shiver and try to make a wish. But what could I ask? For my sister to see sense? For the Italian men to be swept somehow from the island, or struck down with disease? Or perhaps I could wish for something else. Perhaps I could beg for my own memories to be different.

I run my fingers over the hollow at my throat and count my steps until I can breathe easily, until I can no longer feel the sensation of his hands there.

I feel them in my sleep, his hands. Squeezing.

Sand. Darkness. His breath hot in my ear.

I whirl around. There's no one behind me. He's not here. I'm safe.

Then I stop. The silhouettes of the prisoners' huts loom around me in the darkness and, with the stomach-lurching sense of having missed a step, I realize that I am lost.

Lost in a camp of hundreds of men.

With their muscled arms, their strong hands.

The thought is ridiculous – how can I be lost? But the flimsy huts are a maze. Every one of them identical. Like the faces of the men. I imagine them sitting in those huts. Their hot breath, their broad chests. I imagine the sound of their laughter.

My own breath is tight in my throat, my legs suddenly weak, my vision narrowing. I used to think that the idea of tunnel vision was just that – an idea, a myth. But I remember the way my sight had reduced to a single point, a single face. And the thought I'd had: that this would be the last face I would see.

I stop. I lean against the steel wall of one of the huts, drawing air into my lungs, exhaling slowly, watching the clouds of my breath rising towards the star-scattered sky, then disappearing for ever.

I make myself walk onwards, but I have a constant churning dread in my belly, as though the next step might be empty air. If I can just get to the bothy, I'll be safe and Dot will come to find me. Then I'll be able to explain the danger she's putting herself in. Or perhaps I should walk to Skara Brae – the sunken houses on the coast that are over three thousand years old. If I hid there, it would give Dot a chance to look for me. Perhaps she'd feel the terror of losing me, then. Perhaps she'd understand how I feel. Maybe she'd see sense.

It is fully dark now, but from behind the wall of the hut, I can hear voices talking in a language I don't understand. Every word seems loaded with menace.

The darkness is a physical thing as I force myself to walk past the huts, counting each one, trying to find my way out of the labyrinth. From behind one wall there is soft singing. From another, many voices join in a chant that feels like prayer.

The end of the line of huts, and only the barbed-wire fence in front of me. I squint at the grey silhouettes of my surroundings. I've come the wrong way: the gate is on the other side of the camp.

I turn but a noise stops me. Two of the guards are talking and smoking by the fence. The orange glow of the cigarettes lights their faces. I freeze.

It's him.

Again, my hand finds the hollow at my throat. The place where he once pressed his lips.

I want to turn and run, but I'm afraid they'll hear me, so I stand very still as I watch another man – a prisoner – being led out from one of the huts, about twenty paces away.

The guards toss their cigarettes down, walk up to the Italian and then, before I have a chance to turn away or cover my face, they begin booting him. The man cries out, clutches his stomach, falls to his knees. They pull him upright, mutter something into his ear, and kick him again.

One of them laughs as he kicks the prisoner.

This time, the man doesn't cry out, but with every thud of a boot into his body, the breath wheezes from him. No one comes out of the surrounding huts. No protest or protection from the other prisoners.

Who is this prisoner? Was he part of the riot? The guards' kicks are methodical now, their faces expressionless, bored, as if this is simply something that they do to pass the time.

I remember the men in the infirmary – their bruises, their fear-filled eyes. They are so frightened all the time, like me. The only people who aren't scared are the guards. Is everywhere like this? Is most of the world made up of terrified people, with just a few men sitting on top of everyone else, laughing as they boot us, then growing bored, but kicking us anyway?

I watch, my entire body frozen. On the ground at my feet is a rock. Sharp along one edge and heavy enough to crack bone. Heavy enough to smash through a man's skull. I feel the old fury, the old terror – the same mixture of emotions that have kept me sleepless for so many nights since leaving Kirkwall.

And I feel shame. I let him touch me, at first. I led him on.

Bile rises in my throat. I swallow. My eyes water. I close them, pressing my back against the cold wall, counting my breaths, pretending that the rock isn't there. Pretending that I'm not imagining, time and again, how I could bring the rock down. How I could stop the prisoner's pain.

When I open my eyes, it is over: the prisoner has been dragged back to his hut and the guards are leaning against the wooden fence posts, their faces once more lit by the glow of their cigarettes.

I hear the soft sound of Angus's laughter.

I knew it was him. Of *course* it is him. That laughter raises the hairs on the back of my neck, makes me dry-mouthed, rigid with terror. The sound is engraved into me, is part of me.

I've heard it said that every person has their breaking point, although that seems a strange way of describing how someone may fall into violence. There can be no single point when a person breaks, surely. Rather, a person's patience is like the cloth bandage that holds a wound together: over time, it is rubbed thinner and thinner, until the material is all but worn away. The final threads are simply a mesh over the rawness.

The body is a strange thing. It counts out its own time and rhythms with heart and breath and blinking eyes. All these motions are a struggle towards living, but they might as well be grains of sand tolling out the seconds into the grave.

And the dying is done alone.

The guards are smoking, smiling. The soft sound of their laughter could belong to any man, anywhere. There is no way to tell from a man's face whether he is good or bad. There is nothing in his voice or his smile that will let you know if he plans to kiss you or try to kill you, or both.

I drop the rock and walk backwards. I can't kill a man. I can't do anything but back away and try to forget what I've seen. I retreat into the warren of huts – they are all quiet now. The Italians must have heard the prisoner's cries. Perhaps their nights are full of shouts and screams in the dark. Perhaps each morning a different man wakes with bruises and limps down to the quarry, broken before the day begins.

But their suffering doesn't make them harmless. I must remind myself of that. Even men who seem innocent, who seem gentle and affectionate – even they can hurt you. And if you let yourself feel for them, if you allow them to deceive you, they can destroy you.

I don't choose to run – my feet make the choice for me – but it is freeing to be moving quickly away from the men, away from the guards, away from the huts. I break out into the open yard at the front of the camp and wait for a guard to call to me. We're allowed to leave, of course, Dot and I, but if they see me running, they will ask questions.

But all the guards must be elsewhere because no one shouts at me to stop.

I slow to a walk and stand next to the edge of the fence – the part closest to the cliffs. Below, the pulse of the sea crashing against the stone. It never stops pounding, the water beating itself against the stone. Relentless as a heartbeat.

After I crawl under the fence, it will take three steps. The space. The fall. The silence.

I imagine Dot alone in a camp of a thousand men. I count the exhalation of the waves. Implacable, eternal.

I feel the thread of my life, suspended, waiting for the blade. Three steps forwards will change everything. I can do it, if I want. Just as I could have brought that rock down on the guards' heads.

Only I didn't.

I shiver, tears on my cheeks.

I didn't do anything. I let everything happen around me, as always.

Somewhere, in the darkness, I think I hear Dot's voice crying my name.

I force myself to turn, to walk back in the direction I've come from, to go back to the infirmary.

The lights call to me, leading me back to the warmth of the hospital hut, the medicinal smell, the beds of sleeping prisoners. And Dot.

But Dot isn't there. I check our sectioned-off bed,

the cleaning station, the small office behind the curtain, where Bess is drowsing.

I shake her arm. 'Have you seen Dot?'

She startles awake, focuses her eyes on me. 'You're back. I was worried.'

'Where's Dot?'

'Oh, she went . . .' Bess's eyes slide from mine and, for a moment, I think she's going to say that Dot went looking for me. That she's out in the cold now, searching. How could I have run off like that? How could I have put her in danger?

Bess stands, straightens some of the clamps and surgical knives. 'She went to see the prisoner, I think. She took some honey to Cesare. For his cough.' She turns, sees the fear on my face and misinterprets. 'Con! Oh, Con, she hasn't left you. I'm sure she was worried about you. She waited for you to come back. She even shouted for you. She must have thought you'd gone to the bothy.'

I nod, then turn away, my mind a white blank.

As I look around the infirmary, counting the beat of my blood in my ears, I don't see the prisoners laid out sleeping, peacefully, in their pyjamas. I imagine the hair on their bodies beneath the sheets. I picture their hands, which could so easily turn into fists. I think of muscles in their thighs and backs. And I think of Dot, in the Punishment Hut, holding out a trusting hand to a man she barely knows.

Dorothy

Cesare looks smaller when they bring him out of the Punishment Hut after nearly a week. He is filthy, his skin yellowish. When he coughs, I can see the tendons drawn tight in his neck, as if every part of him is struggling for air.

But the sound of his breathing – laboured though it is – fills me with light. *He's alive! He's alive!*

I'd petitioned Major Bates daily during the six days that Cesare had been imprisoned. 'It's cruel,' I had said. 'He's ill.'

Major Bates had shuffled his papers. 'It's not that simple.'

But, in the end, it was. Bess had spoken to her mother in Kirkwall, then bounced into the infirmary one morning, her face bright.

'There's been a meeting. People on the island aren't happy with the prisoners being mistreated.' She'd grinned at me, and I'd tried to share her excitement but found it hard to believe that there had been any sort of protest on the behalf of foreign prisoners.

Still, early the next morning, there was a crowd of guards stamping around the Punishment Hut, looking nervous and resentful, as if expecting a repeat of the riot – although Angus MacLeod wasn't among them.

And now here Cesare is. Coughing, stumbling, but alive.

He chokes, falters, falls. The guards pull him upright again by his arms and he gives a grunt of pain.

'Let go of him!' I call. The guards ignore me, their heavy boots thudding along the path. I follow them up to the infirmary, making a list of the things he will need. Honey, water and sulfa tablets for the infection. Some sort of soup or broth. Perhaps Con can fetch that from the mess.

Con. As if I've spoken her name aloud, she is there, next to me, watching me. Her arms are folded across her chest, her mouth pressed into a thin line.

Don't say anything, I beg her silently. She doesn't, but I can feel her judgement like a cold breeze icing my skin.

They take Cesare into the infirmary and lay him on a bed, where I try to make him drink some water, but he is coughing too much to swallow; his skin is hot and dry, like parchment ready for the fire. I wave the guards away, then sit and wipe a wet sponge over his head and arms and chest to bring his fever down. Under my hand, I can feel the flutter of his heartbeat in its cage, a trapped bird panicking.

Angus MacLeod walks into the infirmary. He stares at Cesare, then at me, his face set in a sneer. 'No firing squad needed. Well done – you've made his death slow and painful.'

I want to launch myself at him, but Con is suddenly there, her hand on my shoulder. I can feel her trembling.

His face softens when he looks at her.

She speaks fast and low. 'Are you looking to have that cut on your head opened up again, Angus?'

He slams the door as he leaves.

Con squeezes my shoulder. 'You don't know this prisoner, not really. He might be –'

I pull away. There is no point in trying to explain anything to her. All I know is that, from the first moment I saw Cesare, from the first moment he smiled, I felt as if I'd always known him and he me. But to say such a thing to Con would have invited mockery or jealousy, and I know it sounds ridiculous – like something from a story: Ferdinand and Miranda in *The Tempest*, or Lancelot and Guinevere, Romeo and Juliet.

'He's not like Angus,' I say. Meaning, also, *I'm not like you.*

Con is still pressing my hand against her cheek, but she stops and stares at me, her eyes wide.

'*What?*' I snap, regretting my tone instantly, as she recoils.

'You don't understand anything.' She drops my hand and stalks from the infirmary.

I don't follow her, though she will want me to. I stay with Cesare, sponging his chest and holding a glass of warm honey water to his lips.

I sleep on the floor next to his bed that night, waking every hour to drip more water from my fingers into his mouth. I can't get enough of it into him: when I try tipping the glass against his lips, the water dribbles down his chin. I think about the lambs and how, when we want them to swallow medicine, we syringe it into their mouths and massage their throats. I climb onto the bed and lie alongside him. It is nearly dark, just the dim, buttery glow from the single lamp in the corner of the room. All the other prisoners are sleeping. Cesare's body is scorching against mine and, as I press against him, I can feel the ridges of his ribs, the hinge of his hips. I can imagine the delicate silk of his lungs expanding, struggling, contracting. When I touch him, his breathing steadies.

I make sure the other prisoners are still sleeping, then take a mouthful of the honey water and press my lips against his. His mouth is hot and dry. I drip the liquid into his mouth from mine, stroking his throat until he swallows. His lips are burning; he tastes metallic and sour. I press my mouth to his again and again, until the glass is empty. Then I sleep, my head resting on the bony hollow next to his shoulder.

It seems only minutes later that Con wakes me by shaking my arm roughly. Her jaw is hard and her eyes blaze.

'Get up! What are you thinking?' She grabs my hand and yanks me upright, but my muscles are leaden and I can't find the strength to stand. I slump against her; she puts a hand to my forehead and curses softly.

'Idiot,' she murmurs, then puts me into the bed alongside Cesare's.

Time bleeds into itself. I try to stay awake, but my eyes keep closing. One moment it is light and the next it is the middle of the night. Every time I open my eyes, Con is there: sponging my forehead, bringing me water, spooning honey into my mouth.

Occasionally I hear her muttering to herself. I'm aware of her gaze on me. Her fear is almost palpable. She rests her head on the pillow next to mine, strokes my hair, kisses my cheek.

'You'll get ill,' I protest.

'I don't care.'

She tends Cesare too. Sometimes I wake to find her gazing at him, watching him breathe; it gives me some relief to know that she wants him to live – why else would she stare at him so?

After an endless stretch of nightmarish light and dark, my fever fades. I wake with a clear head. Con is gone but Cesare is looking at me from the next bed. I try to speak but only a wheeze emerges.

He smiles. 'I think you are angel but you sound like my grandfather.'

I laugh, then cough. 'You are better.' I feel foolish for saying what is obvious.

His face is serious. 'You save me.'

My cheeks heat and I want to hide my face.

'Look at me,' he whispers.

I turn my face towards his. There is intimacy in this, lying down together, within arms' reach.

'I remember . . .' He touches his lips.

Then Con walks in. She stops in the doorway, staring at us. She looks as though she might be sick.

She doesn't return my smile. The lamp casts ghastly shadows on her face and, for a moment, she seems menacing, monstrous. Before I can call to her, she turns and stumbles from the room.

Cesare

It is heat that brings him back to himself. Heat and cold. The heat from Dorotea's body near his, as if she is a lamp held up close to his warming skin. As she drips water into his mouth, something inside him thaws. Everywhere that she doesn't touch is icy, numb, dead.

When he wakes fully, it is as if everything during his fever was a dream – had she really touched her mouth to his? What does this mean? What does he want from her, this foreign woman on this strange island? His mind feels fogged and fuzzy. He drinks and dozes. Gradually, his strength returns.

She recovers from her illness more quickly than he does – the work in the quarry has weakened him.

Once she can walk and move around more easily, she sits by his bed and reads the newspaper to him.

He sees her sister too. Costanza – Con. Her name means steadfastness, but also obstinacy. Her face is more serious than Dorotea's, and she is always watching. If she were a man, Cesare would think that she meant him harm. It is not aggressive, her stare, but it is suspicious. Something about her reminds him of the wary cat in Moena's church: it used to sit above the pews like a gargoyle, glowering, its tail twitching. Sometimes it pounced – Cesare still has the scars on his wrist.

Now Cesare pretends to doze, while Dorotea flicks through the newspaper, recounting stories about war meetings in London and about the movements of the round-faced British prime minister. Her voice, when she reads, is clear as a struck bell. Her red hair falls over her face. The other men lean in to listen too, the whole infirmary quiet while Dorotea tells them everything that is happening in the war.

Occasionally, her eyes skim over an article, her lips compress, and she turns the page, before beginning to read again. The second time she does this, Cesare sits up.

'What is this story?'

'Churchill is meeting –'

'No. The story on the first page. You are not reading to me, I think.'

She looks down at her feet and gives an almost imperceptible shudder. He waits, suddenly fearing what she will say. Her eyes are bright with unshed tears.

'Bombs?' he asks, his voice no more than a whisper. The other men must have heard it too, because a silence falls over the rest of the infirmary. Every man holding his breath.

'Moena?' he asks.

'It . . . it doesn't say here. It says . . . forgive me. It says, *successful attack*. And it mentions Milan. Is that near your home? Your . . .' she swallows '. . . your family?'

He shakes his head and closes his eyes, feeling a rush of relief, and then is sickened by it: if his family is safe, then another man's loved ones will be dead. There will be at least one prisoner in this camp with family in Milan.

There is muffled sobbing from the corner and he looks over to see the man in the far bed with his sheet pulled over his face, his shoulders shaking.

Cesare's thoughts are suddenly back in the desert: the bleached sky, the circling vultures, the explosions and fire. The coppery smell of blood that was impossible to forget. And he thinks, too, about the quarry. About the endless sea, the brutal guards and the barrier they are building for the enemy.

Madonna Santa.

178

He's sick of all of it. He can't even begin to listen to Dorotea again, though he can feel her watching him, waiting. But how can he lie in a bed, hearing war tales as though they're entertainment? How can he listen to this foreign woman talking about a *successful attack* on his people?

'I am tired,' he says, trying not to care when Dorotea's face falls, when she winces as though he's snapped at her. Perhaps he has. Perhaps that doesn't matter when, somewhere, everywhere, people are dying.

He turns his face to the wall, pulling up the covers, over his shoulders, over his head so that he re-breathes his own panicked exhalations in a white tent, which cuts off the rest of the world, which cuts off Dorotea. As he hears her rise and turn to leave, her sister, Con, says to her, 'I *said* you should stay away from him, that –'

'Enough!' Dorotea's voice is sharp. He hears the door open. A freezing breeze scours the infirmary, and then there is stillness, apart from the low whispers of the other men, and the quiet weeping from the bed in the corner.

Later, the sound of movement wakes him. He opens his eyes, still facing the wall, but he knows it is her: he knows it from the sound of her breathing, from the smell of woodsmoke that she often carries with her, as if she's not had long to warm herself properly and has stood, very briefly, too close to the fire.

He can't bring himself to turn, to look at her. He feels ashamed of the way he'd shunned her, the way he'd blamed her for simply delivering the news. The war isn't her fault. She isn't the enemy.

Who is the enemy now? He isn't sure he knows.

He watches her shadow on the wall, watches her reach out a hand, as if to touch him, then sees her withdraw it. He tries to keep his breathing steady, but on each outbreath he thinks, *Please, please, please.*

Finally she touches him. Not on his shoulder, where the sheet covers him: she places two cool fingers on his bare neck. Skin on skin.

He stirs; he turns.

On her face, a tremulous smile. 'I talked to Major Bates. I told him that you – that all of you – must hear news from Italy. I said you should have a companion to read your letters from home. One of the other men to read the Italian. I said – forgive me, but I had to convince him – I said that many of the prisoners probably couldn't read.'

Cesare sits up, with effort. 'He knows I read. What did he say?'

'He said . . . well, he said a lot of things. I think he feels guilty about what has happened.' She looks down at her hands, then glances back at him. 'And he has agreed, as long as there are other guards here to make sure there is no trouble.' She shifts uncomfortably as she says this, but he nods in quick agreement.

'*Sì*. There are many guards after . . .'

'After the riot, yes. Fifty more.'

'Sixty,' says a voice from the shadows, and Cesare jumps. He hadn't realized that Con was standing there. He can't see her face, but her voice is hard. 'There are *sixty* more men on the island.'

'So,' Dorotea leans forward, 'I asked for a man from your hut, Gino, to read some letters to you, and to the other men. He is allowed to come in the evenings. A guard is bringing him now.'

Cesare sits up, just as the door opens and Gino is there, walking behind a stern-faced guard, carrying a pile of letters and grinning. 'You look terrible,' he says to Cesare in Italian.

'English only,' the guard snaps.

Dorotea flashes Cesare a quick smile and then, before he can thank her, she goes to tend the other prisoners. Her sister follows her, like a shadow.

Gino sits in the chair next to Cesare's bed, opens one of the letters and says, '*Mio caro*,' at the same time as the guard says, 'In English, you Italian pig. I've told you.'

Still smiling, Gino turns, and says to the guard, '*Il mio inglese è molto buono.*'

'What's he saying?' The guard glares at Cesare.

'*Stronzo.*' Gino's smile doesn't falter as he says *arsehole*.

'His English is very not good,' Cesare says, although he knows Gino speaks English well. 'He must read this letter for me in Italian.'

'You can't read your own language but you can speak English? That doesn't sound right.'

Cesare shrugs. 'My village is small. I learn English when I help the priest in the church. No time for reading.'

The look the guard gives him is the same expression he's seen on the faces of dozens of other guards: it says, *You are stupid, you are worthless, you are an animal.*

Cesare swallows the rage he feels, then nods at Gino to continue.

'*Mio caro*,' Gino begins again, and then, squinting at the paper as if he is reading the letter, he says, in Italian, 'There has been trouble in the camp. No one would work for a long time and we were fed bread and water. Then the major told us that we were working on *causeways*, not barriers, and that these *causeways* are needed for the islanders in peacetime, so are not part of the war effort.'

'*Stronzate!*' Cesare curses.

'English from you!' the guard says.

'Sorry. The letter is bad news.'

Gino continues in Italian, still studying the letter. 'Some men have started working on these "causeways". Those who won't work are still being given only bread and water. The guards are making them stand all day in the yard in the cold. If we don't do something, then more of us will be ill.'

Cesare struggles to keep his face smooth. The

guard is watching them closely. He finds himself gripping the sheets and forces his hands to relax, his jaw
to unclench, and makes himself nod, sadly, as if he
has heard some unhappy news from home.

He looks at the window, where a lamp casts a sickly
yellowish light on the flakes of snow being whipped
through the air. Something cold writhes in his gut. He
has never been a violent man but slowly, in this place,
he is beginning to understand why some men hoard
scraps of steel that they sharpen until the jagged edges
gleam. He is beginning to understand why, over time,
a man might start to lash out, or might plan something brutal and final.

The sudden comprehension – hot and shameful –
frightens him.

He draws a deep breath. 'We must do something.'

After Gino has moved on to 'read letters' to the
other men – giving them the same news, Cesare
guesses, from the outraged whispers, the shocked
faces – Cesare lies back, his thoughts whirling, as if
some explosion is readying itself inside his skull. The
anger feels like a return of the fever: first he is too
warm; then he shivers. His hands are bunched into
shaking fists.

To calm himself, he thinks of home. He imagines
the green sweep of the mountains, the little houses
crammed as closely as teeth, one garden spilling into
another. Women swept each other's doorsteps, looked

after each other's children. Everyone shared bread, meals, stories. And at the beating heart of the little village, with the bell pulsing out its passing hours, was the church. Cesare remembers the comforting hum of the priest's words, the gleaming censers casting smoke heavenwards, the touch of the holy man's fingers on his forehead as the Communion bread melted on his tongue.

Nel nome del Padre, del Figlio e dello Spirito Santo.

And he remembers the paintings that stretched over the ceiling, so that everywhere was brimming with life. He remembers the church swelling with the music of joined voices. The peace on the faces of those he loved. The hope.

He inhales deeply, filling his chest with a resounding longing for home. It echoes through his limbs, leaves him trembling, on the verge of tears.

When he opens his eyes, he has decided: they must build a church on this island.

March 1942

Orcadians

It is Robert MacRae who first hears from Angus MacLeod that the prisoners are to build a chapel – a *Catholic* chapel – on Selkie Holm.

They're drinking ale in the pub in Kirkwall, hunched over their pints in the corner, listening to the rain and wind batter the blacked-out windows.

'What do they need a chapel for?' Robert asks, sipping his pint. 'Isn't God everywhere?'

'Exactly,' Angus says. 'I tried telling Major Bates it was a bloody cheek that they're demanding a special place to pray.'

'Well, at least that will stop them from trying to sneak into the church in Kirkwall. Neil MacClenny said he saw two of them trying to get into the church when they were supposed to be digging a ditch.'

'Maybe. But still, it's not right, is it? Foreigners building something on our land. I told Major Bates that people on the island wouldn't like it, that the prisoners are here to work, not to spend their time building their own church in a place that doesn't belong to them.'

'What did he say?'

Angus stares moodily into his pint. The major had shouted that Angus was a jumped-up little worm who couldn't find his way out of a wet paper bag and he should stop interfering when he'd caused enough bloody trouble already. *All of this mess is your fault. I should have you sent off to fight and die in Africa, but I suppose you've got some medical exemption or other. What's it for – stupidity?*

'He told me to mind my own business,' Angus says.

'Who does he think he is?' Robert demands. 'The English are arseholes, I tell you. How does Major Bates think they'll get the materials for building a church? Going to ship everything in, is he? Because I'm sure the German U-boats in the North Sea need some target practice.'

'He's using two of the old metal huts and some left-over materials from the barriers –'

'The *causeways.*'

'Aye.' Angus smiles. 'The causeways. And they're going to use scraps of metal and the like. He seems to think that some of the prisoners will be able to work with metal. He's going to let them have a workshop with a furnace. Can you imagine? Think what weapons they could make in there. I told him it'll only be a matter of time before a guard gets used as a pincushion. Those prisoners are angry – there's a lot of rage for them to let loose.'

'You're right! What did he say?'

Major Bates had raised his eyebrows at Angus and asked if he was offering himself as a fucking pincushion.

Now Angus says, 'He didn't agree with me.'

'Well, he's a fool. From everything you've told me, that island is a powder keg.'

Angus nods and, without thinking, he rubs at the irregular semicircular scar that stretches over his wrist. The skin is smooth, now, and numb, but sometimes, when the sunlight catches it, it shines and he's certain he can still feel the warmth of her breath.

Robert watches Angus and, very quietly, says, 'Have you spoken to her?'

'Not for a while.' Angus stands up so suddenly that the chair falls over. The other men in the bar freeze, but don't dare to look over. Best to turn the other way when Angus is in this sort of mood.

Angus downs his pint, bangs his glass onto the table, then stalks from the bar, leaving his chair on the floor and the door wide open to the biting cold and rain.

March 1942

Constance

The mist is massing thickly on the hills when the last lorry clanks past the infirmary, delivering supplies up the hill for the new chapel.

'It'll blow away in the first storm,' I say to Dot. 'Won't it?'

There is no answer, and when I turn, Dot isn't behind me – I'm so in the habit of speaking to her that I'd forgotten she isn't there. I haven't seen her all morning and I'm starting to worry.

I search behind the curtain in the infirmary: our bed is neatly made and bare. Her boots are gone. I walk past the lines of beds, aware of the men's eyes following me. None of them calls but, still, their gaze feels like something heavy pressing on my skin. I keep my head down.

The bed that had been Cesare's is empty too – he was sent back to his hut yesterday evening, still coughing, but without the fever. He had recovered so quickly, after he'd spoken to Major Bates about the chapel. Every time I saw him, he seemed stronger, his limbs filling out, his eyes brightening. He and Dot had sat late into the night whispering. She had laughed and leaned forward over his bed. I had watched from behind the curtain as her hair fell across his face. I had watched him reach out and gather it in his hand, twisting it into a long red rope. My breath had stopped in my chest. I'd imagined him winding that rope of hair around her throat, or yanking on it to pull her in closer.

I stepped forward.

He'd looped her hair over her shoulder and released it so that it spilled down her back. She'd tucked it behind her ear and smiled at him.

Still, the fear swelled like a balloon beneath my ribs. He's pretending – I *know* he is. All the prisoners are play-acting the role of polite gentlemen, but it is a shabby costume. I know how a man can pretend to be affectionate and concerned when he wants something. I know how warmth can deceive.

Now I can't find Dot, the mist is closing in and there are a thousand men on this island, not to mention the cliffs. Not to mention the curse.

I push my face up to the infirmary window, but all I can see is the greyish churn of the fog, pressing against the cold glass like some slick-backed beast.

It's a ridiculous curse, the one they say is on this island. That if two people fall in love here, someone will die. I tell myself it's a story, a foolish superstition. But that doesn't stop the sick twisting in my stomach, and the thought that I cannot escape: the story tells us that *someone* will die, but it doesn't say who. A lover, it says, but which one?

I hear soft footsteps behind me and turn suddenly to find Bess behind me, her eyes wide as if she is frightened of me. I must, I realize, look half wild. I smooth my hair and press my mouth into a smile. 'Have you seen Dot?' I try to keep my voice level.

'No, I . . . Not since I heard you . . . *talking* to her last night about the chapel.'

'Thank you,' I say, turning away, bundling myself into my coat, my scarf.

'You can't go out in this,' Bess says.

'I have to find her.'

'But the cliffs!' Bess voice rises in pitch. 'Con, it's not safe.'

She grabs my arm but I brush her off.

The men are sitting up in their hospital beds, watching me, talking to each other in a rapid patter of Italian. What are they saying? What are they planning? I dig my hands into my coat pockets and push my shoulder against the door. Gasping at the cold air, I call Dot's name.

The mist swirls around me, swallowing the sound. It's like shouting with a cloth pressed over my face. Suffocating.

For a moment, the memory of his hand covering my mouth, and how small my smothered scream had sounded.

What if he's waiting out there for me?

I close my eyes against the nausea. I dig my nails into my palms. 'No time for this, Con,' I say aloud, to myself, to the mist, to whatever creature or human may be listening.

I make myself walk, counting my steps. I can see perhaps two paces in front of me, but any further is a swirling grey blur.

I set off in the direction of the bothy – it is up the hill from the camp, so I know I am walking away from the cliffs. Dot and I have rarely been back to the bothy – when I asked if we might return there, away from the camp, she'd shaken her head. At first, when I was ill, she'd said I needed to be near to the infirmary. Once I was better, she still insisted that we stayed. We both knew why, although neither of us said it.

In the back of my mind, as I walk, is the fear of Dot returning to the bothy alone and discovering the necklace I'd hidden in a gap between the bricks in the fireplace. I imagine her questions – how would I answer them? How can I lie to her? My cheeks burn and my pulse quickens at the thought.

A gust of wind, and the mist clears for a moment. Ahead of me, I catch sight of a dim shadow, a figure moving quickly up the hill.

'Dot!' I shout, into the mist. The figure doesn't stop – if anything it moves faster, then disappears as the fog regroups.

'Dot!' I call again. And I can hear footsteps now, fading, as if someone is fleeing from me.

I begin to jog, blinking against the damp air, then stretching my eyes wide, but it's useless. I can't see or hear anything. I run faster, wishing she'd stop.

She must be thinking of the argument we'd had last night, when she'd told me about the chapel. For two weeks, after Dot had helped Cesare across to Major Bates's office, I'd known something was wrong. The prisoners all seemed suddenly excited, and Dot often talked to Cesare in whispers, both of them laughing. He made quick, expansive gestures with his hands, and I watched, thinking how strong they looked, how easily they could crush her.

'What's he telling you?' I'd asked her, time and again. But she wouldn't say.

Finally, last night, Bess and I had been sweeping the infirmary when we'd watched a lorry drive past, loaded with sheets of metal and skeins of wire, followed by another two lorries, each carrying a metal hut.

'What are they doing?' I asked Bess, expecting her to be as baffled as I was.

'Oh,' she said casually, hardly looking up, 'that'll be for the chapel.'

'The what?'

She stopped sweeping. 'Didn't Dot mention it?'

I waited until the evening, until the curtain was drawn around our little sleeping area.

'When were you going to tell me that the men are planning to build a chapel?' I demanded.

'I thought you knew.' Dot's eyes slid from mine.

Behind the curtain, one of the men coughed.

'So, they're staying here, are they? They're living on the island.'

'I don't know, Con.' Her voice was soft and she held out her hands. 'What's the harm if they are –'

'You don't see it, do you? Or else you see it and you're pretending not to. As long as *he* is here, you'll be happy.'

Dot stepped back, her expression suddenly cold. 'I don't know what you mean.'

'You know exactly what I mean.'

I watched the movement of her throat as she swallowed. If I closed my eyes, I could imagine his hand around my neck. So many times since that day last summer I'd looked in the mirror and traced the invisible outline of each of his fingerprints. He hadn't squeezed hard at first. He'd been so tender when he gave me the necklace – he'd told me he loved me.

I blinked, to bring myself back to the infirmary. 'You can't trust Cesare. You don't know him. You don't know what he might do.'

'I'm not *you*,' she said.

And I knew what she meant: that she wasn't naive, that she wasn't allowing herself to be deceived. That she wouldn't be foolish enough or weak enough to get herself into trouble. I knew she meant that she believed nothing bad would happen to her. I knew she meant that she wouldn't blame herself if it did.

I sat on the bed, closing my eyes. My face felt rigid. Ice in my veins. I pulled my legs up and hugged them, as though I could close myself off somehow. I imagined myself inside a shell. Some creature that is soft and unformed, protected by an armoured carapace. But still I felt the tears on my cheeks.

Dot put her arms around me but I stayed rigid. After some time, I lay down. I could feel her watching me but I said nothing. And, as so often over the past months, at the last moment before I fell asleep, I remembered again the feeling of pushing my coat down over the sailor's face. And I knew that I must be a monster to do such a thing. That I must be a monster to long for that for myself sometimes. The peace, the silence.

In the morning, when I woke, Dot was gone.

'Dot!' I cry now, into the blank, faceless mist on the cold hillside. She will hear me; she will turn; she will run back to me. 'Dot!'

And then my foot catches on a dip in the land and I fall, my ankle twisting, my hands smacking painfully against the rocky ground.

I lie there for a moment, stunned. The mist eddies around me in a silent blanket, no noise except my own sobbing breaths. No movement apart from the rise and fall of my chest.

She's gone.

Pain scythes through my ankle when I stand and, though each step is agony, I continue up the hill, limping and, when the pain gets too much, crawling. My hands are ripped by stones and gorse bushes and, through the thin material of my trousers, I can feel my knees throbbing with a warm wetness that must be blood.

I can't leave her out here.

And then I see a shape moving in the mist. A man. A man, walking towards me. And I know who it is.

He's found me. And we're out here alone. In the fog, no one will hear me cry out. No one will hear me scream.

I stay very still, my body frozen, my face pressed against the cold, damp ground. My breath is tight in my chest, as if something is pressing down on my airway. As if fingers are digging into my windpipe.

And I know that I was foolish ever to leave the bothy at all, foolish to think that I could work in the infirmary, that I could be anywhere near Angus without putting myself in danger.

If I can just stay still, perhaps he won't see me.

I open one eye, then the other.

Stillness, except for the swirling mist. And silence. No sign of the figure in the mist. It wasn't my imagination – I *saw* him, I'm sure of it. And perhaps he's out here, searching for me still.

Gradually, I make my limbs move. I manage to

push myself upright, to crouch and then to crawl forward. Slowly. The rocks dig into my knees. I wince and struggle to my feet, still breathless, still waiting to feel his hand on my shoulder, his fist in my hair.

I walk forward quietly, moving up the hill. Away from the camp, away from the infirmary. Away from the men.

At last, I see a building rearing out of the mist. At first it is distorted by the vortices of whirling cloud, but then it resolves itself into home. Our home. The bothy. The place where I know we're safe.

Before our parents left, before everything with Angus, I used to feel like that about returning to the blue house in Kirkwall – even the sight of it was warmth.

Some tension in my gut uncoils and I drag myself over the doorstep, calling Dot's name, wanting to throw my arms around her, to apologize, to tell her that all I want is for her to be safe.

But the bothy is empty, the fireplace cold. The bed hasn't been slept in.

With a sob, I turn back to face the blank rectangle of mist in the doorway and I shout her name again and again, the sound disappearing into the mist.

There is no reply.

Dorothy

The mist has cleared and it's almost dark when I reach the bothy. My throat is raw from shouting for Con.

My legs ache and my stomach clenches around itself. I've eaten nothing all day. Instead I walked along the beaches and, with my heart in my mouth, I stared into the beating water beneath the cliffs, searching for her pale skin, her red hair.

In the end, I'd returned to the bothy, although I doubt she will come back here as I know the roof reminds her of Angus.

The bothy looks gloomy and skeletal in the dusk, almost as if it is years into the future, after Con and I have gone and the land is rising to reclaim our abandoned home. But as I reach the door, the shadows resolve themselves into the solid shape of the place we left some weeks ago.

My lamp casts shivering shadows on the pockmarked walls. The little table is bare. The stove, when I touch it, is cold. She hasn't been here.

As I turn to leave, I hear a sound. Something like an exhalation from the corner of the room. I wheel around, the lamp swaying in my hands, so that the light flickers and almost dies.

The blanket on the bed is moving.

And I think of the curse on this island, the stories that Con has always been so ready to believe: the talk of dead lovers and restless ghosts and desolate spirits. I think of the Nuckelavee: the skinless monster, half man, half horse, that is said to crawl from the sea, ready to exhale madness and disease.

The blanket shifts and writhes, then sits upright. And, in the shaking lamplight, the monster turns into Con.

'Dot! You're safe!'

'God, Con, you terrified me! What were you thinking, running off like that?'

She rubs her eyes, which look swollen, as if she has been weeping. 'I was looking for you. Where were you?'

'I went to check on some of the patients in their huts.'

Con's gaze hardens and, despite myself, I can feel my heart beating faster, can feel the anxiety, the shame. I had left the infirmary early that morning, while Con was still sleeping. The guards on duty were used to seeing me walk around the camp, so no one stopped me when I approached Cesare's hut. I paused outside the door, hearing movement within. What if the men were getting dressed? And what would they think, finding me outside the hut before first light, asking for Cesare?

Just as I turned to go, the door to the hut opened and one of the men emerged. He saw me, jumped, exclaimed something in Italian, then said, *'Scusi!'*

I held up the bottle of sulfa tablets I had taken from the infirmary. 'Is Cesare here?' I felt ridiculous – what had I been thinking?

But then the man called behind him and, suddenly, Cesare was there, smiling.

'Dorotea. You are well?'

'Yes, I brought . . .' I held up the sulfa tablets again.

'Thank you, but I am not needing. I am better.'

'Oh. Good.'

I could see the men behind him glancing at each other and grinning, and I felt my cheeks heating.

'You are good nurse,' said Cesare.

'Thank you.'

One of the men muttered something in Italian. Cesare snapped a reply and glared at him.

Oh, Lord, what are they saying?

'I must go,' I said. 'I'm glad you are better –'

'The huts are here for building the chapel,' he said, his face bright. 'They are on the hill, I think. You will see them with me?'

'Now? But –'

'Major Bates is letting me see them. He tells the guards to let me see the huts, work on them. We can go now. No hurt, you will see.'

I tried to return his smile. I couldn't say no – I didn't want to – and yet I was aware of the whispering, grinning men behind Cesare, and what they would think. And I was aware of the guards, who would see me walk out of the camp with a prisoner. However much freedom Major Bates, in his guilt, was allowing them, it wouldn't change what the guards would say to each other.

I thought of Con – all the rumours that had started about her. The lewd jokes that were shouted at her in the street before we left Kirkwall.

Cesare watched me, his expression more serious. 'You do not want? You can tell me this.' But something in his face was closing down, as if he'd had a new thought about me, as if I had disappointed him.

'No!' I said. 'I can come with you.'

Now, as I watch the same expression of disappointment on Con's face, I know I can't tell her that I walked out of the camp gates, with Cesare at my side. I can't tell her that I walked up the hill with a strange man, a foreigner, and that, as we walked, the mist began to close around us.

So I say, 'I took medicine for Cesare. And when I got back to the infirmary you were gone. I've been looking for you ever since.' All of this is true, in some way.

'Oh,' she says, and I can see she doesn't believe me. Then she says, 'I think we should come back and live here, in the bothy.' She raises her chin, and there's a defiant set to her mouth.

The lamp flickers; the shadows on the walls shift.

'All right,' I say. 'You want to stay now? Won't Bess wonder where we are?'

'We can go back down to the camp tomorrow.' Con is still watching me, and I know that if I object she'll fire question after question that I cannot answer. I know she'll demand to be told where I really was this morning.

I can't tell her that, as I walked up the hill with Cesare, our footsteps were in time. I can't tell her the joy I felt at seeing him happily tell me about the men's excitement over the chapel. I can't tell her that the mist grew dense around us and we never reached the huts. I can't tell her that I was confused suddenly, that I didn't know which way to turn.

'I'm lost,' I'd said, feeling fear well in me and clutch at my throat. I didn't know if I was frightened of this man, this stranger, or if it was the simple terror of being disoriented. I didn't know if I was scared because – because I *wanted* to be lost with him. I wanted . . . something I couldn't name. And the wanting travelled through me like fire.

Then, with the fog blanketing our eyes and filling our lungs, Cesare had reached out and taken my hand.

'Stop,' he'd said. And he laced his fingers through mine.

I turned to face him. Tendrils of mist spiralled between us.

'You are frightened?' he asked softly.

I nodded, unable to speak past the fear.

'I am frightened also,' he whispered.

We stood like that for some time while the mist shifted around us, while the waves throbbed on the distant beach, while my own pulse vibrated in my ears. I was aware of the warmth of his hands, their size, their strength.

He squeezed my fingers gently and said, 'We must go back to the camp.'

I nodded.

'It is down the hill?'

I nodded again. We turned and began walking slowly back in the direction of where the camp must have been. Neither of us said anything. He kept hold of my hand and, very gently, he rubbed his thumb over my knuckles.

Finally, the shape of the wire fence and the shadow of the guard on the gate emerged from the mist.

'There,' I said.

Cesare still didn't let go. Only at the very last minute, just before the guard saw us and called out for us to identify ourselves, did he give my fingers a final squeeze, then let my hand fall back to my side.

Before he walked to his hut, he said, 'We will see the chapel hut another day, Dorotea?'

I had walked back to the infirmary, my hand warm from his.

Now, as I build a fire in the bothy with Con, I can still feel his fingers through mine.

I am frightened also, he had said.

Con places the last piece of wood in the grate and leans forward to light the match. As she does so, I see a flash of gold at her neck.

'What is that?'

'What? Oh!' Her hand flies to her throat and she pulls up her jumper so that the gold chain she is wearing is entirely hidden.

We stand, looking at one another. A dry log shifts in the growing flames. It is hard to tell whether the colour in Con's cheeks is from the sudden heat or something else.

'It's nothing,' she finally says. 'I must get another log for the fire.'

She pushes past me, out of the bothy, and I hear her footsteps going around the side of the building, past the woodpile. Where on earth could she have got a necklace? It doesn't look like anything our mother would have left behind – she was never one for jewellery, and we sold the rings she had left long ago, during that first hard winter. Could Con have found the necklace somewhere, perhaps, or – and this is a troubling thought – could she have stolen it? I don't recognize it, but I do know the expression on Con's face. It's the look she used to wear after shouting at our parents. It's the expression she wore when she returned to the blue Kirkwall house last year, with her skirt torn and livid marks on her neck.

Shame.

There is a scrape against the wall, and I can imagine her, leaning her back against it, looking out into the swelling darkness.

I place my hand against the wall where she must be standing on the other side. I close my eyes, willing some peace, some calm, to pass through the thin layer of plaster and brick.

When Con returns to the bothy, some minutes later, she isn't carrying a log for the fire. She walks past me and begins undressing for bed. I watch, from the corner of my eye, as she pulls her sweater off over her head.

The necklace is gone – no glint of gold. Around her throat instead, are deep, red scratches, as if something has clawed at her. Or as if, standing there, alone in the dark, my sister has tried to scrape off her own skin.

Cesare

When he first sees the old metal huts, half rusted and moss-coated, Cesare has to work hard to keep the smile fixed upon his face. He and a small group of men, including Gino and Marco, have been released from digging duties to decide what supplies they might need.

All of them stare at the building that is to be their 'church'. A bundle of tangled barbed wire lies next to the decaying huts.

The guard who had accompanied the prisoners up the hill pokes the wire with his toe. He is young and blond and new – just recently put in charge of supplies. He'd introduced himself by name, as Stuart, and then, perhaps worried about seeming too friendly, had shouted at them to *get moving*. When Cesare had met his eye, the guard had given a nervous grin, which he quickly turned into a frown.

But he had soon relaxed, and as they walked up the

hill, he'd told Cesare about his five younger sisters: how much they argued and how much they ate.

'Gannets, they are. Bloody gannets.'

'What is *gannets*?'

The guard had glanced at Cesare in surprise and said, 'You know, those birds. Greedy buggers.'

'Yes.' Cesare had smiled, not knowing which bird the guard meant, but enjoying, for a moment, the familiarity – the companionship in assuming that another person understood what you were saying. *You know, those birds.*

Now Stuart stands, blinking nervously, holding a clipboard and a scrap of paper flapping in the wind, and pokes at the wire again.

'And *this* is a church you're making? A church, from this . . . stuff?'

Cesare nods, more confidently than he feels.

'And,' Stuart says, 'you don't think someone's pulling your leg?'

'He is right,' Gino says in Italian. 'This is a pile of shit. They're laughing at us.'

'Fooling us,' Marco agrees, 'so that we will work on their barriers.'

The other men agree loudly, in Italian, and Stuart watches them, listening to the patter of foreign language, the angry gestures. Cesare notices his hand moving towards his baton.

'Stop!' Cesare says in English, but to the Italians, not

to the guard. 'Stop this complaining. We ask for a place to pray. This is our place. It does not look like a church – it is not a church. It was a prison, this place, or it was used in war. These huts are the dark places. We live in the huts like this. We know. But –' he holds up a hand so the men can't interrupt '– but we will make this a beautiful place. We will bring light to this place. In these huts, there will be no more the war. In these huts, we will make the peace.'

The men nod. Some of them smile. And they follow Cesare, one by one, into the darkness of the first hut.

Like the huts they sleep in, it is cold and draughty. The whole structure is a single semicircle of corrugated steel. In some places, rain has corroded the metal and scrawled curlicues of rust over the ceiling and walls. The air smells sharp and bitter, and Cesare is reminded strongly of the Punishment Hut, of the terror that had gripped him, of the way that the cold air had seemed to squeeze him, like a promise of death to come.

The men gaze around them, their eyes wide, and Cesare can see the despair in their expressions. He feels it himself, but he mustn't show it. If the men object, or rebel, if the mood in the camp plunges, they will all refuse to work again. Once more, there will be lines of men standing in the yard every day, shivering in their thin uniforms, then limping to the mess hut to eat bread and drink water before being pushed out again into the wind and the rain. If there is another riot, no amount of guilt or kindness from Major Bates will save them.

This hut is more than a chapel. This hut is life.

'Listen!' Cesare says. 'Shut your eyes and listen.'

The men look at him doubtfully. Gino raises an eyebrow, and Cesare shoots him a pleading glance. They all close their eyes. Even Stuart, the guard, stands with his arms folded and his eyes shut.

The wind gusts over the sea into the chapel. And as it escapes through the rust-crazed cracks in the roof, it whistles. A high note, at first, when a sudden fierce blast billows in, followed by a lower note as the wind drops, then a higher note again, higher still, and dropping lower once more. Softly, Cesare hums the five notes.

'Listen,' he whispers in Italian. 'It sounds like the *Ave Maria*.'

The men look sceptical. Gino opens his mouth to object, but before he can, Cesare hums the five notes again. They rise through the echoing space, resonating off the metal walls. Unmistakably, the start of the *Ave Maria*.

One by one, the men's faces break into smiles and, when the wind gusts through the chapel again, the men all hum the five notes, then continue to hum the rest of the song.

Ave Maria, Gratia plena . . . Ave Dominus . . .

Even Stuart hums along – somehow this foreigner,

this Orcadian, knows the tune, the Catholic prayer that feels like the sound of home to the Italian men.

Cesare's eyes fill with tears as the men's voices unite in the prayer, the plea. The sound rises, swirls, swells to fill the space. And in this rusted old hut, this piece of discarded war junk, there is sudden beauty. The men's faces fill with wonder and hope as they sing. They must picture, as Cesare does, the vast, beautiful churches of home. The gleaming altar. The arching ceilings, covered with beautiful frescos.

In Cesare's church in Moena, there is a painting of the Madonna and Child above the altar. Maria's face is so peaceful, her eyes so full of warmth and hope, like the face on the prayer card he carries in his pocket.

He will paint the same picture above an altar here, he decides, only Maria's face will look like Dorotea's. He imagines her peaceful smile, as the men sing. He remembers her hand in his as they walked through the mist. Her cold fingers, which had slowly warmed in his. He hasn't seen her since. Perhaps he'd frightened her away, somehow. Their joined hands had felt . . . like peace. It is the same feeling he has now, surrounded by song, full of music, which is swelling out of the chapel and must be echoing through the air, over these islands.

Pray for us now and at the hour of our death.

After the final notes have faded, they walk out into the cold, clear sunlight, blinking. Cesare feels cleansed somehow, as if the few moments in the church have drained some of the anger that has been storing over the past months. The other men's faces are livelier too and they talk to each other – and to Stuart, in English, discussing how beautiful the church will look, how it will remind them of home.

Stuart holds up his clipboard. 'What will you need?'

The men begin to list the bags of cement and sand, the quantities of metal and wood.

'And paint,' Cesare says. 'I need paint.'

Stuart writes it down and scans the list. 'Major Bates has said you can have spare cement from the barriers and any other scraps you can find on the ships in the bay.' He gestures out towards Scapa Flow and the sunken vessels from the last war.

'But,' Stuart frowns, 'paint may be difficult to find.'

Cesare tries not to let his disappointment show, as the glowing church in his mind fades and is replaced by a drab, gloomy building, where everything is the same colour as the barriers.

He forces a smile. 'It is good,' he says. 'We start with cement. No painting yet.'

The next evening the men sit planning in the rusted hut, which will become the chapel. They have been allowed to light a fire just inside the doorway, and although sometimes the wind blows choking clouds of smoke into the structure, no one minds. They are here together, away from the itchy anxiety of the cramped sleeping huts, where fear always lurks: fear of the guards; fear of these strangers, from all over Italy, who must suddenly become something akin to family; fear of the weather; fear of the next morning and the shrill, insistent whistle that will drag you outside to face other, more brutal fears.

Among them is a slightly older man, grey-haired and a little stooped, who had come to Cesare's hut yesterday and introduced himself as a priest.

'Father Ossani,' he'd said. 'You are building a chapel, they say.'

'Yes, Father,' Cesare had replied.

'Well,' Father Ossani said, 'I would like to lead this church, if you do not already have a priest. And I'd like to help now too.'

'With the building?' Cesare looked doubtfully at the small man, his skinny arms and bowed posture – they couldn't have him working in the quarry, surely.

'Not the building,' Father Ossani said, 'but if you need supplies I can apply pressure to the major. No one likes an angry priest.' And then he'd *winked*.

Cesare gave a delighted laugh and assured Father Ossani that he would prove very useful.

Now the priest is here, sitting among the other men in the shell of the echoing building. At first, the men were shy with him, but they are too excited to stay quiet and reserved for long.

They have mixed a small quantity of cement in a bucket, taking turns to stir and mix it with a stick. Cesare watches as Gino beats too enthusiastically, tipping the bucket and splattering cement over Marco's boots. Cesare expects Marco to shout and rage, but he laughs, cuffs Gino over the head and, with his forefinger, wipes some of the cement off his boot then smears it onto Gino's. It is the same cement that they have been using to build the barriers, the same thick grey sludge that, along with the rock from the quarry, has bent their backs and made their muscles ache for months.

But here, in this building that will belong to them, the cement has become something to laugh over, something to share. In the corner of the chapel, two of the men, Vincenzio and Alberto, have started to press a layer of cement against the rusting metal of the inside wall. Cesare has told them already that this will not be necessary, that Major Bates has promised he will find boards coated with plaster, enough to cover the inside of the chapel. 'There will be a shipment in the next two weeks,' he'd said, not meeting Cesare's gaze.

Since Cesare's time in the Punishment Hut, the major's eyes always slide from his, and while he is eager to provide material, he doesn't want Cesare in his office for long. His expression, as Cesare turns to leave, is one of pained relief. While Cesare lies awake in his hut at night, it has occurred to him that the war is horrific for everyone. The captors are almost as damaged as the captives. No one will leave this place unscathed.

Now the two men in the corner are laughing while they try to make the cement stick smoothly to the metal wall, while the others are gathered around Cesare, watching as he sketches an outline of how he envisages the outside of the chapel.

'So,' he says, in Italian, 'we will place the two huts together and we will layer concrete over them. From the front, it will look just like a stone chapel. But you must think how you want the inside to be, and how we will make these things from scraps.'

'We will need an altar,' says Marco, 'and an altar rail.'

'A font,' says Gino, 'and candle-holders,'

Cesare writes it all down, then calls to Stuart, who is dozing in the corner. 'We will have how much metal?'

Stuart stirs. 'Plenty. Plenty of metal, plenty of concrete.'

Cesare nods, imagining a finely wrought metal screen to separate the ornate sanctuary and altar from the rest of the chapel. That is where he will paint his picture of the Madonna, as the central figure behind the screen. To anyone entering the chapel, the delicate metalwork will seem to protect the figure of the Blessed Mother. She will appear enclosed and untouchable.

If he can get paint, of course – Stuart is still doubt-ful about this.

As the men continue to talk, Cesare sketches a quick outline on paper. He captures the curve of her jaw, the upward tilt of her mouth as she smiles. But it is impossible to draw her eyes. Maria should look self-possessed, serene. Her eyes shouldn't carry the intensity he sees every time Dorotea looks at him. The expression that is so close to hunger.

As he finishes the drawing, leaving the eyes blank and expressionless, he makes a decision: if she does not return to the camp tomorrow, he will slip away from the chapel and look for her. He will go to her bothy alone and he will find her. He will speak to her. He will try to tell her how often he thinks of her, how he can't stop wondering about her, want-ing her.

But how is it possible to say such things without frightening her away? How is it possible to talk about *want* and *need*, when those words, in any language, sound like demands?

Cesare knows he won't sleep tonight: he will lie awake, trying to find the right words. Although per-haps the right words don't exist in any language. There's no name for this feeling, just as there's none for the sensation he has as he dips his brush into paint and runs it over canvas.

Still, he has to find a way to tell her, somehow.

Constance

I am woken by watery winter sun creeping under the bothy door, carrying the faintest promise of spring. We have stayed here for three nights, Dot and I, and each night my sleep has been more restless. Each night I lie awake, listening to the laughter from over the hill – the knocking and banging and scraping from that chapel. If I fall asleep, briefly, then the sound turns into the slow, repeated *clud* of a shovel on rock, a grinding rasp, like a wooden box scraping past stone.

Dot has lain awake too, sighing. Occasionally, if there is the sound of laughter, she sits up. Sometimes, when she thinks I'm asleep, she creeps to the door, pulls it open a crack and stands staring out into the night. I watch the silhouette of her back. She looks so vulnerable, so alone.

We don't talk about the men or the chapel during the day. We round up the sheep and the chickens. We sweep out the grate and gather scraps of driftwood. We cut and gather blocks of peat to burn.

Twice, in the quiet, firelit evenings, Dot has said, 'I should check on the men in the infirmary.' And by *infirmary*, she means *chapel*, and the man she wants to see is Cesare. I'm no fool and someone has to keep her safe.

'Not yet,' I've replied, both times. 'The camp gives me nightmares.'

And she nods, smiles at me, but I can feel her retreating from me, hour by hour. I want to tell her to come back. I want to tell her that I'm keeping her safe.

But if I do, I'm worried she'll tell me I'm being foolish, that I need to forget what happened to me, that not everyone is the same. I'm worried she'll tell me that what happened was somehow my fault. And even though I know it was, although I know I'm to blame, I'm worried that, if she says these things, it will sever something between us for ever.

This morning, when I wake, the bed next to me is empty, and I know that she will have walked down towards the camp. I begin pulling on my trousers, ready to follow her, but then I hear a scuffling outside and I realize that it wasn't the light that had woken me.

The sunlight under the door is cut off and there is the scrape of a boot on our step.

A sharp knocking. *Tap, tap, tap.*

I freeze, one leg still in my trousers, breath held.

The shadow shifts. A boot creaks. Angus? Is it Angus, looking for me? Is the door locked? Where could I hide? What can I reach? There is a metal poker for the fire, but I don't know if I will have time –

Tap, tap, tap.

I pull my trousers on, as quietly as possible, then stand very still, my gaze flicking between the metal poker and the shifting shadow under the door.

'Dorotea!' calls a voice.

Cesare.

I stand absolutely still, ignoring the clenching panic in my chest. He will leave soon. He must leave. And then I must find Dot and make sure she is safe.

The boot scrapes again on the doorstep. The slash of light reappears, and then is cut off again, and there is a rockslide beneath my ribs as I realize – *Oh, God!* – that Cesare is kneeling on our doorstep.

I see his fingers – his workman's fingers, grubby-nailed – appear in the gap beneath the door, and I glance at the poker again. It would take a moment. He would never expect it. My panicked breaths are loud in my ears and, for a moment, I'm back within those nights when I'd be woken by the sound of our father's terrified shouts. Dot and I would huddle in our room, listening to him weeping. He would never tell any of us what he dreamed, but I guessed he was back in France, crouched in a trench. Some terror stays with you, in your blood and bones.

Now there is another knock and a rustling as the man pushes something beneath the door. A piece of paper. I don't move. I won't touch it. It's as if he's entered the bothy himself and it takes all my strength to remain absolutely still and silent, when every jolt of my blood tells me I should scream or hide or run or –

That poker!

The creak and scrape of his boot as he stands.

A rasp as he presses his face against the door.

'I am sorry,' he whispers, 'if I have frighten you.'

Is he talking to me? Or has he somehow terrified Dot? Is that why she has stayed here with me for three days? Is she scared of him? Has he hurt her? Some part of me knows that he cannot have, surely. She would have told me. I would have known.

Some terror lurks in blood and bone.

Unbidden, the feeling of hands around my throat. I force air in and out of my lungs and I watch the shadow under the door disappear, watch the sunlight return.

I count to sixty twice, and then I tiptoe forward and snatch up the piece of paper from the floor.

On it are two sketches. One is the outline of a woman's face, and even though the eyes are blank, I recognize the angle of Dot's jaw, the shape of her mouth. We are identical, but this is her without question. Somehow, he has caught the softness of her expression, the vulnerability she doesn't know she radiates. The other sketch is of a pair of hands, the fingers interlaced. I have to study the paper carefully to see, in the confusion of linked fingers, that one hand belongs to a woman and the other to a man. Again, without needing to be told, I know that this is her hand held in Cesare's. I am struck by how much bigger his hand is than hers, by how the veins and muscles and bones of his hand entirely envelop her tiny, pale fingers.

I hold my own hand out in front of me, curling it into a fist.

'Oh, Dot,' I say aloud. 'What have you done?'

It fills me with terror, the thought that she has allowed this to happen – that she's allowed this man to become infatuated with her, that she's placed herself entirely at his mercy. And now he won't leave her alone, just as Angus won't leave me alone.

I should have told her everything. I should have warned her. This is my fault, my fault.

And then I tear the sketches into tiny pieces and I scatter them into the glowing embers in the grate. When I prod them with the metal poker, they flare, flicker and blacken.

Soon, the only remaining sign of the drawings is my own laboured breath and the images in my mind, which I cannot shake.

I finish dressing quickly, pulling on two sweaters and gloves: though it is warmer than it was, the bite of winter still lingers in the air.

Then I walk over the next hill, in the direction of the infirmary. I won't tell Dot about the drawings or Cesare's visit, but I must see her, must see that she is safe and well.

As I near the breast of the hill, I hear men's voices and I stop.

There is banging and hammering, and a shout of laughter. And then, under those noises, the sound of . . . *singing*.

Men on our hillside, the prisoners apparently allowed to roam free. Men laughing and talking and planning . . . God knows what they could be planning. My first thought is to return to the bothy, to close the door and wait for Dot to return, then tell her we must leave – even if it means returning to Kirkwall.

But the singing grows louder. It is a simple melody and reminds me of something my mother used to sing:

> *I would spin a web before your eyes,*
> *A beautiful web of silver light,*
> *Wherein is many a wondrous sight.*

The tune the men are singing is not the same as my mother's, but is similar enough to bring tears to my eyes.

I should have stopped her going, I think. *I should have stopped them both.*

And suddenly I am lying face down on the turf, half crawling to the top of the hill, where I will be able to see the men, the foreign prisoners who are singing this familiar song.

They are gathered outside the two metal huts, seated in a circle on the ground. Most of them sprawl, half lying down, as if they are on a picnic with friends, and they don't look like soldiers. They could be men from anywhere at all.

One man is standing in the middle, hunched over something. He points at a grey lump of cement in the centre of the circle, and the others cheer and applaud. Then he pulls one of his friends to his feet and sprawls in his place at the edge of the circle; the next man takes cement from a bucket and layers it onto the grey lump.

What are they building?

They begin to sing again, and suddenly it is as though I am watching my father, sitting around a fire with his friends as they passed around a ripped fishing net and a jug of beer. I used to love sneaking onto the beach to watch them repairing the nets and boats. Each man was suddenly friendly with the others. It didn't seem to matter which men were there, and how they might gripe at one another during the day. There was something in that *making* that was about more than the net, more than the boat.

And now, watching the prisoners, my stomach pressed hard against the cold soil of my home, I see, suddenly, how lonely they must be, in this strange land, so far from everyone they love. And I feel my own loneliness anew, like the hollow, aching socket from a dug-out tooth.

I touch the spot at the base of my throat where my

breath suddenly feels tight, as if something – some*one* – is squeezing the air from me still and always, long after those fingerprints have faded. But I can feel the ghost of something else there too, as I watch the men. Another presence. Another absence. The trace of the necklace I'd buried three nights ago behind the bothy.

PART FOUR

We never find what we set our hearts on.
We ought to be glad of that.

From *Beside the Ocean of Time*,
George Mackay Brown

April 1942

Cesare

Someone is calling his name. He is back in Moena, running through the streets towards the church, knowing he has to get inside, away from the bombs that are falling. All around, the streets are on fire, but he knows his family are safe in the church, waiting for him. And, somehow, Dorotea is there too. She calls his name again, reaches out her hand and shakes his shoulder. He twists around, trying to catch her fingers in his, trying to put his arms about her, but she moves out of his reach.

He wakes, with a start, to see Gino's face close to his – frowning, his dark eyes worried.

'You can't sleep here. You were supposed to come back to the camp hours ago.'

Cesare stretches, looks around. It is dark outside and he is in the chapel: the new plasterboard wall is cold against his back; there are faint pencil marks where he has etched out the beginning of some of the pictures – when he has paint, they will glow like the walls of the finest churches in Italy.

'Come on,' Gino says. 'You'll get us both into trouble.'

Cesare shakes his head. 'Major Bates has said I can stay in the chapel late. There will be no trouble.'

Gino grins. 'You are his favourite now. When the chapel is finished, perhaps you will marry Major Bates.'

'Careful. There's too much sharp metal in here for you to mock me.'

The floor is littered with scrap pieces that the prisoners have salvaged from the half-sunken boats in the harbour, or scavenged from the barriers. There are shards of corrugated metal that will help to reinforce the concrete altar, spools of barbed wire that Cesare is shaping into a statue of George defeating the dragon, and old beef tins that he will make into candle-holders.

As Gino walks back towards the camp with him, Cesare looks up at the stars and wonders what his family in Moena can see. He wonders if they're still alive.

Gino pokes him in the ribs. 'I saw your girlfriend today.'

'She's not my girlfriend,' Cesare says, and then, too late, he adds, 'Who do you mean?'

Gino gives a low laugh. 'She left some metal near the chapel. A huge chunk of it – looks like it was part of a ship once. She said she'd found it on the beach. I told her she should give it to you, but she wouldn't stay.'

'You scared her off with your ugly face,' says Cesare, but it is a struggle to laugh, a struggle to conceal his worry: Dorotea has been avoiding him, ever since he held her hand in the fog. She hasn't answered his letter and he doesn't want to go to her bothy again; it doesn't feel right to pursue her.

Occasionally, he has caught a glimpse of her in the camp, near the infirmary – or perhaps it is her sister – but he won't approach her.

Instead he has thrown himself into building the chapel. Along with the plasterboard on the walls, there are sections of metal that Cesare will be able to shape into a screen. There are sheets of glass that he will paint to look like an expensive stained-glass window. When he imagines the sunlight shining through, onto the walls and the floor, the thought is transporting. He is, for a moment, no longer a prisoner. His muscles do not ache, his stomach does not gripe. He is a free man, standing in a church in his own country. War and death are things that happen to other people, in other places. The chapel will be a place of peace.

Now Gino reaches out and stops Cesare, breaking him out of his reverie just before they get to the camp. There is a guard on the gate, standing in the shadows, and both of them wait to see who it is. Now that they have shown they can be trusted, the Italians are given a little more freedom to roam, but that is no consolation if Angus MacLeod is in charge. Twice now, he's seen Cesare returning to the camp late, and has given him instructions to come to the quarry the next morning, rather than going up to the chapel.

Tonight they are in luck: the guard is young and nervous. Although he keeps his hand on his baton, he lets them past without stopping them.

Back in his hut, the rest of the men are asleep. Cesare is cold, as he climbs into his bunk – he is always cold in this northern land, but he prays to distract himself. He prays for the skill to make the chapel as beautiful as he imagines it; he prays for his family's safety. He prays for the chance to be able to hold Dorotea's hand again. To be able to tell her that he is sorry for whatever he has done to hurt her.

Some nights, he prays for the war to be over, but then he tries to imagine returning to Italy, leaving Dorotea in this place; everything he pictures is a gaping blank. Without her, returning home would be a descent into darkness.

In the morning, late frost rimes the inside of his hut. The winter has been long and Cesare has almost forgotten the feeling of waking up warm. Now, his muscles are stiff with cold, but he feels no reluctance at getting up. The chapel calls to him, as it does to all of the men in his hut. They grin at each other and dress quickly before starting up the hill in the weak sunlight.

Cesare walks alongside them, feeling comfort and ease, as if he's known them for years. It is strange how this place has brought them together and made them into something new. Before they came here, they were strangers from different parts of Italy who had joined the fight for different reasons: some liked the idea of defending their country, and others were so poor that the regular meals and pay were impossible to ignore. A very few were Fascists, who scrawled *Il Duce* into the rocks on the quarry walls and the metal sides of their huts. But most were just ordinary men, who wanted to make sure their families were safe — safe from this nameless, faceless enemy. And now they are here, and their differences don't matter because they're building something together. And the enemy has a face, but it isn't the face they expected. The enemy is MacLeod with his baton, but it is also Major Bates's kindnesses. It is the nurses who care for them. It is the twin girls with their long red hair and their anxious smiles.

Nothing is as they expected.

The sight of the chapel, on the breast of the hill, never fails to take Cesare's breath away. Although it is only half covered with cement, and looks like some weather-ravaged rock formation, he can make out the beginning of the façade of a church: he can picture the pillars around the doorway, which will welcome weary travellers; he can imagine the pointed arch with its pediment, its cornice. They will paint it white, with flashes of red. It will be visible from miles away; far-off sailors will see it in war and in peace. Cesare will embed a sculpture of Christ's face above the doorway. It will remain on this island long after he is gone.

I can't leave without her. By winter, the barriers will be finished.

He shakes off the thought, instructs Gino and Marco

to continue mixing the cement for the front of the chapel. All the men begin to work happily, and much faster than they ever have in the quarry. Cesare goes into the chapel and continues painting the grey plasterboard white. In some places, he paints over the pencil marks where he has sketched out faint designs. He covers the outline of a hawk, a lion and a crow. There is no purpose in having the images there without coloured paints.

The concrete altar will be finished today – Alberto and Aureliano are hunched over it, smoothing layer after layer of cement over the surface. They flash quick grins at Cesare, and return to their task. Both men are utterly engrossed in creating something beautiful. Far off, from the direction of the quarry, comes the boom of another explosion.

Above the altar, there is a pencil outline of a woman's face. Her expression is serene, but her eyes are fierce. And in Cesare's mind she has long red hair. He puts the brush of white paint to the image, ready to cover it, but stops himself. How can he paint her out, as if she never existed? She is somewhere on this island. Perhaps, sometimes, she thinks of him.

Later, after Alberto and Aureliano finish pressing the last layer of cement onto the altar, Father Ossani leads all the men into the chapel.

Cesare has put lanterns under the altar. From a distance, they look like the most intricate decorated boxes, with beautiful patterns carved and etched into the metal. Cesare has crafted them carefully, so that the light from the candles casts flickering patterns up the whitewashed walls. It is only by examining them very carefully that you might guess that, until yesterday, these decorations were empty beef tins.

The men file in silently, all jokes forgotten as they watch the yellow light licking the clean white walls. The altar itself is still grey, the cement still wet, but the scalloped edges are delicate, curving like the inside of a seashell; it rests upon two fluted cement columns, just as Cesare had imagined. He glances across at Alberto and Aureliano: their faces are flushed, their eyes shining.

Back home in Italy, churches may be collapsing, the land may be burning, but here, in this desolate corner of the earth, they have made something sacred.

Father Ossani stands. As one, the men kneel.

The cement floor is hard and cold under Cesare's knees. He doesn't care – he barely feels the pain. Candlelight falls on the men's faces; they raise their eyes, basking in the glow of it.

Father Ossani begins to recite the praise to God that marks the opening of Mass, the familiar litany a balm of dew in the desert. Cesare puts his head back and recites the words he has known since childhood, the words that acknowledge Christ's conquest of death, and speak of Cesare's own hope of eternal life.

Behind Father Ossani's bowed head, the pencil sketch of Dorotea seems to shift in the flickering candlelight. And, in this moment of exultation, Cesare cannot stop himself feeling despair.

He walks forward with the other men and kneels again to accept the bread and wine that Father Ossani has brought to the chapel – a scrap of bread each and a dribble of watered-down wine.

In nomine Patris, et Filii, et Spiritus Sancti. Amen.

Corporis et Sanguinus Domini.

Body and Blood of Christ.

It is somehow warming, this old bread and weak wine. Somehow filling and strengthening. When Cesare glances at Gino, there are tears on his face. His own cheeks are wet. Father Ossani's voice quakes; his hands quiver as he makes the sign of the cross over Cesare's face.

Body and Blood of Christ.

After Father Ossani has touched his fingers to Cesare's forehead and blessed him, Cesare remains kneeling. He hears the other men rise, one by one, hears them leave the chapel, hears their voices fading as they walk down the dark hill towards the camp and the mess hut, where their dinner will be waiting.

He can't make himself move. This moment feels

like a miracle. How have they built a house of God on this island? How have they begun to craft something so exquisite, when the world is raging and folding in on itself?

To Cesare, it seems that if one miracle can happen, then another must be possible. He bows his head and thinks of Dorotea. He doesn't know what he wants, but finds himself repeating her name again and again – at first in his mind, and then aloud, in a whisper, like a prayer, his whole body full of a longing that feels like worship, a longing that feels almost idolatrous.

He presses his hands to his face and tries to steady his breathing.

A scraping noise from the doorway, like a boot shifting. His breath stops in his throat and he sits up.

'Gino?' he says.

The sound of an intake of breath, and then of footsteps retreating down the path. Cesare stands, runs, his own footsteps echoing around the empty chapel.

'*Fermare!* Stop!' he calls, as he reaches the door. But no one is there. Just the black, blank mouth of the gathering night and, in the distance at the bottom of the hill, the glimmering lights of the camp. He feels as though the surrounding hills are a dark sea, and the chapel is the only thing keeping him afloat.

'*Dove sei?*' he whispers. 'Where are you?'

The night replies with silence. He must have imagined the footsteps. Maybe it was some creature, a wild animal.

But as he turns to go back into the chapel, where he will blow out the candles, something on the ground catches his eye.

He crouches down. Three small jars, each filled with something.

He picks them up – they are warm as freshly laid eggs. On the altar, he opens them and, in the flickering candlelight, he sees three paints. A dark yellow, a bright red and a vibrant blue.

His instinct is to kneel, again, to thank God for this marvel. But he remembers the scrape of boots, the indrawn breath, the light footsteps running away. *Dorotea.*

And as he holds the jars of paint against his lips, he turns around in the chapel, imagining the walls glowing with bright colours, imagining the creatures, brimming with life. And the central picture, above the altar, will be the face of the Madonna, surrounded by angels, her defiant gaze focused on the miraculous Child in her arms.

The night is cold, but Cesare doesn't feel it as he begins to paint, starting with the blue cloth that surrounds the cherubs.

If one miracle can happen, then why shouldn't everything be miraculous?

He knows, from the lectures of the artist in Moena who helped him decorate the church, that blue was once the rarest colour. *Il blu oltremare* was made by grinding precious lapis lazuli into a powder. It was so expensive that Michelangelo abandoned his painting *The Entombment* because he couldn't afford the blue paint.

And yet here, incredibly, in this chilly northern wilderness, Cesare holds a tiny pot of blue.

If one miracle can happen . . .

He brushes it onto the plasterboard gently, delicately. The whole wall lights.

He is trembling. He must find a way to talk to her. He must find a way to thank her. He must find her.

Orcadians

16 April is St Magnus's Day. Nearly everyone in Kirkwall flocks to St Magnus's Cathedral to remember the murdered saint. The red sandstone building has rarely been so full, even before the war and certainly not in recent years. Outside a light mizzle dampens the air, and as the minister recites the Lord's Prayer, steam rises from the wet clothes of the congregation and ghosts upwards, towards the rose window.

'We remember our fallen sons,' the minister says, 'and those who are lost. May they be returned to us.'

'Amen,' the congregation intones. A few people sneak glances at John O'Farrell, whose son, James, is an aircraft engineer and was reported missing in action last month. Along with the pity that everyone feels, along with the horror at the thought of one of their own having fallen, there is an undercurrent of relief.

Not my son. Thank God, it's not my son.

John keeps his head bowed – his hair is even greyer than before, his face more lined. There have been stories about prisoners being sent to German camps. No one knows what happens to them there; no one likes to talk about it.

After the service, the postmistress, Mary Guthrie, goes to give John her best wishes. She, too, looks haggard. At night, when she tries to sleep, her thoughts are full of the hopeful faces of mothers, who have walked to the post office for a letter from their sons. She has handed out one telegram after another, and watched her friends' faces crumple. In the dark, she imagines the men – the boys, many of whom she has known all their lives: she dreams of their pale skin, like candlewax. Until last week, she dreamed of her own son, Robbie, who is a navigator. She didn't imagine him dead, but pictured him, aged nine, laughing at the joke he'd told her.

What do you call a deer with no eyes? No idea!

He was forever telling jokes and stories. He was always prone to clowning; he had an infectious laugh. Every Sunday, from when he was fifteen, he'd got up early and fetched some decoration for her breakfast tray.

Sometimes it was a rose, sometimes it was a trail of kelp or bladderwrack, but he always woke her with two slices of toast and a cup of tea on the tray he'd decorated.

Last week, Robbie returned to her with a limp. He is thin and dull-eyed; he says barely a word. When he is supposed to be asleep, she hears him crying and banging some part of himself – his foot or head? – against the wall. She can't imagine him laughing.

Now, she places a hand on John's shoulder. He pats her fingers and gives a pained smile. 'Give Robbie my best.' The words sound hollow; they both hear it. John's son may be missing, but Robbie is absent too. Some vital part of him was lost in the air over Germany, when he gave directions to help set a city on fire.

As John is leaving the church, Angus MacLeod steps into his path. 'I've been wanting to talk to you about this chapel they're building.'

'Not today, Angus. Can you not find something else to amuse you? There must be someone who wants tormenting. A child, for instance, or a harmless animal.'

'But have you seen the chapel? The time it's taking. I've been talking to people and we agree it's unwarranted, out of all proportion. These men are prisoners –'

'I expect they know that, and I expect their families are also aware. Now, step aside, would you?' John continues walking down the steps but Angus grabs his arm.

'They're *painting* it. One of the prisoners is busy decorating the walls with pictures of people and birds – I've seen the pencil marks. Think of the supplies they need – the paint and whitewash. Not to mention the food and drink they'll be demanding – and for what? To build a *chapel*, when they should be working on the barriers.'

'The *causeways* are well on their way to being finished, from what I hear. They'll be completed within six months and then the prisoners will be leaving. And if you've a problem with them in the meantime, I suggest you talk to Major Bates about it.'

Angus drops his gaze. The drizzle turns to rain.

John gives a short bark of laughter. 'From your expression, I'd say you've spoken to Major Bates already and he gave you short shrift.'

Angus's face twists. 'It's not . . . It's not just the chapel. It's the prisoners and the girls –'

John holds up a hand, his expression suddenly hard. 'You'd best not be talking to those girls – you'd best not even be *thinking* about them. Other people might be willing to give you the benefit of the doubt, but I've neither the time nor the patience to pretend that I trust you. You stay away from those girls, or there will be trouble. Do you hear?'

'But I –'

John steps forward, so that his face is inches from Angus's. 'Do not test me on this.'

Angus steps back, then looks away.

Around the two men, a small crowd has gathered. No one is standing close enough to interfere, but plenty have overheard.

After they have gone, there is a short silence and then a few people go back into the cathedral, out of the rain. Some agree with Angus, that the chapel is ridiculous – a gaudy thing, it will be, full of Catholic icons. There is not a single icon in St Magnus's Cathedral, which has stood since the twelfth century. The pink sandstone walls are heavily etched with nine hundred years of graffiti: the names of sailors and ships are scratched alongside a skull, the eyes blank-socketed. The building carries the chill and reverence of a life longer than human thought.

'Their chapel won't last,' says Neil MacClenny. 'It's made of tin cans and bits of old board, so I hear.'

Everyone nods. No one mentions the cement. No one remarks that, on some nights, if you look out over the sea towards Selkie Holm, it's possible to make out the faint glow of a lamp burning in the darkness.

May 1942

Dorothy

Every night, Cesare paints the chapel by lamplight. And every night, I watch him from the shadows. I don't know if he sees me. Occasionally, he freezes and half turns. Once, I saw him put down his brush and bow his head. Then he said something that might have been a prayer, but sounded like my name, or so I thought – so I hoped.

I leaned forward, stilling my breath, straining for the sound of his voice, for the sound of my name on his lips. He was silent, but I watched his shoulders rise and fall with the rhythm of his words.

I try to leave gifts outside the chapel for him, when I can. Pieces of metal I have found, or paints that I have managed to make using old onion skins, lichen and tree bark. I have boiled up bilberries and elder-berries, which have stained my hands blue for days – I remember my mother making paints for us when we were children. She came from Fair Isle to the north, and knew how to make all sorts from plants: paints, medicines and even poisons.

Sometimes the chapel door is shut and I have to peer through one of the window holes that has been cut in the metal hut. Other nights, it is raining, or a biting wind blows in from the north and I stand in the darkness, shivering, watching him until I can no longer stand the cold. Then I walk back up to the bothy and huddle close to the burned-out fire, drawing a little heat from the dying ashes and trying not to wake Con with the chattering of my teeth.

Time after time, I've asked if she will go back to the camp, to work with me in the infirmary, but she has become more and more solitary. I don't understand why her fear has grown over time. It is as though everything that has happened to her is an old wound, which, although it seemed healed, has hidden an infection under the scarred surface.

'You will feel better if you come out with me, Con,' I say.

'I'm tired.' She looks it, pale and drawn. 'I'll go tomorrow.' And she scratches the skin at her throat until it reddens, until it's nearly raw.

She sleeps long hours and still she looks haunted, jumping at every shift of the wind. She must know that I'm going out to the chapel, although she never asks. I can't meet her eyes when I leave, and when I return. I'm terrified she'll ask me to stay. I'm terrified that I'll not be able to stop myself leaving, even if she begs me.

By mid-May, it is nearly Beltane. There are no bonfires this year, no celebrations – the war has brought so much darkness and silence – but the weather softens. The winds drop, the land brightens, and thin fingers of sunlight stretch through the clouds, making each day longer than the last.

For a long time, Cesare has been painting the walls at the front of the chapel brown, to look like tiles, but one evening in May, he begins to work on the whitewashed walls next to the altar. I peer around the doorway, watching. His back is to me, as ever, but I can see the stern focus in the set of his shoulders. I have watched him long enough now to know every movement of his hands and arms, yet still, as the delicate blue-black arch of a crow's head and neck emerge from under his hands, my breath catches.

I am used to beauty: the shattered sunlight on the sea; the brash purple and yellow of the autumn heather and gorse; two goshawks circling each other in an open blue sky. But I've never watched something so beautiful being created and with such ease. He dips his brush into white paint to add light and depth to the crow's black eyes, and it seems that the bird is staring straight at me.

And what I feel, along with my sense of wonder, is desire. It is an inescapable tide rising through my limbs, throbbing through my veins; in that moment, the cost doesn't matter.

I shift my weight, knowing my boot will creak. Knowing he will hear me. He stops painting. He sets down his brush.

'Dorotea?' he says, without turning. Inside the chapel, his voice resonates, *thea, tia, tear.* Not my name, not part of my name, but an echo of sadness and breaking, and yet I find myself walking forward, into the lamplight.

'Cesare.' His name sounds strange said aloud. I've said it to myself so many times in the dark, but it seems foreign to me now.

I step further into the chapel, my nerves humming, and, to avoid his gaze, I look upwards.

The building is a marvel: each tile has been carefully painted to give the illusion of height and depth. Even though the ceiling is not the arched roof of a church, it gives the impression of loftiness, of reverence. And on the whitewashed wall near the altar, I can see pencil sketches of birds and animals and angels.

'It's beautiful,' I gasp. 'How do you paint the flat wall to look like tiles? They seem so real.'

'It is not finished,' he says. 'But I show you.' He picks up a brush, dabs it in the brown paint, then strokes it in the centre of one of the rectangles he has drawn to be a painted 'tile'. 'In the middle must be dark. And light at the edge, with white. You try.'

He passes me the brush and nods towards the wall. I touch the bristles to the rectangle Cesare was just painting. I'm aware of his eyes on my face, aware of the heat in my cheeks. I dare not look at him directly. My hand is unsteady and I blot the paint, making an ugly smear on the tile. 'Oh! I've ruined it.'

'No.' He smiles, takes the brush from me and, with a deft flick of paint, my mistake is gone. 'See?'

Then he passes the brush back to me and watches as I paint more of the tiles, badly.

'I have not seen you,' he says softly. 'You are hiding from me?'

I swallow. I inhale. I paint a shaky line of pale brown around the outside of a tile. 'Not *hiding*. I have been busy.'

'You are busy hiding.' I can hear him smiling and I smile too, despite the tremor in my limbs, the strange electricity flickering under my skin.

'I think I have upset you,' he says. 'I think I have hurt you.'

'No!' I say, turning to him.

His eyes are dark; his expression is pained. I look away. 'You haven't hurt me,' I say. 'I just —'

At that moment, the air-raid siren screams out from over the water in Kirkwall.

Cesare quenches the lamp immediately and pulls on my hand, dragging me under the concrete altar. My breath is tight in my chest, and his body, so close to mine, feels solid. Comforting and terrifying all at once.

The door to the chapel is open and, down the hill, I can see the lights in the camp being extinguished one by one. The island becomes a mass of darkness, with bone-white moonlight shivering on the sea.

We've had so few air raids: after the submarine attack, an order came from London for gun batteries to be built all along the coast, protecting the naval vessels moored around the islands, protecting the barriers, protecting us.

Over the sound of the siren, I strain to hear the noise of a plane's engine.

'What does a falling bomb sound like overhead?' I ask, my voice high-pitched. 'Will we hear it before it hits us?'

'They will not be bombing us,' he says, and he sounds steady, certain.

'Oh, Con is by herself! In the bothy. I should go to her.'

I try to stand, but he says, 'She is safe.'

'She will be terrified.'

'It is dangerous for you to walk out,' he says. 'When the siren is stopped, it is safe to walk.'

I know he's right but I feel sick. I try to steady my breathing.

He says, 'You want to go? Then I will walk with you.'

I shake my head, then realize he can't see me in the dark. 'No. It's not safe.'

'When I am in the desert in Africa,' he says quietly, 'I am frightened. So many men shooting and dying. I do not want to fight. I must. But I am scared. War is made for fear.'

He still can't see me, but perhaps he feels me

nodding; perhaps he hears my breathing slow slightly as I strain to catch the sound of his voice.

'I must be calm,' he says. 'If I am not calm, then perhaps I make a mistake. Perhaps I die. So I make myself calm like this.' My hand is motionless in his. He turns it over between his own and places his finger on my palm.

My stomach jolts. I don't dare to move.

'I think,' he says, 'what is the shapes of the mountains in Moena? I remember this.' And he traces his finger in a curve over my palm. The hairs on my arms rise, but I am not cold.

'And then I think,' he says, 'what is the shapes of the birds and the trees? I remember this.' With his finger he sketches towering trees with arching branches; on my arm, he picks out the outline of a soaring bird. '*Albero*,' he says, '*uccello*.' And I know these must be the words for 'tree' and 'bird'.

Then I feel him hold out his own palm for me. 'Draw something. A thing you are remember.'

So, hesitantly, I trace the outline of the caves to the north of this island. I sketch the path that leads to them. I draw the sea that crashes around the cliffs below them.

I can't hear the air-raid siren any longer, and I don't know if it has stopped, or if everything has disappeared apart from us. His skin is warm. I reach for him. His neck, his face.

His breath brushes my cheek. In the darkness, his mouth finds mine.

'Dorotea.' He exhales my name against my lips.

Constance

In May, each day stretches out longer than the last. The sun rises high in the sky and the light touches everything. Even the bothy is bright, the dark shadows banished, so that I can no longer doze my way through the days, even if I barely move from the bed.

And the lighter days seem to draw Dot out more often, too, and for longer. Even when I ask her to stay with me, she waits until I'm asleep – or until she thinks I am – and then she slips from the bothy, like a shadow. I watch her from the window, pulling the old sailcloth to one side to see her going towards the chapel. And I know that she must be going to see him.

Sometimes I pretend to wake up as she's leaving and I cry out so that she will stay, at least for a while. It's not only that I feel safer when she is with me, not simply that her presence exorcizes the darkness or softens the glare of the sun. It's also that if she's with me I know that no harm has come to her. I used to watch our mother feigning illness if a storm was coming so that our father would stay with her rather than going out on the boat. She would be doubled over, clutching her stomach, but if she caught my eye, she would flash me a brief smile and I would know: she was keeping him safe. She was keeping all of us safe.

That was when Dot and I were young, before our mother truly became ill. Before the pain kept her confined to her bed. Before she had to go out on the boat with our father to try to reach a bigger hospital, to try to find some stronger medicine.

If I could lock Dot in the bothy with me, I would. If I could make her follow me to some deserted island further north, I would.

One May morning, after Beltane has passed, the fires unburned, I pretend to be asleep, so that she will leave quietly, so that she will not suspect anything. As soon as she has shut the door, I get out of bed, fully dressed, and I follow her.

The land is green and painfully bright. I squint as I walk over the next hill, in the direction of those huts they are using for a chapel. If she isn't there, I will go down to the infirmary.

When I round the hill, I gasp.

The last time I saw the chapel, it was two ramshackle metal buildings, half rusted, looking as though they would blow away in the next storm. Now, the huts are part of a new creation, something entirely foreign and beautiful. The chapel is smooth-backed, as if it has grown out of the earth, and with a concrete frontage that looks as though it has been taken from a fine sanctuary in another country. It reminds me of pictures I'd seen in newspapers of churches in lands to the south; the same churches that the radio tells us are being bombed now, and are in flames or crumbling, but this is whole and elegant. Some of the men are painting it white and, in the bright summer sun, the building radiates light.

I can't see Dot, but I can't make myself leave. Instead I find that I am walking towards this shining building, walking towards the men who are outside, painting, talking to each other in Italian.

They have no reason to harm you. I remind myself of the prisoners in the infirmary – not one had tried to hurt me. But then I'd been around other people. Now, I'm alone.

My shadow falls across the white-painted wall and the two men stop talking and turn, dropping their brushes. They squint, the sun in their eyes, and, for a moment, their faces are full of fear.

Then they relax into friendly recognition.

'Bella!' one says. 'You are well? Where have you left Cesare, eh?'

'I . . .' *I don't know what you mean.* The words die in my throat as I realize that these men must believe that I'm Dot and they seem pleased to see me: their smiles are welcoming, their faces open as they push a brush into my hand.

'We have not painted the tiles by the door,' one of the men says, still grinning. 'You are doing this very fine.'

Then they shove open the door to the chapel and, brush in hand, I walk inside.

The sight knocks the breath from me. I'd expected the drab cold grey of the men's sleeping huts – the glimpses I'd caught before they arrived had been of chilly corrugated metal and bare boards. An icy breeze had whistled through some unseen crack and every hut had smelt of rust and damp.

But the chapel is full of light. Sun pours in through the four windows to reflect off the white walls near the altar, and the painted tiles near the doorway. Around the altar itself are splashes of colour in half-finished paintings: a peach-skinned cherub is wrapped in blue cloth; a crow cradles an open book in its outstretched wings. On the ceiling, the outline of a white dove soars through an impossibly blue sky.

'It's *beautiful*!'

The men look at me strangely, and I remember that they think I'm Dot, and that she must be used to seeing all this wonder. And, suddenly, it's too much: the thought of all the life that is passing me by while I stay locked in the bothy, locked in my own memories. I don't know how to escape myself.

Footsteps outside the door and Dot is there, Cesare behind her. When Dot sees me, her jaw drops. 'Con! What are you . . .' She glances at Cesare and flushes. There are blotches of colour on her neck and chest and, for a moment, they look like fingerprints. But her eyes on mine are lively; she looks happier than I can ever remember seeing her.

I may vomit.

The memory envelops me like a wave. It is the moment that returns to me in the dark when I try to sleep and in the morning when I wake. The memory that lurks in the silence between heartbeats. Time folds in on itself.

I'm back with Angus, his hand in mine. He had taken me for dinner and then for a walk along the beach in Kirkwall in the half-dark. For weeks, I had been grieving for our mother and father and had refused when Angus asked me to walk with him. I didn't know him well. In school, he had been two classes above and popular, but prone to wild outbursts and touches of cruelty towards younger boys. His sudden interest in me was as baffling as it was flattering. I didn't know then how drawn he was towards people who seemed broken.

Dot had asked me, time and again, not to go. But the Kirkwall house was heavy with memories and my grief felt crushing. So that evening, when Angus knocked on my door and asked me to walk with him, I said yes. What could be the harm?

As we walked, he gave me a gold chain. He fastened it around my neck and then touched the point where the clasp touched my skin. My blood jolted and I didn't dare to move. But when he asked me to walk along the beach, I felt I couldn't say no. I didn't want to upset him, or to be ungrateful, when he'd been so kind to me.

The beach was dark and empty away from the harbour. Angus took his shoes off and jumped down onto the sand.

'Come on.' He held out his hand and I didn't know how to say no. So I didn't.

He put his hand around my waist. I was intensely aware of the pressure of that hand, so it was hard to swallow, hard to focus on anything else. But I felt it would be rude to push him off.

We walked away from the harbour lights and further along the beach, where the only sound was the rush of the waves, and the only illumination on his face, when he turned to me, was the pale, silvery glow from the moon.

My chest felt tight. When he wrapped both arms around me, I kept my hands by my sides. He kissed my neck, where his chain lay cold against my skin. His mouth was warm, but it left a cold, damp trail as he brought his lips to mine.

I recoiled and he stopped.

'Have you been playing games with me? Leading me on?'

'I . . .'

'You want to be here, don't you? You liked dinner? And the necklace?'

'Yes.' It was true: he'd been kind, had listened to

me. When I'd told him I missed my mother and father, he'd reached out and held my hand.

'But now you want to go?' he asked.

He looked contemptuous and a muscle pulsed in his jaw.

Mutely, I shook my head.

'Good.' He kissed me, his mouth wet. He pushed his tongue against my lips and I knew he expected me to open my mouth, but everything in me clamped together; my muscles were rigid.

He pulled away from me and, even in the half-darkness, I could just make out his frowning confusion and the hard anger in his gaze.

'I thought you liked me,' he said.

'I do.' This seemed like the right thing to say, the polite thing to say, the way to stop him getting even angrier.

'Kiss me, then,' he said.

So I did.

I let him kiss me, and I let him lie down next to me on the sand. When he tried to shift his body onto mine, I froze again and pushed him away. But he was so much bigger, so much heavier, so much stronger than me. My arms pressed against his chest made no difference. When I turned my face from his kisses, he put his lips to my neck. His teeth grazed my skin. And I could feel his hands gathering my skirt, pulling it above my hips.

'No!'

'Don't be like that, Con.'

'Get off me!' I shoved him. It was like pushing on a rock, like heaving a wall off my body.

He didn't move. He kissed me again, harder.

'Get off!' I shouted, with the little air I could gather in my lungs. 'Get –'

And then my words were cut off by his hands around my throat.

I choked and coughed, beating my legs on the sand, batting my hands against him, trying to claw at his face. My chest burned; my vision narrowed to the single point of his features – eyes, lips, teeth.

I'm going to die here. I'm going to die.

I tried to slap his face again. He grabbed both my hands in one of his and then tried to press his other arm on my neck to hold me down. His arm brushed my lips. I opened my mouth and bit down, hard, until I tasted iron, until something crunched between my teeth.

He yelled and jumped off me. I drew in a lungful of air and stumbled to my knees, crouching, retching.

'You bitch!' he shouted, clutching his arm. 'You *bitch*!' His voice was full of fury, his face twisted, and he moved towards me. I began to run.

I don't know why he didn't chase after me. When I got home, Dot had fallen asleep on the sofa. I crept past her and filled the kitchen sink with cold water, then washed myself. I scrubbed at the livid scratches and purple bruises until my skin felt scorched. I threw away my ripped skirt, knowing she'd ask questions if she found it.

In the following days, I wore a scarf. I refused to tell Dot where I'd been. And, as more bruises bloomed maroon and blue on my neck, I stayed inside the Kirkwall house, shut away, safe from prying eyes. But the rumours started anyway.

Dot came home from the grocer's, her face flushed. 'You need to tell me what happened with Angus,' she said.

I stared out of the window, wrapped my scarf more tightly around my neck. 'I don't need to tell you anything.' The thought of her knowing how stupid I'd been, the thought of causing her pain . . . The shame was more than I could bear.

'I found your skirt. The one you threw away.'

I bit the inside of my cheek, fighting the burning behind my eyelids.

She took my hand between hers. 'People are saying – Angus is saying that you led him on. He says you went onto the beach with him. That you kissed him and then . . . He says you *bit* him.'

I flinched, blinked, breathed. I didn't deny it. There was nothing in what Dot had said that wasn't true. I felt her watching me. I felt her expression change.

'I still love you,' she said. 'No matter what.'

My cheeks burned, but I didn't say a word.

Three weeks later, Dot and I left to come to Selkie Holm. In my pocket, I took the gold chain Angus had given me, as a reminder not to trust anyone, as a reminder of my disgrace.

Now, in the chapel, looking at the bright spots of colour on Dot's neck, I can't escape the idea of Cesare's fingers there, of his mouth there. I can't rid myself of the thought of his body on hers.

Bile rises in my gullet. The chapel, sunlit as it is, feels suddenly dark and airless. I feel my throat narrowing, as if I have swallowed a stone, or as if someone's arm is pressing down on my windpipe.

'I have to go,' I manage to choke, and then I shove past Dot and out into the glaring sun.

But before I can run back to the bothy and lock myself away, Dot grabs my shoulder.

'There's nothing to be scared of,' she says. 'We're safe here. I promise.'

I stare at her bright eyes, her earnest expression. She believes her own words. On her neck, still, are red marks – from his lips or his fingers, I can't tell – and yet she truly believes what she's saying. And it's impossible to know what to do.

There are so many pathways to disaster: I walked out with Angus and I can still feel his hands around my throat; I rowed out to rescue the drowning sailors and I can still sense the dying man's shuddering last breath beneath my hands as I pressed the coat down on his face. It's so easy to make the wrong choice. Easier just to hide away, where I can do no harm.

I look at Dot: her wide eyes, her face full of hope and life. She is everything I once was and I can't leave her here alone.

I'm still holding the brush, my hand white-knuckled around it. Dot follows my gaze. 'You could help me paint?' she suggests softly.

My head aches. 'I'd like that.'

As I follow her into the chapel, I can see Cesare and the other prisoners watching us. I can feel the guard's eyes on us – I don't know him. I don't know what he's thinking, what he might be planning. My breath balloons in my chest, my legs tingle with the urge to run.

I can't leave her here.

I force myself to follow Dot. I force myself to copy her movements, dipping my brush into the brown pigment and lifting it to the wall. She shows me how to paint the centre of each tile dark brown, and then to make the outside paler. She shows me how to use white paint at the edges of each tile.

'It'll give the illusion of light, from a distance,' she says confidently.

I glance sideways at her, my sister, the other half of myself, as she speaks in a voice I don't recognize, telling me things I don't know, and for a moment, I feel a surge of bitterness at the way these prisoners have pulled us apart. But I also know that the separation started long before they arrived. It started after Angus held me down on the beach and I wouldn't tell Dot the truth. Or perhaps it started before that. Perhaps it started the night our parents left and I blamed myself. And she blamed me too, I'm sure of it.

My hand trembles and my brush blotches the paint. 'It's all my fault,' I whisper.

Dot pauses in her painting. 'Oh, don't worry about mistakes,' she says brightly. 'It can all be corrected. See?' And she takes her brush and paints out the blurry smudge, before going back to her own tile and running a dark streak across it.

'You try,' she says.

Carefully, my hand still shaking, I paint over the ugly brown line, blending it into the surrounding tile, so that no one would ever know there had been a mistake at all.

'Now stand back from it,' Dot says.

I step back three paces and look at the wall, which is simply flat plasterboard. But from a distance, each painted tile looks real, as though it is part of some living, breathing building.

Behind us, Cesare and the other two men give a small round of applause and I can feel myself beginning to smile. I can feel some tension inside me loosening, as though a hand that has grasped me for so long is finally releasing its grip.

July 1942

Dorothy

Usually, July would be a time for working on the land and at sea. There are fish to be caught and salted; there are blocks of peat to be cut and dried out, ready for burning in the winter. But this year, there is a constant supply of food, sent from the south for the prisoners, who are happy to share with us.

The barriers are coming on fast: huge cages full of rocks act as stepping stones between the islands now, and the prisoners are busy tipping more rocks into the gaps. The sea roars between these spaces and the currents around the islands are unrecognizable, dragging everything far out to sea.

The chapel, too, is nearly finished. Major Bates lets the men scavenge scraps of metal from the ships lying in the bay. Cesare wants real tiles for the chapel floor and I have started to go with him, helping to lever up the tiles from the head in one of the half-sunk ships.

Con watches me leave from the chapel doorway, her face anxious. 'Come back before the tide turns.'

'Of course.'

As Cesare sets off towards the shoreline, I glance

back over my shoulder at Con. She looks thin and pale-faced, but she lifts her hand and waves.

The chapel is more than just a building for all of us. Somehow, it's a bridge. Somehow, it's an outstretched hand.

The land is brash with new growth. The wind buffets the grass and the tiny petals of the sea pinks; bees buzz drunkenly from flower to flower, the hum of their wings lost in the hushing whisper of the sea. From the rain-softened earth, the damp smell of life pulses.

Cesare walks ahead of me, turning back occasionally to smile. We have been on this journey twice before, and we know there is no time to linger.

The nearest ship is the easiest to reach: it is only partially submerged, its raw metal skeleton rising skywards from the water, while some of it rests on bare mud during a low tide. But it is so close to the shoreline that is has been almost completely stripped; the ship beyond it is the one that contains the real treasure.

The sea is cold around my legs as I wade out, gathering my skirt in one hand and lifting it clear of the water. Cesare's trousers are rolled above his knees, but the material on his thighs soon darkens. I watch the water creeping up his legs, laughing when he gasps at the chill.

'You are cruel,' he says. 'This sea is cruel. It wants to kill me with cold because it did not drown me.'

I laugh, but it feels strained. 'You shouldn't jump into the sea if you can't swim.'

'You will teach me to swim,' he says. 'And I will not need to be frightened of the sea.' He reaches out for the lowered side of the sunken ship and pulls himself up, then holds out a hand for me.

'Everyone should be frightened of the sea,' I say.

And I can't help thinking of the night when our mother and father left on the boat. There was a storm brewing but Mammy was in pain again – her stomach had swollen so much over the past months, as her arms and legs had grown thin, her face gaunt. Daddy had been planning to take her across to the mainland to ask about stronger medicine than we could get in Kirkwall, but Mammy wouldn't leave without saying goodbye to Con, who was out walking.

Con didn't want them to leave at all, so stayed out as long as she could. By the time she got home, darkness was dropping, the wind was howling and the waves were wild. Mammy was doubled up with pain and groaning, but Daddy wouldn't take out the boat in such bad conditions.

'Take her, please,' Con had begged, her voice tight with fear and guilt.

At first, Daddy had refused and I'd argued against it too. But Con had begged and pleaded, while Mammy had writhed in pain. Eventually, Daddy relented and set off in the smaller of our two boats. Con and I watched them row away.

They didn't come back.

He'd been out fishing in worse, I consoled Con. Perhaps they had sheltered on one of the other islands. Perhaps they would return one day, I said desperately, knowing they wouldn't, finding it hard to keep the anger from my voice.

I never blamed her out loud.

Con wouldn't talk about it, barely spoke to me at all, barely left the house. And then one night, with no explanation, she had gone walking with Angus MacLeod.

Now, with one hand on a sunken ship, the other held out to me, Cesare says, 'You look sad.'

I force myself to smile. 'No, not sad at all.' Maybe I will be able to tell him one day, but not yet. Not until I'm certain I can trust him not to judge Con, not to criticize her.

We gather scraps of wood, bits of metal and old tiles in silence. Whenever I catch Cesare's eye, he smiles and, gradually, the feeling of darkness recedes.

'Your family,' I say. 'Are they like you?'

He pauses, his head on one side, and puts a piece of wood into his bag. 'They are different but the same also.'

I wait.

He bends to pick up more wood. 'They believe

sometimes things that are different, I think. They talk about *Il Duce* – I think they believe this, in here.' He points to his head.

'And you?' I don't dare look at him.

'I do not believe this. And this makes me angry, what they are believing. But now, I think . . .' He wipes the salt water from his hands and takes my arm. 'I think there is a belief in here,' he touches two fingers to my temple, 'and a belief here.' He touches the fingers to the centre of my ribcage and leaves them there. 'And this is the belief that matters.' He taps his fingers against my chest, like a heartbeat.

I nod, thinking of Con, who believes that the men are terrifying, but cares for them anyway.

'You're right,' I say. 'It's easy to get swept up in imagining all sorts of things. But it's the heart that matters. That's who you are. That doesn't change.'

When both our bags are full, he takes my hand and kisses me, very gently.

'We can go back to the chapel. If you are not wanting to go to the cave.'

I shake my head. 'I want to.' I kiss him back. He smells of leather, of wood, of the sea.

We have been to the cave twice before but, as we walk back along the cliff path, it still sets a deep pulse in my stomach. I'm intensely aware of Cesare alongside me: the sound of his breath, the sweat on his skin. We have to skirt around the camp to avoid being seen.

I keep my eyes focused on the boggy ground, the tus-socks of grass, the rocks and gorse, but still, from the corner of my eye, I can see him looking at me, can feel his eyes on my face. Twice, he trips and nearly falls, pulling laughter from both of us.

Once we are on the north side of the island, there is no need to stay out of sight: no one comes to this treacherous land, with its hidden sinkholes and marshy ground. In Kirkwall, they tell of how the Nuckelavee roams the seas around this part of the island, of how this is the ground where cursed women – too many of them to count – have buried their dead lovers. With each telling, the tales get taller. Con and I had chosen to believe none of them, although Con is reluctant to come out this way when the mists roll in from the sea.

Now the day is bright and clear, and I know exactly where the track is. My feet find the solid path and, behind me, Cesare places his own feet in the exact spots where I've trodden.

'One day,' he says, 'I will show you the hills around Moena. There, I can lead you. It is beautiful.'

'I'd like that,' I say, but the words are painful because how can that be? How could he ever show me his land? It feels like the myths of the dead lovers, like the stories of the Nuckelavee, like a made-up tale. It feels like something you might believe, for a short time, in the sleepless dark, knowing that daylight will make it dissolve. I worry, for a moment, that he will have heard the hesitation in my voice, and that he may think I don't care for him.

He says nothing.

The land drops away before us. To someone who has never been here, it would look like the edge of the cliff. Far below, the sea shifts against the sharp rocks. But I've been this way enough times to know where I must place my hands and feet, lowering myself into something like a tunnel, where I half crawl, crouching, until I reach the cave.

There is a blanket on an old wooden pallet laid out in one corner, alongside an unlit candle. Below the single gap in the cave roof, a spill of daylight shows the burned-out ashes of our fire from last week.

We are both breathing hard as he kisses me. We fumble with each other's buttons, our skin pimpling in the chilly air of the cave.

'You are cold.' He rubs my arms.

'I don't care.'

The heat of him, the weight of him. The closeness of him as we kiss again and again. His back is hard and smooth. His eyes on mine are wide, serious.

'*Ti amo*,' he says.

I kiss him again.

And everything in me rises to meet him. His mouth on my mouth. His breath in my lungs. For a stretch of time, nothing else exists.

*

As the sweat cools on our skin, he lights the fire, then lies back on the blanket, his arm across me. He runs his fingers over my neck, my breasts, my ribcage, down to my belly and back up, watching the pattern of goosebumps, then pressing his lips to smooth my skin again.

Then he lays his head on my chest.

'I mean this, about the mountains in Moena,' he says, and I know then that he heard the hesitation and disbelief in my voice earlier. 'I will show these to you. After the war, I will take you home.'

'After the war?' I say. 'But the barriers are nearly finished. And who knows where you will go afterwards, what will happen?' *And it won't be my home.*

I close my eyes and breathe in slowly to quell the panic I feel at a world without Cesare. It's a foolish idea that I can't survive without him, that when he goes, my world will be a washed-out grey. Before I met him, I didn't know that I was missing anything at all. I could have lived very happily without him. But now . . .

'Major Bates has said that you will be sent somewhere else, in England or Wales.' It is painful. A physical ache in my chest.

'I will come back for you.' He kisses my neck, my jaw, my mouth.

'How do we know when the war will end? It could be months or years.' I stare at him, trying to hide my fear. But in his eyes, I see the same terror, the same longing.

'Then I will wait for you,' he says. And he kisses me.

We cannot stay long in the cave: people will talk and Con will worry. There is a track, to the east of the cliffs, which leads down to the sea, where we rinse our bodies in the cold water, gasping, and where Cesare tries to swim.

I've shown him every time we've been to the caves, and although he can't stay afloat for more than a few strokes, he's able to turn onto his back now.

'Relax,' I say, my body floating underneath his. 'As if you're lying down.'

'I don't lie down in water,' he says irritably.

At first he panics and tries to stand up, but eventually he lets his weight rest on me, and then, as I swim out from under him, he stays floating, looking up at the sky, smiling.

Afterwards, we let the heat of the sun pull the water from our skin and then we tug on our clothes and start to walk up the path and back towards the camp, the bothy, the chapel.

Cesare presses something cold into my hand.

'What is that?' I open my palm and, in it, I see a jagged piece of metal, which must have come from somewhere on the ship. It looks like a miniature gabled roof, or the arch of a small bird's folded wing.

'What is it?' I ask again.

His eyes are warm. '*Cuore*,' he says. 'This is a heart.'

'Oh!' I turn it over, not knowing what to say. 'It's . . . sharp.'

He laughs. 'I pick it up on the beach before. It is part of a ship, perhaps. Or a bomb. I will melt it and make it a better shape in the forge, if you like?'

'Thank you.'

He takes it back from me and tucks it into his pocket.

The hour is late, the air cold and I worry about Con, so Cesare and I hurry the remaining distance back to the camp. The sun sits low on the horizon – in midsummer there is no such thing as true darkness – but the strange light makes weird shadows and we stumble more than once. There are no jokes this time.

There is a faint glow from the chapel, but inside it is silent and still, as if the building itself is praying. I never grow tired of the feeling of worship in this place. It is partly the closeness of the wind and the sea and partly the way that every painted brush-stroke and every curve of metal seems made from hope.

Cesare and I are both panting and I have gorse scratches on my legs.

'I must go back to the camp,' Cesare says, kissing me quickly.

I watch him walk down the hill, until I can no longer see his shadowy shape moving through the gathering darkness.

Then there is a hand on my shoulder. My blood jolts and I whirl around, hands raised, ready to claw at whichever guard –

It is Con. Her face tear-streaked and pale.

'Heavens, Con! What's wrong? You scared the life out of me.'

'Sorry, I'm sorry. It's just – I think I saw him. I think he's out there, somewhere, waiting for me.'

She doesn't have to tell me who *he* is.

My throat is dry and I pull her close. Her body feels thin and frail, smaller than mine, somehow, more fragile, even though we are exactly the same height. I can feel her fear, can feel her panicked heart. I wish she would talk to me about it, but every time I try to ask her to tell me exactly what happened, her face closes. I can't help thinking she must have done something terrible that night on the beach. I can't help suspecting – only sometimes, and only for a moment – that what people say is true, that she led him on, then attacked him. Why else would she refuse to tell me what happened? And I hate myself for thinking this of my own sister, for doubting her, even for an instant.

I squeeze her hand. 'Do you think . . . Are you *sure* it was him?'

'I'm not mad, if that's what you're asking.' Her voice is hard. 'I'm not imagining things.'

'I didn't say you were.' I feel a stab of guilt. 'Come on, let's go back to the bothy.'

'Can we just . . . Can we wait here for a while? Until we know he's gone. Until we're sure?'

'Of course.' I sit next to her on the cold chapel floor, pulling open the bag of wood and tiles that Cesare and I had gathered from the ship. 'We can start laying these tiles in a pattern on the floor. We've no cement, but we can see what they'll look like.'

She takes the tiles gratefully from me. Gradually her hands stop shaking and her breathing steadies.

As she sets down a tile, she says, 'Does Cesare . . . He doesn't ever hurt you?'

'No. Never.'

There is an awkward silence and I wait for her to ask something else.

We lay out the tiles in diagonal lines, creating an inverted arrow, which will draw people towards the altar and towards that picture of Mary holding Baby Jesus – the picture that looks so like Con's face, so like my own.

As Con lays the last of the tiles, she says, 'I won't let Angus hurt me again.' It's the first time in an age that I've heard her say his name.

Nor I, I think, and I clench the tile in my hand so tightly that it leaves a thin red line of broken skin.

It must be three in the morning when we walk back at last to the bothy, the land filled with the strange blue glow of the midnight sun.

Con's breathing is easier and she smiles at me in the pale light. Sometimes I have a painful glimpse of the person I've lost, of the sister who I feel I'll never see again. I miss her so much – it's like a knife twisting in my chest. And I have to remind myself that she's recovering, still. I have to remind myself that most injuries heal, in the end.

Outside the door of the bothy, my foot brushes against something. I bend down and pick up what feels like a stone, except that it is warm.

I hold it up to the ghostly, cloud-strewn sky.

He must have gone straight to the forge, rather than walking back to the camp.

'What is it?' Con asks.

It is part of a bomb, or part of a foreign ship that was ripped away and washed up on this beach. It is the best gift I've ever received.

Cuore.

'It's a heart,' I say.

August 1942

Cesare

Late one afternoon, towards the end of August, Cesare puts the final touches to the painting of Maria over the altar. She is nearly perfect. In the end, he decides to have her eyes downcast – this makes it easier for him to shape Dot's high cheekbones and the upward curve of her lips, without having to capture the hunger in her eyes when she looks at him.

As he paints, he remembers the feeling of her breath against his ear. The warmth of his name, exhaled into his mouth.

He imagines her working in the small hospital in Moena, if she wants to – hadn't she always said she wanted to be a doctor? It would be possible, surely. He imagines her walking with him in the mountains, swimming alongside him in the lakes. He will show her the church, where he painted the beautiful ceiling. He imagines introducing her to his parents.

Dorotea. Mia moglie. My wife.

His mother will gasp and take her hands. He imagines Dorotea at the table he sat at when he was a boy; he imagines her eating strong cheeses and soft bread, which she will dip into olive oil. He imagines her laughing, and drinking his father's red wine.

He refuses to let himself consider that Moena may be gone. The hospital, the church with its ceiling. The table he knows so well. His mother. His father. If he thinks of it, he feels sick and enraged. He doesn't sleep or, if he does, his dreams are bloody, muddled and vengeful.

Footsteps behind him. Cesare turns, brush in hand, half expecting it to be Dorotea. This happens sometimes: he will be thinking of her, and then she will appear, as if she has felt his thoughts calling to her. Sometimes, they finish each other's sentences; his English is improving all the time, and he has begun teaching her Italian.

But it is Angus MacLeod, now, standing behind Cesare in the chapel. He is sweating. Through the painted glass of the chapel window, coloured sunlight glints on his forehead, his nose, his unshaven cheeks. He licks his lips.

'What is it?' Cesare asks, his heart beating faster. He has only a paintbrush in his hand, and would be no match for MacLeod's baton and muscle. No match for his gun. His eyes are red, as if he has been crying, but surely that can't be right. Perhaps he has a fever. But then why come here, to the chapel? Through the whole process of building, MacLeod has kept away, having been warned and threatened by Major Bates.

'If you are ill,' says Cesare, 'you must go to the infirmary.'

'How did you do it?' Angus says.

Cesare looks around at the chapel, at the intricate rood screen, at the images that fill him with reverence, as if he hasn't created them himself, as if he decorated the entire chapel in a dream.

'I have painted much before,' he says. 'In Italy –'

'Not the bloody chapel, damn you!' MacLeod snaps, his curses cutting through the jewelled stillness of the place. 'How did you get . . . her?'

Someone must have been talking. One of the other prisoners, perhaps, or a guard. He and Dorotea still try to hide their visits to the concealed cave, but everyone knows of their relationship, or so Cesare had thought. Gino teases him about her all the time, and even Stuart the guard refers to her, with a wink, as 'your lady friend'. But somehow, it seems, everyone has kept it from MacLeod until now.

The man is sweating more heavily. A droplet forms above his lip and he wipes his face with his sleeve.

'How?' he demands again.

Cesare decides he must be honest. There is no point in feigning ignorance or lying – he still remembers the thud of MacLeod's baton on his back as he dug in the quarry. He has no doubt that this is a man who, even in his right mind, would be capable of murder. And MacLeod does not seem in his right mind now.

There is a wildness in his bloodshot eyes; a muscle near his mouth twitches, as if he might laugh or weep.

'She loves me,' Cesare says, and for a moment, he can feel Dorotea's breath against his cheek, whispering the words in his ear.

MacLeod's lip curls. 'Loves *you*? She can't. Look at your face, your skin – you don't even speak the same language.' He gestures at the chapel. 'Wrong bloody religion too. She can't love you. You've tricked her, somehow.'

Cesare swallows. How many paces to the chapel door? How much time and distance to outrun a bullet?

Quietly, he says, 'I love her too.'

He waits, muscles tensed, for MacLeod to raise his baton, or reach for his gun. Cesare could shove him backwards into the metal rood screen, perhaps. Or he could try to reach for the gun himself, try to grab it.

But then he sees MacLeod's eyes fill with tears. He steps closer, staggering a little, as if drunk. 'You think I don't love her sister? I've loved her for –'

'They are not the same,' Cesare says, half smiling.

This is a mistake, because MacLeod lunges for him then, wraps his hands around Cesare's head and pulls him in close, so that their foreheads clash painfully. MacLeod seems not to notice. His breath is sour with drink.

'I know that, you *fucking* Eyetie. I know they're not the same. But I've tried with Con. I took her out, after their parents disappeared. I was there to support her. I listened to her go *on* about how guilty she felt. And I still loved her. I gave her a *necklace*. And I've been watching her, making sure she's safe. God!' He pushes Cesare away. 'Perhaps she's trying to taunt me. Leading me on, still. I've heard of girls doing that – pretending not to care. Perhaps Dot will do that to you, eh? Ever think of that? Perhaps she won't talk to you next month . . .' He scrubs his hands across his face, sniffs. 'Oh! I've just remembered.' He laughs suddenly, the sound high-pitched as he stumbles, then fixes Cesare with his red-rimmed eyes. 'You won't be here next month. The barriers are nearly done. By the end of September, they'll be finished, and you'll be sent off to some camp. Major Bates said they're think-ing of Wales. Never mind. I'm sure Dot will find a way of keeping herself warm until the war's over.'

He leers and Cesare has to remind himself of the baton, of the gun, of the Punishment Hut. He breathes out, slowly. He grips the paintbrush until it snaps. He imagines stabbing it into MacLeod's eye socket. He breathes in.

MacLeod watches him, smiling, waiting. Cesare stands very still.

'I'll look after her for you,' MacLeod says.

Then he turns and walks from the chapel, a slight stagger in his step. Cesare forces himself to remain still; he fights down the white-hot fury that surges through his veins. He reminds himself that MacLeod won't be able to touch Dorotea – she'd never go anywhere near him.

But, still, Cesare will be leaving. He has not much more than a month left with her.

Five days later, lying in the cave, he is distracted and restless. He has walked the usual path in silence – he could walk it in his sleep – and, now, with Dorotea's head resting on his bare chest, he still says nothing. Twice, she has asked him what is wrong – the first time, she'd poked him teasingly in the ribs; he'd glared at her, then felt guilty at the hurt in her face. But he still can't tell her about MacLeod's threats. He can't tell her that he will be leaving so soon – even if she has her suspicions.

Today, she had looked out towards the barriers – at the few shrinking gaps, where the tide still surged – and she'd said, 'It won't be long.'

He'd said nothing. He knows his mood is ruining the little time they have left, but he can't shake himself out of it.

Will she wait for him? Will she follow him to Moena, one day, as she's promised? Or will she stay here with Con, who seems so much brighter and happier these days? She has talked about working in the

Kirkwall infirmary after the prisoners have left. Cesare can imagine Dorotea staying with her sister — or, at least, he can't imagine her leaving.

'I should go.' She sighs, standing up. Her face is tense and he wants to hold her, to kiss her. He wants to apologize, but then he would have to explain, would have to talk about leaving.

He watches her pulling on her dress, watches the elegance of her movements, her long pale limbs. Why would she wait for him? MacLeod is right — she deserves something more than *an Eyetie*.

Her hand, he notices, is curled around something.

'What is that?' he asks.

She opens her hand. In her palm is the metal heart he'd made for her. He'd pulled it hot from the forge and lifted it from the bucket before it was fully cooled. The skin of his right palm is slightly smooth, a scar the shape of half a heart or in the curve of a question mark.

'You like it?' he says.

'I carry it everywhere,' she says.

Something inside him crumbles. How could he have doubted her? He curls her fingers around it and kisses them.

'I'm sorry I am a *bastardo* today.'

She strokes his cheek. 'You are worried about leaving?'

Grateful to her for understanding, he nods.

'You should be,' she says, kissing his mouth. 'I have your heart.'

He laughs, returns her kiss. He's never known anything like the love he has for her. The closest feeling was when he was painting the chapel. It's a sense of reverence. A feeling like worship.

He kisses her again and then she pulls away.

'I have to go. Con will be worried.'

He nods, kisses her once more. 'You go. I'll follow. *Ti amo.*'

'I love you too.'

And she is gone.

He dresses slowly, enjoying the soreness in his limbs, the smell of her body on his; he is always reluctant to swim afterwards, but Dorotea insists that he practise, teasing that she won't always be there to rescue him. Now, the thought of her not being with him is too painful, so he is grateful for the way the cold sea clears his thoughts. His swimming strokes are basic – Dorotea laughs that he looks like a dog – but at least he won't drown. He dries himself quickly and walks back along the route to the chapel, trying not to look at the near-finished barriers. There are rumours that it's possible to walk across some parts of them now. Perhaps, after he has gone, Dorotea will be able to walk back to the old house that she'd spoken about, in Kirkwall – she says she misses it. Perhaps she'll try to buy it back. Perhaps she will find an Orcadian man to live with and they will have children, while he is miles away in Wales or somewhere else. Perhaps –

Stop!

There is a darkness creeping down from the sky and a few stars glimmering. It's still warm at the moment, but he hasn't forgotten the winter chill. Will it be as cold in Wales?

He is nearing the chapel when he hears a cry. High-pitched, then quickly cut off, like the calls of foxes he remembers echoing over the Moena hills. But there are no foxes on this island. The cry rings out again and, for a moment, he thinks of the stories Dorotea has told him about this place. The beasts that come in from the sea. The skinless creatures that breathe over the land, and the selkies, who cast off their skins and, underneath, are the most beautiful women anyone has ever seen.

The hairs rise on the back of his neck. The shout again – a woman's voice, certainly, and then a man's growl, afterwards.

The sounds are coming from behind the forge.

When he rounds the metal hut, there is a shadowy figure with many limbs writhing against the wall. He cannot, at first, make sense of what he is seeing. And then, all of a sudden, he can.

A man – a guard – is pressing a woman against a wall. He is trying to hitch up her skirt. The woman is batting at the man's face, but it seems to make no difference.

Cesare cannot understand why the woman is silent, and then he sees that the man is holding her by her throat.

He doesn't think, but barrels into the man, fists swinging. The man is knocked off balance and sprawls flat on his back. The woman doubles over, gasping, her long hair falling over her face. And she steps into the moonlight, choking, hands at her neck.

Dorotea!

Everything happens so quickly that it is only afterwards he can piece together the fragments, and even then, he is unsure of what exactly happened. It is a series of images, each like a photograph branded onto his memory: Dorotea coughing and retching, her hands at her throat. His own hand, reaching out for her – numb, as if it is not his own, as if this is not happening. The man launching himself at Cesare, landing punch after punch on his chest, face, skull. Cesare's ears ringing with the sound, but, through the sound and the pummelling fists, the awareness that the man sitting on his chest is Angus MacLeod.

Then a final thud, which Cesare does not feel . . . and Angus slumps on top of him, as if, in the midst of punching, he has fallen asleep.

And, standing behind Angus, with a baton in her hand, is Constanza. She raises it to strike again, to bring it down on Angus's skull.

'*Fermare!*' Cesare shouts, and then Dorotea cries, 'Stop!'

Time slips back into itself, like a joint into a socket. Cesare crawls out from beneath MacLeod's unconscious body and checks his pulse.

Alive.

Then he stands and pulls Dorotea to him. She is weeping.

'He was just . . . He was there. I couldn't –' She chokes.

He strokes her hair. 'You are hurt?' He examines her throat, where there are faint bruises emerging, but no other marks. 'He hurt you?'

And he takes the baton from Con and stares at Angus's body. He lifts it.

'Stop!' Both women speak at the same time.

Blood trickles from Cesare's forehead into his eyes; his mouth tastes of copper. He spits, then looks at MacLeod's prone body again.

'What shall we do?' he asks.

Con says, 'We could roll him off the cliff.'

The women stand side by side. They look uncanny, otherworldly. He thinks again of the selkie myths. The stories of those mysterious women, who can drown sailors without remorse.

Dorotea sighs. And Cesare doesn't know what she would have said, doesn't know if she's capable of murder, because, at that moment, MacLeod stirs, swears, rubs the back of his head, sits up.

He blinks at Con, at the baton in her hand.

Then he looks at Cesare, at Dorotea, and back to Con, with the baton. He sits upright, licking his lips nervously.

'Con, I'm sorry,' he says. 'I didn't mean to go near Dot. I thought . . . I thought she was you.' His story doesn't make sense, but he carries on, his face earnest. 'She tried to kiss me and she told me she was you. And it's *you* I love. You have to believe me.'

Con doesn't move. 'Don't touch my sister.' Her voice shakes.

'You stay away from them,' Cesare says. And he's aware of a threatening growl in his voice that makes it sound like someone else's. He's aware that it wouldn't take much for him to kill this man. The thought feels calming and clear, like a drink of cool water when you're parched with thirst.

MacLeod stands, looks at Cesare. 'What will you do if I don't?' MacLeod touches his head. His hand comes away bloody. 'Tell you what,' he says, 'if anything else happens to me, you should remember I've got friends in Kirkwall. And soon they'll be able to walk across to this island. They're not worried about stupid stories of a curse any more. And they can bring others with them to redecorate your chapel, to take down some of your flashy *Catholic* decoration. They might talk to your Eyetie friends, too – Gino, is it, and Marco? And that priest, Ossani? No one will object if prisoners get hurt in another riot.'

Cesare feels sick. 'You cannot –'

'I can do what I like.' MacLeod steps in close to him, until their faces are almost touching. 'I belong here. I've got a uniform that says so. I'm part of this land. What are you? Some piece of dirt from a place that probably doesn't exist any more. And these girls, they're not yours. You've no right to touch them, do you hear?'

Cesare imagines grabbing the baton from Con and bringing it down on this man's face again and again.

He imagines the Punishment Hut, the firing squad. It would almost be worth it, to keep Dorotea safe.

'Please,' he hears Dorotea whisper. 'Please don't touch him.' And he doesn't know if she's talking to him or to MacLeod, but a heartbeat passes, and then another, and then another. Finally, MacLeod steps backwards, snatches the baton from Con and begins stumbling down the hill.

As soon as he is out of sight, Dorotea turns to Cesare. 'You have to leave.'

His stomach lurches. 'I can't.'

The bruises on her neck are darkening. He can almost make out the shape of MacLeod's fingers. 'You have to leave,' she repeats, 'or he will kill you.'

Con nods. 'She's right.'

He swallows. 'How?' he asks.

'We have a boat,' Dorotea says. 'You can row out, before the barriers are finished. There's still room between them for a small boat. It's ten miles to Scotland.

Or if you don't go to Scotland, if you go to one of the other islands, south of Kirkwall . . .' She draws a shuddering breath. 'Anything is better than staying.'

'I can't leave you.' His chest swells and his throat aches with everything he can't say, everything he can't put into words. That to leave her here would feel like leaving part of his soul. That to leave her in danger, with MacLeod, is unthinkable.

'Come with me,' he says.

'I can't.' Dorotea's eyes are full of tears as she takes Con's hand.

But Con steps away from her. 'You should,' she says.

'What?' Dorotea steps back, confused.

Cesare doesn't understand either. Why would Con tell her to go? It makes no sense.

'You have to go,' Con says, her voice steady.

And Cesare can see the effort this costs her, can see the way she balls her still-shaking hands into fists behind her back, so that Dorotea won't see.

He can see how she is taking her terror and turning it into something better. He remembers crawling, dehydrated, across the desert in Egypt, dragging the injured Gino with him, knowing the strain might kill him in that heat, knowing a bullet might hit him at any moment. Knowing that none of it mattered, as long as Gino was safe.

'You should go with him,' Con says.

Late August, Early September 1942

Dorothy

The days grow darker but no one sleeps. Cesare explains the cuts and bruises on his face to the other prisoners by saying he fell one night on the way to the chapel.

'Do they believe you?' I ask. His lips are cut and one of his eyes is half shut, blackened by Angus's fists.

'Gino does not,' he says. 'But I cannot be truthful about this.'

He doesn't need to tell me why. I imagine the prisoners turning on the guards in revenge. I imagine the retribution that would follow.

I run my fingers over his scabbed lips, thinking of everything we have to hide.

Each evening I stay in the chapel with Cesare for as long as I can. Often, we don't speak at all, but he rests his hand on my cheek or my leg. I can feel him looking at the marks on my neck; they are fading, but the feel of fingers there never leaves me. Sometimes, as if sensing the bleakness of my thoughts, he wraps his arms around me. Each gesture is one of comfort, with no hint of demand in it. We haven't been back to the cave.

When my eyelids are starting to droop, Cesare walks me to the bothy, where he kisses my cheek gently, then goes back to the camp. Angus must have gone to Kirkwall hospital to have his injuries tended, because he is not in the infirmary. I dread to think what he must be planning in Kirkwall, with his friends who hate the prisoners and resent the chapel.

I lie awake in the darkness of the bothy, my mind humming. When I close my eyes, I see Angus's face pressed close to mine; I feel the crush of his lips, the heat of his breath. If ever I do sink into an uneasy doze, I startle awake with the sensation of his hands around my throat. Con strokes my hair when I gasp upright, or rubs her hand over my back if I weep. 'It will get better,' she whispers.

She can't sleep either, so much of our time is spent planning how we will get Cesare away from the island without anyone noticing. I still can't decide what to do. If I go, I will be leaving Con alone. She tells me she will return to Kirkwall, that she will work in the hospital there. She tells me she has befriended Bess Croy, who also wants to work in the hospital after the prisoners have left.

'What about *him*?' I ask.

Her jaw tightens, but her eyes are clear. 'I will stay away from him,' she says, even though we both know that in a place as small as Kirkwall, that won't be possible.

In the chapel, Cesare says to me, 'I will escape alone. If you want to stay with your sister, I will go

287

first. You can follow soon.' His expression is pained as he says this, but I know he means it.

And I think of how this war has shown everyone's true nature.

I imagine Cesare on the boat alone, sailing through the rough autumn waters, and then I think of our parents setting sail in the dark, never to return. And I know that my decision was made long ago, when I picked up a wind-whirled piece of card and gave it to a man I didn't know.

The question is, how we will get away without being noticed. We need a distraction.

On the first day of September – five days after Angus held me up against the forge wall by my throat – Cesare knocks quietly on the bothy door in a quick pattern of five raps, which we'd all agreed on, so we would know it was him.

I'm lying on the bed, but Con gets up to answer.

Cesare's cheeks are flushed from the walk up the hill, and there's a tension around his eyes.

'What is it?' I ask.

'Major Bates says we are having a feast. For . . . Michaelmas?'

'But Michaelmas isn't until the end of September.' Con frowns.

'He says we will not be here then. The barriers will be finished and we will all be gone. But now there is much spare food to use and he wants to celebrate the chapel and barriers also. He will bring people from Kirkwall.'

My mind whirls. People from Kirkwall . . . That will mean Angus. My stomach drops. But with all the disruption, people coming and going from the island . . .

'This is our chance to escape,' I say. 'When is the feast?'

Cesare hesitates. 'Tomorrow,' he says.

I look at Con. She's trying to smile but her eyes have filled with tears.

'It's good you don't have many things,' she says. 'Packing will be quick.'

I pull her in close. 'Thank you,' I whisper.

The next day dawns grey and bleak. September is the time of Gore Vellye, the autumn tumult, when the weather turns vicious and the sea batters the land. Tales tell us it is the time of the battle between the Sea Mither and the monster Teran. Every spring, the Sea Mither battles the vicious Teran and imprisons him at the bottom of the ocean. But each autumn he rises again and banishes her. Then he begins his six-month winter tyranny: he buffets and pounds the islands, and pauses only to listen to the gurgling cries of drowning sailors.

It is a year to the day since our parents disappeared.

I don't mention it and neither does Con, but her face is anxious and, when she thinks I'm not looking, she wipes tears from her eyes. There is little time to grieve, though: we rise at dawn to stuff clothes and food into a bag. Con makes some dry oat biscuits and wraps them in greased paper – enough for Cesare as well as me: he won't be able to take food with him from the camp without arousing suspicion.

After we have fed the chickens, Con disappears behind the bothy and I hear the scraping sound of her digging. I remember all those months ago, when I'd heard a similar sound after the night of fog.

I don't look at her when she returns: I don't want to pry. But she places a small material bag in my hand. It contains something cold, which jangles lightly, like far-off bells. I go to open it, but she places her hands on mine.

'Don't,' she says.

'What is it?'

'Something I don't need any more. I'd like you to throw it into the sea, somewhere far away from here.'

I nod and tuck it into my pocket.

As she turns away, I murmur, 'I didn't ever blame you.'

And I don't know whether I mean I didn't blame

her for our parents, or for Angus, or for the life we had to build here. I don't know if it's true. Perhaps I did blame her sometimes. Perhaps I thought her guilty or weak or frustrating. Perhaps I thought she'd brought all this upon herself and had dragged me into it too.

But I don't blame her now. Now, finally, I understand.

People start arriving from Kirkwall just before midday. We watch them setting off from the far shore; some walk along the barriers as far as they can, then decide that the gap in the centre is still too big and they must take their boats. The sea is whipping up a fury and the route across is nearly impassable. As soon as the barriers are finished, that won't matter. For thousands of years, this island has been cut off, private, cursed. Now those old tales are dying out.

The faces of the Orcadians in the boat are eager, expectant. Some of their owners point across at the chapel on the hill, and the place where Con and I are standing. We have positioned ourselves here intentionally. So much of today's success will depend upon us being seen.

Angus MacLeod must be among the people in the boats – he wouldn't miss this. Standing on the hill, letting him look at me, but unable to see him, I feel as if everything is being flayed from me. Clothes, skin, flesh. I stand, shuddering in my bones.

Con slips her hand into mine.

After the boats have moored in the bay, she and I walk across to the chapel to wait. I wonder where Cesare is, in the camp. I hope he doesn't meet Angus when he is alone. My chest contracts in fear.

The chapel is cold and filled with a light the colour of old paper. While we are waiting, I offer up a quick prayer to whatever force for good there may be in this world. Then I stand, alongside Con, just inside the door. My legs feel weak and I'd like nothing more than to hide in the bothy. I know from her uneasy expression that Con feels the same, but it won't do: we have to be seen by as many people as possible.

We hear them coming up the hill: their shouts and laughter. It is a feast day, after all, and for many of them, it'll be the first time they've been to the island. They hesitate outside the chapel: we hear them marvelling at its beauty, its elegance, at how like a real stone building it is.

I feel a swell of pride and wish Cesare could hear them. Except that they probably wouldn't say it to him.

John O'Farrell is the first into the chapel. His hair is greyer than I remember it, his face pouched, his skin pale. Bess told me the rumours about his son, James, and my heart aches for the boy I remember playing with, and for the man standing before me now – the man who was once my father's best friend. He stares at the walls and ceiling in gape-mouthed wonder – he doesn't notice me, or Con, standing just inside the door.

'Hello, Mr O'Farrell.' I feel suddenly shy, meeting this man from my old life, who helped teach me my times tables and how to hold a pen.

'Oh, hello there!' His eyes flick from me to Con, and then he looks at my skirt and her trousers and says, 'Dot.'

I nod, wondering how much we've changed to other people. How is it possible to be entirely transformed on the inside and still look like the same person to the rest of the world? I thought the same after our parents disappeared when people would say, approvingly, *You look well*, as if they expected me to be constantly wailing or tearing out my hair. As if they expected sorrow to have bent me double, or aged me, or twisted my features. As if, because this hadn't happened, I must be coping.

And I would think, *What do you know about grief? About loss? About anything at all?*

John O'Farrell shifts awkwardly and looks down at his feet. 'I'm sorry if things have been ... difficult here.'

I wonder how much news from the island has reached Kirkwall, how many made-up stories. And I think of the promise John made, to our fisherman father when our mother was so ill, that he would always protect us if he had to.

'I think . . .' I say, and I can see John bracing himself, I think war makes everything difficult, everywhere. One way or another.'

He smiles gratefully. 'You're a good girl, Dot.'

I return the smile. And I think, *What do you know?*

After John has moved to the front of the chapel to look at the paintings, other people file in: old Mr Cameron, coughing; Neil MacClenny and his family; Bess Croy's mother, Marjorie, with all her young brood. The children gasp and gawk at the pictures. They run their fingers over the plasterboard and stroke the rood screen. Laughter echoes through the chapel. Every face is filled with wonder and delight.

Then Robert MacRae comes in, his face set in a sneer. And behind him walks Angus MacLeod. Nausea rinses through me, but I do exactly as we'd planned. I go to Con's side, straight away, standing close enough for our arms to touch.

Angus stops in front of us.

'Well, aren't you a doubly fine sight on a terrible day?' he says.

'Hello, Angus.' I force the words out. There are so many reasons that I must be friendly to him today, but the most important one, at the moment, is that he must be calm when Cesare arrives. Because I will not be here to keep the peace.

He looks me up and down, smiles, then leans in close. 'I'm sorry about . . .' He touches his throat briefly. 'I didn't mean to hurt you. Truly.' His eyes are wide and earnest.

I want to shout, *You held me against a wall by my neck. You forced your tongue into my mouth. You tried to tear off my underwear. How could you not hurt me?*

I swallow. I nod. I can hear my heart beating in my ears. If I say anything, I will vomit or scream. I force myself to smile. My muscles feel rigid, wooden.

'Con.' Angus says, and I see the same stiff smile on her face.

'Hello,' she says, and her voice sounds high-pitched, as if fingers are pressing against her throat.

Angus looks us both up and down again, then moves on into the chapel. I hear him whisper something to Robert and both of them laugh, loudly.

My skin crawls.

I turn to Con. She is pale, her breath coming fast.

'Right. We can go now. You're ready?'

Wordlessly, she nods and we walk back towards the bothy. The wind is whipping more strongly now. Down in the camp, the prisoners are lining up, ready to march up to the chapel for the blessing. Cesare must be among them, but I can see only a mass of those brown uniforms with their red targets. My mouth is dry. We can't afford to fail.

Inside, the bothy is warmer, with the last faint ashes

of the peat fire still glowing in the grate. I hold my hands up to it — who knows when I will next be warm?

Then I take off my skirt and give it to Con. She pulls off her trousers and passes them to me. They hold the heat from her skin still. I put them on, experiment with bending down in them, then try lifting my legs high, as if I'm climbing into a boat.

'This is so much easier!' I exclaim.

'I know.' Con pulls on my heavy woollen skirt with such distaste that I can't help smiling, despite my fear, despite my dread. Despite the electric stretch in the air, like a thread ready to snap.

I turn to take a last look at the bothy, imprinting it on my mind. Then I tuck the bag under my coat and Con and I walk out of our home into the gathering storm.

Constance

No time for tears, although I can feel the familiar ache in my throat, the bubble of grief swelling in my chest as we walk towards the camp. Dot says nothing, but flashes a quick, tight smile at me.

What will I do without you?

The thought echoes what our mother used to say to us, after she became ill and we moved back into the Kirkwall house to nurse her. We would sponge her cheeks and chest; we would hold a glass of water to her lips. We were twenty-three and all our lives she had been the strongest person we knew. She lay in bed, weak as a child, her eyes burning. And she would say to us, *What would I do without you?*

The words wheezed from her; the house echoed with the rattle of her breath. On the day she and Daddy were supposed to go on the boat to Scotland, to get her some better medicine, I stayed out late walking, because I didn't want to say goodbye to her. I didn't want to watch her go, knowing I might never see her again.

But she wouldn't leave without saying goodbye to me. So they waited for me to return. They waited and waited and, all the while, the wind rose. And by the time I arrived home she was grey with pain but the waters were too rough for rowing across to Scotland. But I felt guilty, so guilty. I couldn't stand the thought that I'd increased her pain. And so I persuaded them to row out on those rough waters. Daddy had been out in worse, I knew. I told them to go so that I wouldn't feel so guilty for being selfish and not wanting to say goodbye to her.

I screamed at them.

They never came back.

It won't be like that today, I tell myself. Dot will be safe; she will return. This isn't for ever, it's just for a short time, just until the war is over.

If the war is ever over.

I crush the thought.

Dot is walking next to me, deep in reflection.

I don't know what to say to her. The wind whips tears from my eyes. The sea heaves, covered with white caps. It is a grim and sickly grey.

'Are you sure you won't come with us?' Dot asks.

My stomach twists but I shake my head. 'The hospital in Kirkwall needs nurses. There are always people brought in after storms – I'd like that, I think, helping people.'

I think of our parents: of how I wish I could have taken them from the sea and cared for them. How I wish I could have kept them safe. I clear my throat and say, 'There's a life for me here.'

I keep my voice level because I can't allow her to guess at my uncertainty and fear. I can't allow her to suspect the other part of my plan for today, the part I've barely allowed myself to think about. The part that will allow me to be free. If Dot suspects, she will try to stop me. If she suspects, she will not leave.

And if it works, I will be able to live in Kirkwall again. I will refuse to feel shame. I will face people again. I won't run away.

The camp is deserted, apart from a single guard, who is red-faced and squinting in the wind, and keeps looking up towards the chapel. His body stiffens when he sees us walking down the hill. I feel a flash of fear and have to remind myself that he won't hurt me.

I don't think he'll hurt me.

'Shouldn't you be up at that get-together in the chapel like everyone else?' he asks resentfully.

I force myself to smile. 'We have to come to the infirmary and check on the patients,' I say. 'So we're working, just like you. But it doesn't seem fair on you, when the other guards are all having fun. Are you here alone?'

He scowls. 'We drew lots,' he says. 'So it's fair enough, I suppose.'

I step closer, making my voice light, despite the fear I feel at being so close to this man, this stranger, who is so much stronger than me. 'Why don't you go up to the chapel with the others? It seems a shame for you to miss it. There are hardly any prisoners here, only the men in the infirmary and we'll be watching them.'

'I can't leave my post without getting a court-martial.' He eyes me suspiciously, then looks at Dot, at the bag she's carrying, full of her things for the journey.

'What's that you've got?'

I curse myself, wishing we'd hidden it better. But I've underestimated Dot.

'Incontinence pads, for the soldiers whose cathe-ters have come out. I've brought some of the cloths I use for my monthlies. Here.' She holds up the bag; he turns away with an expression of disgust.

'Get on with you.'

I hurry towards the infirmary, exhaling some of the jittery fear I've felt, and Dot follows.

'If Bess is there,' I say, 'I'll sidetrack her.'

But the infirmary is quiet. There are only three men in the beds and all of them are asleep. Bess must be out at the chapel, or else she'll have gone into the mess hut to get to the food before all the prisoners arrive back.

'Quick,' I say to Dot, and turn to keep an eye on the door, while she goes to the supply cupboard. I hear the clink of bottles dropping into the bag, and the rattle of pills.

'Take as much as you can,' I say. 'You might need to trade.'

She stuffs two extra bandages and another bottle of sulfa tablets into the bag, her face tense.

'I don't like doing it this way.'

'You've no choice.'

When we go back outside, it's raining. The guard by the gate stands with his back to us, hunch-shouldered.

'I'll distract him,' I say. Because I can do this for her. I can.

She nods and pulls me into a hard embrace. I wrap my arms around her, concentrating on the rhythm of my breath, on keeping it steady, in time with hers.

I mustn't fall apart now.

'Be careful,' I choke.

'You too.'

What else can I say to her? How can I say goodbye to half of myself?

I let her go. She turns and steps into the shadows behind the infirmary as I crush my nerves and call out to the guard. I tell him I heard a noise. I ask him if someone might have come across to the camp from Kirkwall, instead of going to the chapel.

The guard grumbles in irritation, but he dutifully searches the other side of the infirmary, and down between two of the first empty huts. And while I help him to check, Dot slips out from behind the infirmary and towards the gate. She doesn't turn to wave, or for one last look, but puts her head down against the rain, walking quickly in the direction of the bay.

Something inside me cracks and collapses.

And as I thank the guard – who cannot find anyone skulking near the infirmary – and walk back up the hill towards the chapel, I feel a ripping sensation in my chest, as if my lungs are being squeezed and I cannot draw enough air. Or as if a hand is reaching into my ribcage and placing a cold finger next to my heart.

The wind snaps my hair across my face and drowns the sound of my sobbing.

By the time I reach the chapel, my breathing has steadied.

The Italians are massed around the outside of the building – and perhaps some are inside, too, with the people from Kirkwall. Maybe those prisoners who helped with the farming work on the mainland have also been allowed into the dry and the warmth, or perhaps not. I'm sure that allowing the foreigners to work on their land feels very different to the island people from being alongside them in a church.

At first, I worry that I won't be able to find Cesare, but after the first few prisoners turn and see me, the word travels through the crowd, and soon they are all turning to look at me.

Like a pack of hungry dogs, I think, and the old fear washes over me again. I nearly turn away, nearly walk back over the hill to the bothy. But I cannot. Because of Dot. Because I am being brave.

My cheeks flame as the prisoners step to one side. As I walk through the crowd to try to find Cesare, I am aware of the closeness of these men, watching me. The size of them, the musky smell of them, like something feral and waiting. I imagine all of them with Angus's face, with his greedy eyes and his crushing hands.

And I stop, staring at my feet, at the size of them, surrounded by these men's boots, the smell of their sweat, the heat of their bodies, the boom of their laughter. I want to be with Dot, walking down towards the boat. I want to be back in the bothy. I want to be back in the house in Kirkwall, before our parents left.

'Dorotea!' a prisoner's voice shouts. And I turn, hope rising in my chest, expecting to see her coming over the hill. But the prisoner calls again, and someone grasps my hand. And I jump and recoil and look up into Gino's face. He has a cap pulled down low over his head.

'Dorotea?' he asks.

I remember. I swallow my fear. 'Yes,' I say.

'Cesare is here.'

I nod, unable to force any more words past my dread.

Cesare is standing just behind Gino. He, too, is wearing a hat, where most of the other prisoners are bare-headed.

Cesare smiles when he sees me, and says, *'Bella,'* but there is another question in his eyes. Something like, *Is everything all right?* Or, *Is she safe?*

I give a tiny nod and watch the relief tug his smile wider. And there is no name for what I feel then, for the mixture of jealousy and loss and release. She has someone who loves her absolutely, and without question. I have only her in this world, and I have to let her go.

Cesare stands next to me until the people from Kirkwall begin filing out of the chapel. They flinch as they walk into the blasting wind and rain, but still, I see Angus emerge from the building, searching, ignoring the weather. His gaze travels over the crowd of prisoners, finds me, standing next to Cesare, and stops.

His mouth sets in a thin line and he begins moving towards us, just as the guards blow the whistle for the prisoners to walk down towards the mess hut.

The Italians give a whoop and I'm carried along with them, down the hill. Cesare is next to me, within arm's reach, and Gino is walking three steps ahead of us, although I notice he has taken off his hat. Somewhere behind us, Angus is watching. He will be trying to fight his way through the prisoners, trying to get to me.

My neck and back feel exposed but I daren't look back.

Cesare turns to look at me. 'You are ready?' he calls.

I nod, although I don't know the details of this part of the plan, don't know what to expect.

Gino lifts a guard's whistle to his lips and gives a short blast. Then I hear shouting off to our right, a scuffle and a yell: some of the prisoners have begun fighting. Everyone stops and turns as one prisoner shouts and swings his fist at another. More guards blow their whistles; the men all around me roar and, in the midst of the confusion, Cesare gives my fingers a quick squeeze, takes off his hat, and pushes away to the left, out of the crowd, away from the chaos. In less than three heartbeats, Gino is next to me, his hat pulled down low over his ears.

'Now we are to stay away from that *bastardo*

MacLeod,' he says, 'and we will make him believe that we are Dorotea and Cesare.'

I nod. I search the crowd anxiously for Angus and catch a glimpse of his face. He is watching the fight, looking on with satisfaction as the guards drag the two fighting men away, and off towards the Punishment Hut.

'Do not worry,' Gino says. 'They will have extra food and cigarettes after.'

But I'm not worried about them – not truly. I'm thinking of Dot, waiting for Cesare. I'm imagining him running down the hill towards the bay. I'm picturing them stepping into the small rowing boat. I'm trying not to think of the danger that lurks under the grey-green surface of the water. Sea the colour of illness. The colour of drowned bodies.

I close my eyes and hold my breath, as if my hope and longing could carry her safely past the barriers.

And then the crowd begins to move forward towards the mess hut, and I walk alongside Gino, hoping we can fool Angus for long enough.

Food is laid out on all the tables. Bread and beans and tureens of steaming stew. There are plates of eggs and even a little bacon. The prisoners exclaim with joy and, in spite of my anxiety, my mouth waters: it is more food than I have ever seen and I've been too nervous to eat for days.

'This is all the food for two weeks,' Gino says. 'Because we are finishing the barrier quickly. Just one gap and then it's finish. We are leaving soon, I think. They say we are going in Wales? I do not know but I am eating all this food today, until I have a fat stomach!'

He laughs, but I can see tension around his eyes and I know that he must be thinking of Cesare, wondering if his friend is safe. He must be pretending, just as I am, must be gripped with terror, just like me.

He piles his plate high and offers to do the same for me, but I shake my head. He leans in and says, 'You must try to eat, *bella*. Remember, you are Dorotea and I am Cesare. People must believe this. We are in love.'

'I know,' I say faintly.

His gaze is soft with pity. 'We do a good thing for them. Now, you tell me if you see the *bastardo* and I turn my face from him. We must give them much time to escape.'

I nod and pick at the bread roll he gives me. It is like chalk in my mouth.

Around us, the prisoners shout and sing and eat. I can't see Angus, and then I spot him, over in the corner of the mess hut. He isn't eating either; his eyes skim repeatedly over the prisoners. I incline my head, so that Gino knows where he is standing. Gino moves his body so that Angus will see only his back, and I position myself so that Gino hides my face from view.

There are other people from Kirkwall in the hut

now, other people who are not in uniform and will make me harder for Angus to find.

I keep my eyes fixed on Gino, watching him eat, and on Angus, but I can feel the assessing glances of the Orcadians. Blood creeps into my cheeks as I'm flooded with shame once more.

Dot had asked me once, just before we left Kirkwall nearly a year ago, if I thought I was punishing myself by hiding away, by refusing to look at my face in the mirror. And, in a way, I suppose I was torturing myself for what I'd allowed to happen – I felt I deserved to be unhappy.

But now, seeing the smug expression on the Orcadians' faces when they note me blushing, I understand that I punished myself because that was what people expected. There was something reassuring to them in my shame, in my guilt, in my self-loathing. When I condemned myself, when I hid myself away, I made them feel safer – as long as I felt disgraced, then all was well in their world. Every time I looked in the mirror, I didn't see myself through my own eyes, but through theirs. I saw my humiliation.

I'm tired of feeling ashamed.

And that is when I step away from the protection of Gino's body. He is talking and laughing with another prisoner, so he doesn't notice me moving to one side, into Angus's line of vision.

I wait, feeling a jolt as Angus's eyes lock on mine. I

don't know if he realizes it is me, or if he thinks I'm Dot. Either way, I know he will want to follow me.

Quietly, I squeeze through the crowd of prisoners until I am near the door.

Dot and Cesare must be in the boat. They will be moving out of sight, rowing towards freedom. There will be no one to see me, or Angus, now. There will be no one to stop me.

I turn back, to make sure he is following me, and then I push out into the cold and the growing darkness.

There are still some people from Kirkwall and some prisoners waiting outside the mess hut, but they are so keen to get inside and reach the food that they barely notice me.

I don't look back again, but walk briskly across the yard. My boots tap on the stony ground. The sound is certain, definite. I listen to the rhythm of my footsteps, imagining that they belong to a more confident woman, a fearless woman. Imagining that they belong to someone like Dot.

I picture them together, passing through the barriers, out of sight of the island. The night will be closing around them, like a fist, hiding them – hiding everything.

The sea will be wild. The rocks are sharp. And if I am ready for Angus, if he doesn't suspect anything, I will be able to surprise him.

I imagine the single hard push against his chest. I imagine him falling. I imagine the splash.

I am out of the yard now, out past the guard, out of sight of the camp. My fear is an animal thing, a writhing sickness that threatens to overwhelm me, but it mustn't. I mustn't stop now. I look back once more, to see that Angus is following.

And I begin to run.

Dorothy

Twice, while waiting for Cesare, I nearly go back to Con. But then I remember the thud of Angus's fists against Cesare's skull. I remember the pressure of his fingers around my neck. And I stay by the boat, waiting. In my pocket is Con's gold chain. I will find a place to fling it into the sea, once Cesare arrives.

I imagine him changing his mind. I picture him going into the mess hut with the other prisoners, staying with Gino and the rest. He is giving up everything for me. And I am giving up everything for him. But what if it's not enough? What if everything we have to give and all the things we sacrifice are not enough?

I run my hand over the metal heart again and again, thinking of his hands making it, picturing the smooth, scarred skin on his palm.

The hill is blank and bleak. From here, I can't see the chapel. I can't see the camp or the bothy. The island looks deserted, as though it has been plucked out of time. As though no one is alive here any more, apart from me, standing on the beach, waiting, my heart in my hand.

And then I see him. He is running down the hill towards the beach. For a moment, I worry that someone is chasing him, but there is no one. He is here. He has come for me and all will be well.

He wraps his arms around me, lifting me briefly off my feet. His cheeks are cold.

'I thought you were going to leave me here,' I say.

'I will not leave you ever.' But he doesn't meet my eyes, and though he sounds sure, and though he is here with me, I see how much it's hurt him to abandon his countrymen. And I feel the same dull thud in my chest at leaving Con, at leaving part of myself on this island.

'You are ready?' he says, eyeing the greenish sea, the dark waves, the white-caps.

'Yes.'

Together, we push the boat into the water, battling against the surging waves, and scramble in, soaked and shivering. The clutch of the cold sea gives me a moment of doubt, but I push it away. There can be no return now.

I pass him an oar and we begin to row together, heaving the boat away from the shore. He rows awkwardly at first, but he is strong, and soon we find a rhythm, although the wind and waves make it hard to keep time against the pitching boat and the rolling swell of the sea. Salt spray stings my eyes and fills my mouth; my skin is cold and rain-slicked but I pull on the oar with all my strength. A savage energy courses through me. Soon, we will be safe; soon, he will be free.

There are many small towns along the north coast of Scotland – Con and I visited them once with our parents, spending a week travelling from John o'Groats to Wick and down to Crowbie. Inland, I remember a wild landscape of rocks and heather and gorse – whole areas without a house in sight. And I remember old, deserted farmhouses and fishermen's cottages with collapsed roofs. Con and I have lived in the bothy on Selkie Holm for almost a year: Cesare and I will be able to find somewhere to shelter, at least for a while – somewhere isolated, away from people, where his accent and dark hair and tanned skin won't matter because no one will find us. And perhaps, if we stay in an area close to the shore, I will hear news of Con from people in one of the villages. And perhaps, after the war is over, I will be able to convince her to come with me to Italy.

Perhaps. Perhaps.

I know these are fairy stories, so I don't say them out loud to Cesare. I pull on my oar, and every stroke makes my muscles burn and my heart ache.

'Was Con safe when you left her?' I ask.

'Yes, *bella*.' He is out of breath but pulls hard on his oar. The boat pitches with every wave. 'She is safe with Gino.'

We are nearing the barriers now: the water crashes against the rocks and cement, and torrents through the last small gap. I heard Neil MacClenny saying in the chapel that the barriers have changed the current. Everything is dragged northwards now – to who knows where? For a moment, I allow myself to imagine our rowing boat being hauled towards the blank expanse of the North Sea. If we were lucky, we might reach the Shetland Islands, or Fair Isle, where my mother was born. More likely, we would die of thirst.

The boat rocks and pitches. Salt water burns my eyes.

I imagine Con, waiting for me to return. I imagine her alone.

I hear a shout on the wind. A voice that sounds like hers. A word that sounds like a cry of despair.

No!

At first, I think it's my mind playing tricks on me, but then I hear the cry again and I see a figure on the barrier, running.

No! No, it can't be.

A figure wearing a heavy skirt, and with long red hair, which is snapped around her face by the squall.

She has stopped, her hands shielding her eyes, staring out towards the boat. Then she turns and begins moving back towards the land, running away from the barriers, away from the sea and our tiny vessel.

And then I see why.

Another figure is running along the barriers towards her – towards us. A man. He has seen our boat and gives a cry, pushing past Con and moving towards the end of the barrier, the part we will have to pass through to leave these islands.

I'm not close enough to see his blond hair or that sneering, handsome face, but still I recognize him. Even if we do get past him, Con will be left alone with him.

'Shit,' I say.

Cesare follows my gaze and says something in Italian that I don't understand.

'I have to go back to help her,' I shout above the wind.

'I will come with you –'

'No! No, you mustn't. He will kill you.'

'I will not leave you,' he calls. And he is already trying to turn the boat, trying to row away from the current that surges between the two halves of the barrier. And I love this man so much. This man who will risk his life for me without hesitation. This man who says, *I will not leave you*, with utter certainty, as if he is telling me that the sea is wet, or the sun is hot.

On the barrier, Angus is running still, but Con is following him, is running behind him. And I see what she intends.

I pull on the oars harder. We have to reach the barrier before she gets to him. But it is hopeless. The current has gripped the boat and is dragging it towards that gap between the piled rocks and steel and stones, where the water roars. We will be carried through and will leave them behind. I will be leaving Con alone in the darkness, on the lonely blockade, with him.

'Con!' I call desperately. But she has already reached Angus. She shoves at his back, but he doesn't move, doesn't waver, doesn't stumble. I watch him grabbing at her arm, see him shouting something into her face. I see her shake her head and try to fight him off. But he won't let go. And our boat is being dragged further away from her.

And then I'm standing up and the boat is plunging, and the sea is surging.

Cesare calls out and grabs my hand, but I shake him off.

And I see Con pushing her hands against Angus's chest.

I watch him lose his balance and flail backwards.

I see him grab hold of her.

I watch them begin to fall together.

I hear her shout my name.

I jump.

The water hits me and I go under, fighting upwards to the surface, fighting against the current that is dragging everything towards the barriers. A wave crashes over my head and takes me under and twists me around. For a moment, everything is a mass of roaring water. There is no air.

I swim desperately towards light and life, but there is nothing except bubbling confusion. My lungs burn.

I surface briefly and gasp a lungful of air, fighting to see Con or Cesare. But the boat is gone and the wild water around me is empty. Terror and panic swamp me. I have to find them. I swim towards the direction of the barriers, towards the place where I might be able to drag myself out. But another wave crashes over me, taking me under.

And then something grabs at my leg, pulling me further down, pulling me deeper, in towards the rocks and metal under the barrier.

And I know that the hand must belong to Angus, and that he is trying to drown me. And I know that the only thing to do, the only thing that will keep me alive, the only thing that will keep Con alive, wherever she is, is to drown him first.

PART FIVE

These violent delights have violent ends.

> From *Romeo and Juliet*,
> William Shakespeare, Act 2 scene vi

Constance

After we have put the body in the quarry, after we have put the metal heart on the chest, we sit near the barrier for the rest of the rain-soaked night, hollowed out and shivering.

My clothes are damp and stiff with salt and my fingers are raw from where I'd scrabbled at the rocks. Dot's are bloodied too, and she shudders violently.

She's lost so much. I can't allow her to face any punishment for this. None of it was her fault. And in the morning, there will be answers to give.

So, as I watch the sea shifting from pewter to silver to white, I plan what I am going to say.

And when the guards come to fetch us, to take us away, I hold my hands out and I say, 'She didn't do it. I did it. It was me.'

But Dot says almost exactly the same thing, her words blurring with mine and she holds out her own wrists to be taken away.

'Don't!' I say to her, and try to grab her, but a guard seizes her and, to my horror, they begin taking us in different directions. They lead Dot over towards the camp – and I suppose they will put her in the

Punishment Hut. But they push me in the direction of the hill and the chapel.

Before Dot disappears out of sight, I call, 'It wasn't your fault. None of it was your fault.'

And I hope she hears me. I remember what Dot had told me about the darkness of the Punishment Hut. I remember she'd told me about the chains and the damp soil and the smell of rust and rot. Why would they put her in there? Is it because she tried to escape, because she tried to take Cesare away?

Cesare. Something inside me fractures.

'It was all my idea,' I say to the guard, but he ignores me and inclines his head for me to walk up the hill. I don't recognize him and I can see no hint of mercy in his face when he looks at me.

'What about the prisoners in the camp?' I ask.

'They're being sent south later,' he says, tersely.

'If I could just see –'

'You're seeing no one,' he says, in a flat English accent. 'The prisoners have all been confined to their huts since last night, when the weather was so bad, and then we noticed people were missing. Everyone was cooped up in the camp – people from Kirkwall were all shut in the mess hut. And now we've found you and it's a right bloody mess. So there's a boat coming up to take them south. Good riddance, I say.'

I think of all the men who will be sent away, who I will never see again. Gino. Aureliano. Father Ossani.

'But we need them to finish the barriers!' I say, my voice too high-pitched.

'That's not your business,' the guard says. 'You should be worrying about yourself.' And something in his expression chills me. He sounds angry, but his face softens and I recognize that look: I've seen it so often in Kirkwall. Pity and fear.

The chapel is as beautiful as ever. A thin ray of sun washes over the outside walls and makes the inside of the building glow with golden light. But still, when the guard closes the door, it is cold. I huddle against the wall with my knees up.

My head aches. Where is Dot now? And Cesare? Grief bubbles up in me and I wipe the tears from my cheeks.

I wanted to save you, I think. *I wanted to save you both.*

Perhaps I sleep then, because when I wake, the chapel door is opening and Major Bates is standing in the doorway. His face is severe and I remember that, for all his kindnesses about the chapel, he is an army leader who has killed men, or ordered them killed. He is the man who commanded that Cesare be put in the Punishment Hut.

I would like to stand up, but I can't make myself move.

He stands in front of me, hands behind his back, his expression thoughtful.

'Constance, isn't it?'

I nod, my blood singing in my ears.

'I don't think we've met, Constance. But you're in the midst of quite a problem.'

'It's all my fault,' I whisper.

'So I've heard.' He crouches down and looks me full in the face. His eyes are dark grey and tired. His skin is pale and pouched. He looks, suddenly, like an older man than he once seemed. I wonder if he has children – or grandchildren. I wonder if he sits them on his knee and reads them stories. And I wonder if he sleeps well at night, knowing that he has locked prisoners in the Punishment Hut – knowing that my sister is in there now.

'It was all my idea,' I say desperately. Perhaps if I can convince him of this, he'll let her go.

'So you keep saying.' He scratches his head and sits on the floor, watching me. 'Can you tell me what happened?' he asks, his voice gentler than I expect.

But perhaps this is a trick, this gentleness.

'I . . . I can't remember.'

'Well,' he smiles, not unkindly, 'if you can't remember, then how can you be so sure it was all your idea?'

'I just know it was. But I can't remember some of it.'

He leans forward. 'What do you remember?'

Water. Screaming. The rocks. The body. The terror.

It feels like a dream now, all of it blurred and unreal. The more I try to remember, the more everything slides away from me. It is like trying to pick up water between my fingers.

I look down at my scabbed hands, folded in my lap.

'I remember trying to swim,' I say. 'But nothing else, until the guards brought me here.'

He sighs, stands up, brushes his hands over his trousers. I wait for him to leave, but he's looking around at the chapel and he doesn't know I'm watching him. In that moment, his expression is full of astonishment, as unguarded as a child's.

'Incredible,' he says softly. Then he looks down at me, and in a harder voice, a more impatient voice, he says, 'What happened last night was a tragedy. You should work on getting your memory back.'

He slams the door behind him, and then I hear something being slid across the wood, like a bolt. I hear him talking to someone outside, a man, and then, as I hear his footsteps receding down the hill, a shadow blocks the light under the door.

I'm locked in, with a guard outside.

I watch the pale sun pouring through the window, casting a wan square on the opposite wall. It moves across the delicate rood screen, the pictures of the birds. I imagine Cesare's hand making every brush stroke. I imagine the other men who painted most of the tiles behind my back. Are any of them still on the island?

I slide my body closer to the door and press my face to the gap in the wood next to the hinge. If I close one eye, I can just about make out the hill outside, but I can't see the camp, beyond a blur in the distance, which may just be a trick of the light.

I imagine the prisoners leaving: I picture them climbing aboard a boat and sailing around the island, around the barriers, past the vicious current that drags everything away. In my thoughts, I don't allow the boat to stop in Wales. I let it continue south, sailing around France and Spain, through the narrow Strait of Gibraltar and onwards through the Mediterranean Sea. I allow the boat to carry the Italian men safely home.

I restore their bombed houses and their broken churches. I call their families back from the grave. I let them step from the boat and wrap their mothers and their sisters and their wives in their strong arms. I let them tuck their children into bed, kissing their foreheads and lulling them to sleep with tales about a far-off island to the north, where strange creatures shift beneath wild seas.

*

I wake with my cheek pressed against the cold, tiled floor. My face is still near to the door, but the light is different now: brighter and harder. It must be nearly midday.

There is a scraping at the door – that is what woke me, I realize. I can hear the lock being pushed back. The door opens and a sudden burst of sun cuts through the dim glow from the light in the window. I am standing already, but I throw my arm up to shield my eyes against the moment of sun-dazzled blindness.

'Hello, Con.'

John O'Farrell steps into the chapel.

'Hello,' I say, my voice creaky, as if I haven't spoken in days. I wonder if he's here as Mayor of Kirkwall, or as my family's friend, but I can't bring myself to ask.

Like Major Bates, John looks tired, his face drawn and his eyes spidered with tiny veins.

'Aren't you going to invite me in?' he asks, and I give a polite smile, although the expression feels strange. And I wonder if I shouldn't smile, even when someone tries to make a joke, because perhaps if I look happy after all that has happened, I will seem heartless. And perhaps that will make me seem guiltier.

John walks into the chapel, looking around in awe, as everyone does. I wonder if beauty ever becomes ordinary. I hope not.

'Major Bates tells me you've lost your memory,' John says.

'Yes.' I keep my eyes downcast, in case something in my expression gives me away.

'But he tells me you're certain that you're to blame. And I have to say, Con, that doesn't sound right. Is it possible you're confused? Is it possible that it was all someone else's idea, and you simply went along with it?'

I say nothing. John turns to look at the stained-glass window. The colours cast light and shadow in weird patterns on his face.

'Could it have been Angus's idea, for example? Or that prisoner, Cesare – could it have been his idea? Or Dot's idea?'

'Not Dot's idea!' I say. 'She's not to blame at all.'

A bird clatters onto the roof of the chapel. Then I hear it flitting away, its wingbeats like the thrum of a panicked heart.

He nods slowly, and walks along the back of the chapel, running his hand over the altar and taber-nacle, brushing his hand across the font, which looks like stone, but is really an old car tyre and exhaust pipe, covered with cement.

Earlier, I had run my own hands over that font, remembering the feeling of cement between my fingers. And then something glinting at its base had caught my eye. And from under the font, I had pulled out a length of scrap metal. It is the size and width of my little finger, but as sharp as a knife. I'd hidden it in my sleeve.

John O'Farrell's expression is still full of wonder as he looks at the chapel. And I remember how this makeshift building felt like safety, how it felt like home. I remember the sound of the prisoners' laughter, echoing, as if we were in a high-ceilinged church.

My head throbs.

'But you must understand,' John says, 'that this is a very serious matter, with serious consequences. You're talking about . . . *murder,* Con.'

I think of long ropes tied around wooden beams. My body swinging. The pressure around my throat, like hands that won't let go.

My breath comes in noisy rasps.

The people will gather and watch a hanging, the way they watch fish being dragged in or animals being slaughtered. Afterwards, they will return to their houses and talk about it over dinner. The story of my death will warm their bones.

I clutch at my neck, curling my body into a tight ball.

'Breathe deeply,' John says. 'Slowly, now.'

But I can't. My airway is narrowing, my vision contracting.

John puts his arm under my elbow and pulls me to my feet, walking me out of the chapel. A burst of brightness makes me shut my eyes. Vaguely, I'm aware of the guard objecting, of John shouting at him, of the guard recoiling.

He steers me down the hill, away from the chapel, away from the camp and the Punishment Hut, away from the barrier, and in the direction of the bay. I walk next to him blindly, my breaths loud and ragged, as he says to me time and again, 'Slowly now. Steady. Easy now.'

It's the voice you might use with a frightened animal, but gradually, my breathing slackens, and my senses come back.

The tingling in my hands and feet fades and I'm able to see the gulls bombing the ocean, the clouds muscling over the horizon. I fill my lungs and close my eyes and turn my face towards the sun so that everything is red.

'I'm sorry,' I say. 'I think I would be calmer if I could just see Dot.'

He turns away from me, shaking his head. 'Not yet.'

And I wonder what I have to say to be able to see her. I wonder what she has to say about me. Do we need to tell the same story? I won't do it: I won't blame her, and I know she won't blame me. Perhaps we will be stuck here for ever, telling opposite stories.

A peregrine falcon sweeps past in the direction of the cliffs. It will sit like a church gargoyle. When it sights its prey, it will launch silently and smash into the bird mid-flight. Burst of feathers, then blood and bone: fierce life and sudden death.

O'Farrell stops walking and tugs gently on my elbow. 'I have something for you. I nearly forgot.' He reaches into his pocket and I have a moment to brace myself before he places something in my hand. Cold metal with a weight to it. I know what it is, but I force myself to look anyway.

The metal heart.

'I thought it might help you remember.'

A duck thuds skywards. The peregrine falcon plummets.

'I don't remember anything,' I say. The heart – Dot's metal heart – is cold and heavy in my hand. I remember the first time she had held it and passed it to me: it was warm and we'd both laughed with delight at finding something so beautiful.

It's a promise, she'd said.

I didn't have to ask what the promise was for. But now that promise is chill against my fingers.

The peregrine strikes. The duck doesn't make a sound.

John's smile wavers. 'Tell me about when you saw Angus last night.'

I close my eyes and picture grappling with him on the barrier. I imagine his hands around my arms. His voice was loud. Then the push, the drop, the cold water.

I don't want to remember more than that.

The heart is about the size of my clenched hand.

Cesare told me that each man's heart is the size and weight of his own fist. My heart cannot be the same weight as this, surely. It feels so much heavier, thudding relentlessly in my chest.

'When did you last see Angus?' John asks. His expression is earnest, kind. Perhaps I could tell him everything I remember. But then what? Once you've told part of your story, it so easily grows and changes in other people's minds, in other people's mouths. Once you have told your story, it no longer belongs to you.

'I can't remember,' I say again.

John O'Farrell walks away and I follow him, even though I feel light-headed now.

'I feel faint.' I turn away from him and from the thought of the heart. Then there's the sea: waves like a heartbeat, bubbles of air, the smooth surface, as though nothing has happened. My mouth is parched. I close my eyes. I feel a surge of nausea.

'Are you well?' O'Farrell takes my arm. 'Here, sit. This heather is dry.'

I sit and he crouches next to me, his eyes creased with worry. I take deep breaths and keep my eyes closed for longer than I need to. I can feel him watching me.

'Are you strong enough to walk on the beach? I know you want to rest, but I need the truth from you. You must try to recollect, Con.'

I nod and he helps me to my feet.

As we start to walk, the peregrine sweeps past, towards the cliffs, where its scrape will be. In its claws, the limp, dark shape of the duck it has killed. The peregrine soars, elegant and beautiful: from this distance you cannot see the blood masking its beak and face.

The sea has dropped, sinking back onto the mud flats, exposing the wrecks of old ships and leaving a broad line of seaweed to mark the point of high tide.

I step onto the sand and walk down towards the sea, stopping between the line of seaweed and the sea – between the tide lines.

O'Farrell doesn't follow me but stays back above the seaweed that marks the high tide.

'I didn't know you were superstitious,' I say.

There is an old proverb that things of the devil have the most power in the stretch of sand between high and low tide, because the land there belongs neither to the earth nor the sea.

I can feel O'Farrell watching me carefully as I walk over the smooth patch of sea-scoured sand. Back where O'Farrell is standing, there are strings of bladderwrack, as well as things the sea has heaved up: pieces of metal, a scrap of cloth from a shirt, a man's leather boot, dug into the sand as if mid-kick. It seems to me that the superstition is wrong: the high-tide line is the thing that should be feared. That's where all the bad luck lands. That's where things lost in a storm would wash up. My skin crawls.

I beckon to O'Farrell. He hesitates, then shakes his head and walks down to stand next to me.

'I want to know what happened,' he says. 'If you tell me the truth quickly then I can help you.'

'I don't know the truth.'

I don't tell him that no one can help me. It is only a matter of time now, and I am spinning out the hours like gold, hoping to save my sister, hoping to avoid the rope.

'Come on, Con,' John says, and there is a touch of impatience in his voice. His hands clench for a moment, although when he sees me notice, he puts them into his pockets. I fight down the quick, dark terror that clutches at me. I remind myself that he means me no harm. He is simply a man, with a man's big hands and strong muscles. He doesn't understand how the slightest movement from him might seem like a threat. He doesn't know how a man's muscles might frighten a woman into silence, or might make her nod *yes*, when every nerve in her body is howling *no*.

John's eyes are fixed upon mine, and I know he is frustrated, though he thinks he's hiding it. And he won't understand how my whole body is thrumming with the knowledge that he could, if he wanted to, crack my skull like an egg, or cut off my airway with one of his hands. He may say things to me, like *Quickly, Con*, or, *Come on, Con*, and he may not mean them as threats. But threats they are, all the same. If I wanted to make myself equally menacing to an angry man, I would need to carry a knife. I would have to remove it from my belt during conversations, and slowly sharpen it while he trembled.

John reaches out to me now. 'You're not well.'

I tense my arm and flinch away. 'Don't touch me!'

'Con,' he says, his eyes shocked, his voice soft. 'I would never hurt you.'

And he reaches for my arm again, and my breathing is loud, because all I can think of is Angus. His face, his breath, the weight of him.

A memory clicks into place.

Oh, God, the weight of him. The weight of his body as we dragged him, imagining his eyes staring at us. I'd refused to look properly at his face, afraid that it would come back to me in nightmares. Instead, I'd tried to see him as a set of body parts. Feet. Hands. Chest. Mouth. Eyes.

I put my hands over my own eyes now and I know I have to confess, fully. I have to tell John everything I've remembered, or Dot will never be free.

I swallow. I breathe.

Very quietly, I say, 'I didn't mean to kill him. It was an accident.'

John takes his hand from my arm. 'Kill *who*?'

I can't say the name.

He pulls my hands from my face. 'Kill who, Con?'

'Angus,' I whisper.

Now he jerks from me. 'Angus is dead?' His face is stunned, his eyes wide and wary.

My eyes fill with tears and my throat aches. I know that my next words will condemn me, but I have to speak out. I have to take the blame.

'It was an accident,' I say. I close my eyes and I try to explain it, just as I remember it.

'Angus ran along the barrier. I was so frightened. I wanted . . . He grabbed and I . . . We fell. But he got caught in the rocks. I put him in the quarry. It was nothing to do with . . . It was all my fault. I'm the one to blame.'

I wait for his rage. I wait for him to call the guards, for them to drag me away and lock me up.

But he doesn't look angry as he puts a hand upon my shoulder. He looks devastated. His eyes are red, as if he is trying to ward off tears. He swallows twice and then he says, 'The body. The body in the quarry. You . . . believe it was Angus?'

I stare at him. I do not understand. It is as though he is trying to tell me something but I have lost the ability to make sense of language.

'It *was* Angus,' I whisper. 'I saw him.'

'Oh,' he says, and he pulls me into a tight embrace.

'Oh, you poor wee lassie.' His pullover smells of bitter wool and the sea and, for a moment, it is like being embraced by my father, or by Dot, who loves me more than anyone else.

Dizzy, I close my eyes and lean against him. I brace myself, although part of me knows what he is going to say.

'That body in the quarry,' he says. 'That wasn't Angus. We don't know where Angus is.'

John takes me back to the chapel to lie down. My head is pounding and twice I have retched and spat sour vomit into the gorse.

He will send a doctor to see me, he promises. He just needs to talk to Major Bates, to try to understand exactly what happened. In the meantime, they've dragged a mattress into the chapel, and I must stay here for one night, just while they discuss what they should do next.

I nod, barely hearing him. I go in whatever direction he leads me: up the hill, into the chapel, over to my bed, where he leaves me, with a promise to return tomorrow.

Then he shuts the door behind him and I am alone again in the darkness.

John's words rattle in my head like sea stones.

That body in the quarry. That wasn't Angus . . .
You poor wee lassie.

Time pools, unspools, unravels. I run my finger over the smooth edge of the metal heart. I heft it like a stone. I tap it lightly against my skull, then hold it to my temple. The beat of my pulse hammers up the metal into my fingertips.

I watch the chapel window. Light, then darkness – the true darkness that signals the end of summer. Darkness is the first promise of winter, when everything clamps shut for ever.

Across the water, in the Kirkwall morgue, lies a body and I cannot allow myself to think of it. Every time I do, my panic rises, like acid in my throat. Instead, I focus on the light in the window. Outside the chapel, there will be stars, like scattered seeds across the night sky. There is a glow in the window as a crescent moon sharpens itself against the night.

But it is no good. There is a body in the morgue and I'm not safe. I know it. Something is coming for me.

Constance

I jolt awake again and again, but each time I fall back into a dream that is worse than the last. Water bubbling over me, hands holding me under.

O'Farrell is in Kirkwall; he says he wants to save

me but I am certain it will be a hanging. What else would they do with me, now I've confessed? My head aches. In the half-darkness and the spill of moonlight from the window, I try to catch sight of my reflection. The face that stares back at me is wide-eyed and pale. I can't look into her deep-socketed eyes.

I curl around myself on the mattress.

I wake. I sleep.

I am trying to swim but my limbs are lead. On the sea floor is the wrecked hull of the *Royal Elm*. The dead sailors wave their bony fingers at me and grin their skullish grins. This is where I should be, cold on the ocean floor.

I wake. I sleep.

In my dream, Cesare and Dot are standing in the boat, talking about me.

It wasn't her fault, Dot says.

Cesare answers, *She is mad, I think*.

Dot says, *Throw her overboard and see if she floats*.

They wrap their arms around me, and for a moment, I am close to them again. I cry out, reaching for them, *Don't let me go!* They drop me into the cold water. I sink like a stone.

I wake. I sleep.

Seals circle me, laughing. Under their skin, each one is a beautiful woman.

*

When I wake again, it is dark and the door is opening. My heart leaps in my chest. A figure is walking towards me and the face is in shadow. I lie very still, pretending to be asleep. My blood beats in my ears but I keep my breathing steady. Under my bed, somewhere, is the sharp piece of metal I'd found under the font.

Who would sneak into the chapel at night? Is it the guard, come to check on me? Was I crying out in my sleep, perhaps? The nightmare returns to me: Dot and Cesare's arms releasing me as she threw me into the water.

The figure moves closer and I open one eye. It is too slim to be John O'Farrell; it must be one of the guards – the boots squeak. I hold my breath.

Please go away. Please leave me alone.

A spill of silver moonlight casts his shadow onto the chapel floor. He looms over me, huge, then takes another step. He is standing right next to my bed. I can feel the heat from his body. I can hear the rasp of his breath.

Please. Please. I lie very still, hoping, waiting.

The figure leans over me. There is a moment of silence and then he grabs me, clamps his hand over my mouth, using his other arm to pin me down by my throat.

I open my eyes and try to scream, but the sound is muffled, as if I am underwater.

'Wheesht!'

Angus MacLeod's face is close to mine. There is blood on his forehead and his face is bruised and covered with dirt. I buck my body, squirming under him, struggling to breathe, struggling to scream, but I can't gather enough air. There's the smell of sweat and something darker – a feral, animal stench, as if he's emerged from under the ground, as if he's crawled here from some dark grave.

I swing my legs, trying to kick him, trying to fight free of his weight, but his whole body is on mine now. He presses down harder on the arm that is across my throat.

'Lie still,' he says. 'Or you'll be sorry.'

I do as he says. Dark spots cloud my vision; the blood hammers in my ears. I know that it would take only a little more pressure for him to crush my windpipe.

My vision blurs and I stare at him, begging with my eyes.

Air, I think. *I need air.*

'If I let go,' he says, 'you won't scream?'

I shake my head.

He releases me and I cough and cough, gasping deep lungfuls, my throat burning.

'How . . . ?' I choke, my voice a strangled rasp. 'You fell into the sea. I thought –'

'Thought I'd drowned, did you? Or been carried out to sea? I washed up on the north of the island. Hit my head. It took me some time to get back. And I overheard some of the guards say they were keeping you here. So I thought I'd come to see you.'

'Go back to Kirkwall,' I say, coughing. 'Your friends will be worried.'

'I don't care about them,' he says. 'I want to see you.' He runs a finger down my cheek, down onto my neck.

'Did I hurt you?' he asks. 'I didn't want to hurt you, but I thought you might scream.'

'You didn't hurt me,' I lie.

He strokes my neck. My skin crawls, but I don't want to make him angry by flinching away, so I stay very still.

Leave, I think. *Please leave.*

'Are you happy to see me?' he asks.

I nod. The slightest inclination of my head.

He smiles. 'Say it.'

'I'm happy to see you.' My voice cracks.

'You hurt me on the barrier,' he says. 'I could have drowned.'

'I'm sorry,' I say. I turn my head towards the door. Surely the guard will have heard our voices.

As if reading my mind, Angus says, 'The guard? John O'Farrell took him back to Kirkwall. I watched him go. So we have some time.' He smiles and strokes my cheek again. A chill runs through me.

'Don't look like that,' he says. 'Don't be frightened.'

I try my best not to look frightened. My teeth are chattering. I clench my jaw.

'Relax,' he says. 'Smile.' He strokes my face.

I force my mouth into a fixed rictus.

'That's better,' he says. 'Doesn't that feel better?'

I nod. My throat aches. My head is pounding. I feel a tear running down my cheek and I try to stop crying, because he wants me to seem happy. And perhaps, if I do as he tells me, he will leave me alone.

'There's nothing to be scared of. We're old friends, aren't we?'

I nod.

He leans in and kisses my cheek. His stubble scratches my skin. I close my eyes and hold my breath, trying not to inhale the stale, mushroomy smell of damp and darkness.

'Look at me,' he says. I open my eyes and force myself to look at him.

There are tears in his eyes. 'I love you,' he says. 'But you've hurt me so much. You kept hiding from me and pushing me away.'

'I'm sorry,' I whisper.

His hand is on my neck, caressing me. 'I said I love you, Con. Did you hear me?' The pressure on my neck increases slightly.

I nod. 'Yes,' I whisper.

'So, say it.'

My head aches and acid rises in my throat. My breathing is loud and fast.

Words, I tell myself. *They're just words.* And perhaps, if I say them, he will let me go. Perhaps that will be enough for him and he will let me be.

Except I know he won't. And I hate him. I hate his hopeful, tear-streaked face. But I can sense the pressure on my neck increasing again. And I remember the weight of his arm on my neck. I remember the way my vision narrowed, the way my chest burned. I remember that he hadn't looked angry at all. The expression on his face had been calm, focused. Cold.

'Say it,' he says.

I hate you, I think.

'I love you,' I gasp.

'Oh, Con,' he says. 'It's going to be perfect. We're going to be perfect. You'll see.'

He crushes his mouth against mine and, as he forces my lips open and pushes his tongue past my teeth, my stomach twists with nausea.

Under my back, between my shoulder blades, there is something hard and cold. I recognize the shape: the metal heart. I shift my weight and he thinks I'm responding to him.

He is breathless; he stares at me with tenderness, stroking my neck again, caressing my throat, running his finger gently along my collarbone. His hand cups my breasts and he presses his face against them, moaning.

My eyes are squeezed shut.

'Look at me,' he demands.

I open my eyes. His face is bright and eager, full of anticipation.

'I'd like to make you happy,' he says earnestly. 'I know I can make you happy. You just need to give me the chance to show you. You'd like to be happy, wouldn't you?'

I can't speak.

'*Wouldn't you?*' His voice is hard.

I nod, once.

His hand moves from my breasts to my thigh. He strokes me through the thin material of my trousers. I tremble, but I know I mustn't recoil from him. If I recoil, I will make him angry.

His hand moves to the waistband of my trousers. He pulls them down over my hips. He is gentle. He is smiling at me.

'Tell me again,' he says.

'I love you,' I whisper.

'Smile,' he says.

I want him to die. I imagine a blood vessel bursting in his brain. I picture his heart stopping in his chest. I smile.

His hands are on my hips, his breath warm against my cheek.

He smells of rot and soil.

Grave. I think. *Grave, tomb, crypt.*

He moves his body over mine, kisses my neck, my mouth. I lie very still. I count to ten again and again. He pulls my trousers down further. I press my thighs together, but his fingers feel stronger and more forceful now.

'Come on,' he says. 'I won't hurt you. I promise.'

I clamp my legs shut, at tight as I can. I grit my teeth and put everything I have into closing myself off. I shut my eyes as he prises my thighs apart.

The metal heart digs into my back.

'We're going to be so happy,' he says.

Something inside me snaps and an animal panic surges though me.

'No!' I shout, and I try to push him off, kicking and clawing at his chest. I try to slap his face.

He hits me, hard. My head rings with the sound. He hits me again. I try to turn my face away from him, but he grabs a handful of my hair and shakes my head back and forth. I feel him rip a handful of hair from my skull, and I cry out.

'Look what you've made me do,' he snaps.

My eyes are watering so I can barely see him. I blink, frozen, my head pulsing with pain.

He waits, watching me. 'I didn't want to hurt you,' he says. 'You've made me hurt you.'

'I'm sorry,' I whisper.

'Don't *ever* try to slap me,' he says. His eyes are cold. 'You can't slap me and expect that nothing will happen. If you try to hurt me, I will hurt you. Do you understand?' My hair is still wrapped around his fingers. My scalp throbs.

I nod.

'Do you understand? Answer me. Say it.'

'I understand,' I whisper.

'Good.' He puts his hand on my hips.

I know what will happen. My body freezes now. My thoughts scramble and retreat into some dark corner of my mind. I'm numb. I don't feel his hand moving. I don't feel anything. I make my body go completely limp.

'That's better.' He kisses me again, puts his hand between my legs.

Again, that animal panic, but I know there is no sense in struggling.

But I have to move.

With my free hand, I try to reach under myself. He thinks I am moving for him and he presses himself against me, groaning. His flesh is hot against mine. I can't hold him off any longer.

I move my hand further up, to where the metal heart is still digging between my shoulder blades.

I grasp it and pull it from under me.

And then I bring my hand up high and smash it into his skull.

I feel his body jolt, his lips go slack against mine and he collapses on top of me, a dead weight.

I heave him off me and he slumps back onto the bed, unmoving.

He's dead, I think. *I've killed him.*

But he's breathing still.

I scrabble off the mattress and search around for the jagged piece of metal that I'd found under the font earlier. The ragged strip of scrap that is no longer than my finger, but it will have to do.

I retrieve it from under the mattress. I hold it, trembling, and I wait.

Angus snorts and groans, as if waking from a deep sleep. His eyelids flicker.

I kick his leg. 'Get up.' My voice is high-pitched.

He groans again, and then his eyes focus on mine. The rage is instant, but then he sees the shard of metal in my hand. I wave it at him.

'Get out,' I say. My voice shakes.

He blinks and frowns, but he doesn't move. I can feel my heartbeat in every part of my body. My blood thrums in my ears.

'Get out,' I say again. I grasp the piece of metal harder, white-knuckled, and point it at his throat.

He rolls to one side and heaves himself upright. For a moment, he stands, swaying, and I think he will collapse backwards. I think he will drop dead, on the mattress, and I will have to explain everything to John O'Farrell in the morning.

He eyes the piece of metal and I brace myself, ready for him to lurch at me and try to snatch it from me, ready for him to try to hit me again, to hold me down again.

'I will stab you in the throat,' I say.

He sways again, a baffled expression on his face, as if he can't remember who I am or why he is here. And he begins to walk, unsteadily, towards the door.

I yank my trousers up, covering myself. I'm shivering convulsively now, my legs quivering.

Angus stumbles, clutching his head, then staggers from the chapel, leaving the door wide open.

The night crowds in, black and starless.

I shudder. And my heart pounds in my chest, in my throat, in my fingertips. And I can still feel Angus's weight crushing me, the cold, dead-fish touch of his skin. The smell of him. I close my eyes, counting my breaths. I swallow the vomit that rises into my mouth.

On the bed is the metal heart. There is a smear of blood where I hit his head.

I curl around myself, wrapping my arms around my chest and stomach, tight. Tighter. But I still can't hold myself together. I hunch in the corner, gripping the metal heart so tightly that my hand shakes. My whole body shakes. My teeth chatter.

347

I have never been so aware of being alone in this world. No Dot to stand beside me. Not now and not ever.

Never.

I remember John O'Farrell's words. The grief on his face.

That body in the quarry. That wasn't Angus

And, seeing him again, my last hope is gone. Somehow, when I'd remembered dragging the body to the quarry, I'd pictured his face. I'd thought of him, broken and bloodied. I'd imagined him, lying dead. And even when John O'Farrell had told me that Angus's body hadn't been found, that he'd disappeared somewhere, I still, somehow, hoped that he was wrong.

I'd refused to believe him when he told me that the body I'd dragged to the quarry had been my sister's.

Now Dot lies in the morgue beneath the hospital in Kirkwall.

O'Farrell had wept as he had told me.

I had shaken my head. Some sound had come from my mouth, but it wasn't words. I'd collapsed to O'Farrell's feet, slapping at his legs when he tried to pick me up, because no, no, no. No one could help me, apart from her. And how could she be gone? She couldn't be gone, any more than my hand could be gone. Or my eyes or my own heart in my chest. Or my soul.

But now I'd seen Angus, I believed it at last. Dot was alone, her body alone, lifeless. Cold.

I remember again, her chilly skin, those icy lips. The blank eyes, unseeing.

No.

She had never liked being cold. I think of her laughter, the warmth of her hand in mine. At night, when we lay, back to back, I hadn't known whose breath was whose.

Now, if I close my eyes, I can still hear her voice calling to me. Like our mother's, like our father's. All their lost voices, whispering to me from the sea.

I hunch further into the corner of the chapel, my body still quivering.

I'll never see her smile again.

She used to like resting her head on my shoulder. I can almost feel the weight of it, feel the ripple of laughter that would travel from her body into mine.

How is it possible for someone to stop existing? To step out of the world, as if they had never been, and for the world to go on turning, the sun to go on rising? How is it possible to go on breathing, now that she is gone?

If I stay here, they will hang me. Angus will make sure of that. He will tell them that I tried to kill him. He will tell them that I killed my own sister, that I drowned her. He'll pretend that he saw it all. And they'll hang me.

And there's an appeal in that thought. A relief.

I close my eyes, and some voice inside me, that might be hers, might be mine, whispers, *No.*

I don't want to live without her. But mine is the only life we have, now.

I walk to the open door of the chapel, the thin slash of grainy light.

Angus is limping along the barrier, clutching his head. The moon emerges from behind a scarf of cloud. He must be bleeding heavily. Even from here, I can see the gleam of his blood, which forms a trail away from the chapel.

I step outside. A breeze shoves into me, gathering around me, pulling me from the building. For a moment, it is next to me, full of fury, urging me on.

If I had her with me, we would leave the chapel now, and we would stalk Angus along the barrier. We would watch him trip and stumble along. He would turn and see us following him and would walk faster. I imagine the fear squirming inside him. I know, as all women do, how fear can turn your muscles to water, how terror can twist your gut, rise into your throat and choke the breath from you.

Every woman understands that fear of the dark, fear of being followed, the white-eyed hysteria that makes your heart – your poor, startled-rabbit heart – leap uselessly in your chest. There is no point in running because you will always be too slow, and your heart knows that.

We know the dry-mouthed chase in the darkness. We know how the story ends.

But the fear will be fresh and unfamiliar to Angus. He is a man – rich, strong, young, handsome. Every day of his charmed life, the world has opened up to him, like the split in a ripe peach. He could smash it or devour it or leave it to rot. Whatever he wished.

But not now. Not at this moment, as he trips and staggers, bleeding, across the barrier, with a nightmare creature chasing after him.

I am not a woman to him now: I am some age-old monster. I am a selkie, risen from the deep to rip out his heart. I am the Nuckelavee, stepping from the water in my fleshless bones.

I will run up behind him, my body strong, my hands bloody.

I will push him, hard, and I will watch him fall from the barrier.

I will hear his cry cut short as his head hits the rocks.

I will stare at the blood seeping from his smashed-egg skull as the water laps at his body.

And I will feel nothing at all.

I will walk back up to the chapel, carrying handfuls of sand, which I will sprinkle and scrub over the bloodied ground.

Later tonight, the wind will rise again, blowing the sand and blood away.

*

I slam the chapel door behind me, shutting out the wind and the blood and the rage. I sit down on the floor, panting, and I close my eyes. I can still feel his hands on my skin, can still feel his weight on me, can hear his voice in my ear.

'He's gone,' I say, aloud.

And then I think, *She's gone.*

In the darkness, I wrap my arms around myself and I say goodbye to Dot.

I imagine her saying, *You did the right thing.*

I imagine her saying, *I never blamed you.*

I imagine us holding each other, rocking back and forth, back and forth. Like the tide, like the twin chambers of the heart. Like the swelling of the light that always returns.

Constance

I barely sleep that night. In the morning, I'm awake enough to hear the footsteps before the door to the chapel opens. It is John O'Farrell, his face sombre.

'How did the chapel door come to be unlocked?'

I blink, my eyes gritty, and shrug. I can't make myself look at him, but I can feel him examining my face.

'No one came here last night?'

I shake my head.

'You didn't hear anything?'

'No.'

He kneels on the floor, next to my mattress.

'There's been another body found.'

'Oh?' It's all I can say, my breath tight in my chest.

'Angus MacLeod washed up in Kirkwall this morning.'

'What happened?' My voice is high-pitched. Do I sound shocked enough? My stomach twists and plummets. I keep my gaze fixed on the tiled floor.

John sighs and settles himself next to my bed, at my feet. I can feel his eyes on my face, watching my reaction.

'Well,' he says, 'it seems he fell into the sea. But . . . there were some things found with him. He had . . . I don't know how to tell you this, Con, but he had a handful of Dot's hair wrapped around his fingers. And there was . . . There was skin found under his nails.'

I hunch my shoulders to hide the scratches on my neck.

'What . . . ?' I clear my throat. 'What do they think happened?'

'Well,' he says, 'there's an opinion that, on the night of the storm, he must have taken Cesare out onto the boat and perhaps Dot too, by force. I know you can't remember anything very much, but does that sound likely? That he meant to do them harm?'

I swallow, nod. 'He's always been violent,' I whisper.

'Aye. A nasty piece of work, although I shouldn't speak ill of the dead. Cesare's body hasn't been found yet, but can you remember seeing him after the boat tipped?'

I shake my head. I bite the inside of my cheek to stop my telltale tears.

He sighs. 'Some of Angus's friends are trying to start rumours that Dot killed Angus on the night of the storm, or that ... well, that *you* somehow managed to do it, given that the body's fresher than might be expected.' He pauses. I can feel his gaze on my face.

'Of course,' he says, 'to do that, you'd have had to leave the chapel ... There are no witnesses because I had the guard with me – he hadn't been well. What can you tell me of last night? You really didn't see or hear anything?'

I pause. My hands are shaking again. On the tips of my fingers, beneath my nails, are reddish-brown stains. We both watch as I hide my trembling hands by sitting on them.

O'Farrell will have seen the unlocked chapel door. Perhaps he saw the blood along the barrier, leading up to the chapel, which I couldn't have scrubbed away properly in the dark.

'Darkness and cold,' I say. 'That's all I remember.'

'You can't tell me anything that happened to him, then? You hadn't seen him since the storm?'

'No.' I lean my head forward.

It occurs to me that he will be able to see the bare patch of my scalp where Angus ripped out my hair. And perhaps he can see the livid scratches on my neck.

He gives a sharp intake of breath. I wait for the accusation. I brace myself.

He pauses for a moment, then leans forward and gently kisses my forehead. 'Of course you couldn't have left the chapel last night, Con. The door was locked when I arrived just now. I'll tell everyone that.'

I exhale, then look up at him. His eyes are warm and sad. He touches my cheek, very gently. 'Do you need a doctor?' he murmurs.

I shake my head.

'Did he –'

'No.'

John nods, kisses my head again, very softly. 'I hope you will be warmer tonight in Kirkwall. You can come with me now.'

I blink at him.

'Angus MacLeod's body clears you of any guilt, Con. People might try to accuse you of being involved with Cesare's disappearance, or what happened to Dot, but it's clear where the blame lies.'

His face blurs as he takes my hand.

'Follow me,' he says, and we walk out of the chapel into the bright sunlight.

Constance

We hold her funeral some days later. She is buried on Selkie Holm, near the bothy. Most of Mainland Orkney comes across, walking over the barrier to reach us – in the days after the prisoners left, the people from Kirkwall finished the barrier themselves, piling in the last loads of rock from the quarry, and layering cement on top.

Now, they stand apart in a group and they look at me and they mutter.

Above and around me, the blue sky – too bright and too blue for a funeral –arches like the lid of a bell jar; with all these eyes upon me, I feel pinioned, like a specimen on display, with everything and everyone inspecting me from outside the glass. I know they will be talking about Dot and about Angus; about the hair found around his fingers and the skin beneath his nails.

I pull my scarf more firmly around my neck.

I feel sick and guilty and lost. I try not to meet anyone's eyes. I lower my gaze to the gorse growing at my feet. This plant must be years old. It has been wind-battered and frozen. It has been showered with salt water and pelted with hail, but still it grows, still it flowers. It hopes for light and fair weather.

I feel a hand on my shoulder. When I turn, Bess Croy is standing there, tears in her eyes.

'I'm so sorry,' she says. And she pulls me into an embrace.

After she has released me, her mother, Marjorie, puts her arms around me.

'I'm sorry, my love,' she says. She holds me away from her, at arm's length and looks into my eyes. 'We did you wrong.'

She steps away and then Neil MacClenny is standing there, eyes bright.

'I'm sorry,' he says. And he touches my shoulder briefly, then moves on to allow the rest of them to come, one by one, to apologize. Artair Flett, Finley Anderson, Moira Burns – even Robert MacRae, who was Angus's best friend, and always sneered when he saw me.

'I didn't know,' he whispered. 'I never thought he would have . . . I'm sorry.'

An ache builds in my chest and my throat burns with unshed tears. I hear the word again and again. *Sorry. Sorry. Sorry.*

And the voices blur until they sound like a blessing or a prayer, until they echo like the hush of the wings of many birds, travelling south.

They look at me expectantly, and a small part of me wants to rage and rail at them. Of course they should be sorry, but why should I forgive them? Why is it up to me to console them? Forgiveness feels too easy for them, and too heavy a burden to carry – the weight of those words: *I forgive you.* I don't know how to say them.

I turn away from them, breathing slowly. I don't know what to say to these people who want something from me that I can't give.

Up on the hill, the chapel gleams in the sun. I imagine the light pouring in through the window. The pictures on the walls will gleam with life. And, on the ceiling above the altar, a white dove soars through a bright blue sky.

How does something so beautiful come from such darkness?

The tears are flowing freely now, as I turn back to the people watching me and I force myself to say, 'Thank you.'

Because building something is hard. Because building something is a choice. Because hope is the only way we can stop the darkness swallowing us. Because people who came from another country have shown me how to find my way home.

And I allow these people – my people – to take my hands as we stand around the grave and we say the Lord's Prayer. I'm not religious, but I join my voice with theirs.

Forgive us our trespasses, as we forgive those who trespass against us.

'I'm sorry,' I whisper to the grave.

All across Europe, bodies are falling from the sky

or into the sea, or are being blown high into the air. Every explosion is a name. Every lost life is carved on someone else's heart. Every death takes more than a single life. It takes memories and longing and hope. But not the love. The love remains.

They let me see her body, yesterday, in the morgue in Kirkwall. I couldn't make myself go into the chilly room. Seeing her would make it final. Seeing her would make it true. For a moment, my knees buckled. I made myself move forward, one shaky step at a time, like a child learning to walk – although even then I'd had her to balance against, walking alongside me.

Her body lay on a cold slab, covered with a sheet. I reached out slowly.

That sheet was the heaviest thing I've ever lifted – all the weight of the years between us. Our shared smiles, our tears, the way we woke giggling from the same dreams. My name in her mouth.

Her voice silent now. Her breath stopped.

How can she be gone? It isn't possible.

I pulled the sheet back and something inside me ripped wide open.

She was pale and still. She might have been asleep. Her skin was like marble under my lips. I kissed her again and again. I held her. Said her name.

I'm sorry. I'm so sorry.

I sank to the floor. I wanted to howl, but no sound came from my mouth. Just as after our parents disappeared, I felt unmoored and desperate. The grief felt too heavy to carry by myself, and yet I had never been more alone.

But now, on the hillside, next to her grave, half of Kirkwall stands alongside me: holding my hands, praying with me.

And it makes no difference: she is still gone.

And yet. And yet, it makes all the difference.

Onto her coffin, I drop an old dandelion stalk, left over from the summer. I have always liked the way that dandelions can be two things at once: yellow flowers and then, once they seem to have died, they become balls of white seeds, which can be carried far and wide by the wind. New life, somewhere else.

Every beat of my heart aches in my chest.

One by one, the people from Kirkwall come forward with their grave offerings. Marjorie Croy sprinkles salt over the coffin, and her daughter, Bess, puts in an ear of corn. Mr Cameron drops in a sea stone, and John O'Farrell scatters a handful of peat.

Gifts from land and sea, to help her rest peacefully. Years ago, bodies were bound tightly in sailcloth before being lowered into their graves, to stop the spirit returning to haunt the living. I would give anything for her to haunt me.

After everyone has stepped away from the grave, I drop in two more things. The jagged scrap of metal feels small and insignificant. It is barely longer than my finger, but it is sharp – sharp enough to threaten to cut a man's throat, and to mean it. Sharp enough to make him leave you alone, to make him stumble away from you, to make him flinch from you when, for all his life, everyone has flinched from him.

But I don't want the piece of metal any more. It's done its job and I release it. It thuds against the newly turned earth. The second object I drop lands silently. The thin gold chain is too fine to glint in the darkness of the grave.

I nearly threw it into the sea instead, but I want to know where it is. I want it buried.

'You don't need to be scared of him any more,' I whisper.

I close my eyes and open them, but the grave is still there, the new, dark earth a wound in the ground. After they cover the coffin with soil, the grass will grow. In the spring there will be flowers. It will be summer, then winter. Sunshine and snow and rain. Other deaths, other births. In time, people will forget who, exactly, she was. This will all be a story – something to be told around the fireside, like the tales of the selkies or the Sea Mither or the poor woman from a hundred years ago, who is said to have drowned her lover, but always denied it.

We will never know the truth.

Bess Croy puts a gentle hand on my shoulder. 'You are welcome to come to our house for tea and a bannock. It's noisy, with the children, but we'd like to have you.'

Behind her, Marjorie Croy is nodding. 'You'd be welcome.'

'Thank you,' I say. 'But I'd like to . . . I want to see the other islands. Places we went together. I'd like to . . .' My voice cracks.

Marjorie nods. 'I understand. To say goodbye.'

'Will you be coming to the hospital in Kirkwall? To work?' Bess asks.

'Not yet,' I say. 'Maybe one day, but I want some time alone first.'

Bess nods unhappily, her face hurt. I'd like to explain to her, but I can't – not without risking everything.

I walk up to the chapel alone. The sun is dropping now; the light on the walls is gilded. Outside is the statue Cesare had made, of St George defeating the dragon. The dragon, he said, stood for war and St George battled it daily.

'And one day,' Cesare had said, 'there is peace.'

'There can't be peace *everywhere*,' I'd said.

'We can hope,' he'd said, looking at the chapel. 'We must hope.'

I have to hope.

Now, in my hand, I have the metal heart. Inside the chapel, it is cool. The mattress I slept on is gone and everything is peace and silence once more. No traces of Angus's blood on the tiles. No hint of everything that happened here. There is only light and beauty.

Between the two halves of the filigreed rood screen, there is a gap in the floor – a dip in the cement that has been chipped and dug out with a piece of metal. It is a hollow in the shape of a heart. As I sat and waited for them to pass judgement on me, I had hewn and scrabbled and dug away at the concrete floor. My fingers are raw and sore and there are bashed edges all along one side of the heart.

I press it into the gap in the concrete. It fits almost exactly, like a key in a lock.

I stand and I force myself to turn and walk away from it. I don't want to leave it, but I must appear to be content to turn away from the heart.

I have to leave it, for it never belonged to the person I am. It never belonged to Con.

The heart was given to Dot and, as far as everyone knows, Dot is gone. As far as everyone believes, Dot drowned in the storm. Dot is buried in the hillside grave with salt sprinkled on her chest.

And now I must pretend to be Con.

At first I didn't realize, I didn't remember. They saw my trousers and they called me Con. All my memories were so foggy that, when they called me by my sister's name, I answered. I knew that Dot was alive, somehow, somewhere, but I didn't understand how I could know that. The memories came back slowly.

I remember swimming from the boat, leaving Cesare to get to Con. But the water was a shifting, swirling mass and I couldn't see her anywhere. I swam to the barriers, where I'd seen her fall in and I dived beneath the waves again and again, reaching out.

Every time I surfaced, I called Con's name.

Then something below the water grasped my foot. Hands around my ankle. I cried out and then dived down again, one last time.

Con was next to the rocks of the barrier. Relief washed over me and I tugged on her hand. Her body came towards me, but something snagged, keeping her under. It was then I realized that her skirt was caught in the rocks.

My skirt. The skirt she had worn to pretend to be me, so that I could escape with Cesare. I yanked as hard as I could, but she was stuck.

No!

I swam to her face and, pressing my lips against hers, breathed a lungful of air into her mouth. Then, chest burning, I surfaced again, before diving back below the water and pulling on her skirt. The material wouldn't rip and I couldn't get her free.

Mind whirring, I swam to her face again, the water battering against both of us.

I went to breathe into her mouth again, but she shook her head. She fought me off, turning away and pushing my hands from her face.

No! I thought. I tried again, but again she pushed me away. She reached out and stroked my cheek. She placed her hand on my chest, just for a moment.

Then she put her hand in mine and I watched as she let the air bubble from her lungs.

No, no, no! I could see what she was going to do. I could see she'd made a decision to let me go, to let me escape with Cesare. I could already feel the chasm opening between us, could feel her drifting. I wanted to pull her back, wanted to swap places, wanted to change everything.

Please.

She breathed in.

The water blurred everything, but I could see her face, faintly – a moment of struggle, of terror, and a final squeeze of her hand on mine.

Then she was still. And everything crumbled. I swam up to the surface and I screamed. The storm carried my cries away. The waves pushed me against the rocks again and again, battering my body against the barrier. A rock hit my head and I nearly fell back into the water, nearly let myself go under. But no. I had to carry on. I had a choice and I had to take it. I worked to get her body free from the rocks. And I pulled my sister from the water.

I don't remember dragging her to the quarry. It seemed, somehow, that she was with me then. That we were dragging Angus between us. I wanted so much for him to be dead and gone that I imagined his lifeless face. We were glad he was gone, but we knew we would have to pay for his death, somehow.

But I didn't want Con to be guilty for ever. I wanted her to prove that she was innocent. I wanted her to be free. I wanted her to be able to live, without the shadow of Angus, all those rumours and all the guilt. I just had to find a way to help her to live.

So when they came to take me away, I said to them, 'I did it. She didn't do it. It was me.' And then I stopped being Dot and I told them I was Con.

I walk back to the bothy slowly, to pack up the life we shared. I have given away the chickens and the sheep to people in Kirkwall. I have told them I need some time before I come back – if I come back. They haven't questioned me too deeply. They are used to Con hiding herself away.

The bothy is cold; the ashes in the grate are grey and dusty. Perhaps someone else will make a home here, one day. I pick up the case that the two of us brought over, a year ago, and I fill it with our clothes: my skirt and her trousers. I'd like to keep something of hers close to my skin.

*

It is light still outside, and everyone has gone back to Kirkwall. Down the hill, the camp is deserted. I close my eyes, imagining it full of life again. I picture Gino, Marco, Father Ossani. And Cesare. Always Cesare.

The waters around here carry everything north.

Behind me, the chapel is a reminder that there is always hope.

I open my eyes and inhale. Sky and sea and gorse as clean as freshly sawn wood. Uprising sap in the air. For the first time in an age, I am free.

I am free, and it feels like some part of me will always be drowning.

A crow circles overhead, cawing mournfully. Far off, the peregrine calls.

Mine. Mine. Mine.

A sudden crushing in my chest. The years without her will stack up like loose change, uncountable, unending. Everything will remind me of her. Every moment without her will be half lived.

There are some sadnesses too heavy to carry, but still I must keep walking, I must keep breathing. For now, I have to live for the twin souls inside me.

I bundle up my fishing line and lift my case, with its few bits of clothing and food. The place I am going to is not far. If I don't find him there, I will keep searching. I won't ever stop searching.

Before I go north, I walk out onto the barrier for the last time — at least for the moment, although I don't doubt that my feet will bring me back this way one day.

There is a clear path now, all the way to Kirkwall. Anyone who wants to come to this island will be able to walk across the waters. No one is alone any more. That's just one of the things that war gave us. It crammed all of us together, one way or another.

I look across the water at the things on the horizon that may be gathering clouds or pieces of land and, for the moment, it does not matter which they are. I think over all the old stories and rumours about lost souls and drowned lovers.

I wonder which ones are invented and which ones are the truth. Perhaps this doesn't matter either. Perhaps it only matters what we believe. And perhaps this is a choice.

I lean over the side of the barrier and I allow my fingers to trail in the water. There is a dark shape below me. In the past, we used to think monsters lived in the sea, and so it may be. But there are monsters on the outside too, in the real world, walking among us in their human skins. And there are the monsters within us that we will never show to another soul, that we will hide even from ourselves.

And then there are the things we leave behind for the people who follow us: the stone tombs and the stories. The pieces of metal buried in the earth. The chapel on the hillside and the tale of how it was made.

The sun comes out from behind the cloud and the outline of a shadow emerges in the water next to the barrier. It is my own reflection but I can see so many faces in it: I see my parents, my sister, myself. I have a single life to live for all of us.

Out in the bay are the shadows of the long-dead ships from past wars. Our mistakes are everywhere; the skeletons of our past ghost us daily. We can only try to stay above them, to remember them.

Orcadians

In the latter years of the war, there is a tale told about the northern part of the newly named Chapel Island, where it is rumoured that a selkie lives with her mate – somewhere within the land. There are tales told: that she has taken him into the sea with her and taught him to swim, which is not the usual way of things. Sometimes, on a clear night, people walking across the barrier towards the island have heard splashing and shouts of laughter. A child, wandering too far north, says that he saw two people swimming in the sea, like seals – his mother scolds him for stirring the gossip pot, then passes on the story to all of her friends.

A tradition quickly grows: it is good fortune, people say, for those who are in love to walk across the Churchill barrier early in the morning, before the sun is up or when it is still low in the sky, and the sea mist still swirls around the islands. You must travel northwards with your beloved, past the old camp and the Italian Chapel, and you must lay an offering of food on the furthest tip of the island. Then you must both walk away, holding hands, without looking back. By the next day, the food will be gone: this is a sign of the blessing on the couple in love, who have travelled on this journey together.

Afterwards, the couple must go into the little Italian Chapel and kneel. They will listen to the hush of the sea, with its secrets; they will look at the chapel walls and they'll marvel at the beauty of it all. They will press their fingers to the metal heart in the chapel floor and they will hope.

They confess their sins; they beg forgiveness; they vow to change. They promise to be faithful and true. They think of the terrible acts that people commit, during war and peace, and they promise to hold their loved ones closer. They promise to make every breathing moment an act of worship.

Then they walk out into the sunlight and they feel the blessing of the sky and the sea all around them. And they thank whatever god they believe in for the prisoners who conjured hope from war.

September 1942

Dorothy

It takes me less than an hour to reach the northern tip of the island. On every step, I feel torn between anticipation and terror. What if he isn't here? What if he has been carried far out to sea? What if the storm has left his broken boat and shattered body lying on the jagged north rocks?

It is a place of swelling hills and serrated cliffs, with a freshwater loch nearby. There are rumours of a great snake that twists in the depths. It's not an area that anyone visits often: when Con and I were much younger, we used to sneak up here with some of the other children – sometimes with Angus MacLeod – but then one of the boys fell down a gorge and cracked his skull. He lived, but he was never the same afterwards, and no one liked to go too far north after that; the boy's friends said that the gorge had appeared out of nowhere, as if the ground had opened under his feet.

Slowly, the myths about the place grew, and it had been years since anyone had visited here – anyone except me and Cesare.

I walk up the path – my feet know the way, each

step in my bones from the number of times I walked this path with him, my hand clasped in his.

I imagine Con alongside me, walking in easy silence, her hand in mine, or my arm around her shoulders. I have trodden the same ground as her for so long, breathed the same air, I don't know how to continue without her.

My heart is flesh. It will not melt or crack or rust. It throbs onwards. My lungs take in air, my blood circles my body, my legs drive me forward and upwards.

Con. Con. Con.

I am not whole but I am not broken. Part of my life is lived for her.

I miss her the way a tree misses last year's leaves.

I walk towards a mound that is surrounded by reeds and bog on one side and the cliff face on the other. Only if you know the way is it possible to pick a path over the safe patches of grass, to a rocky overhang. Even then, until you crouch by the rock, the mound looks like any other.

But behind the rock, hidden from view, is the tunnel into the mound. Thousands of years ago, people might have worshipped here, rising each morning to greet the sun and the sea that gave life. Or perhaps they buried their dead here and visited once a year, to remember the people who shaped them and made them who they were. Grief can feel like worship.

The grass has recently been crushed underfoot,

and there's the faint smell of a fire burning, or perhaps that's just my imagination.

My hope rises.

I crawl through the tunnel on hands and knees. Con and I used to lie in the tunnel, planning what we would do when we left the islands. We talked about which countries we wanted to see. The world seemed so bright, from the close darkness of that tunnel. If I laid my head on the stones now, perhaps I would hear the echo of her laughter. Perhaps these stones hold the warm memory of her skin still. I run my fingers over the smooth rock and whisper her name, like a prayer.

Then I whisper his name, under my breath – I don't have the courage to call out for him.

Everywhere, people believe in things they cannot see.

Please, I think. *Please, please.*

The main chamber is lighter than the tunnel and, for a moment, I think everything is just as we left it when we last visited, weeks ago. The cave is bare, the floor clean and the small hole in the roof allows a few rays from the sun to shine on the blank stone.

My heart plummets. He is not here.

Then I see the pile of blankets in the corner of the cave.

He is lying on a broken pallet, with old sheets pulled up to his chin. His eyes are closed.

My mouth is dry. *What if . . . ?*

I step fully into the chamber and stand upright, watching him.

He doesn't move.

Oh, God, I think. *I can't, I can't . . .*

His chest rises and falls; beneath closed lids, his eyes move back and forth, as if, even in his sleep, he's searching.

Relief tingles through me. I crouch next to him and put my hand on his shoulder. He's warm. He's solid. He's alive.

His eyelids flicker and then he looks up at me. Those dark eyes, which somehow always know me, have somehow known me from the first moment I saw him.

Cesare.

At first, he doesn't move. His eyes travel over my face, which is more bruised than when he last saw me, and the scratches on my neck, which are new. He will only be able to see me dimly in this light. What if he is angry that I left him? What if he doesn't understand, or if he, too, has been knocked on the head and has forgotten me?

'I am dreaming?' he whispers.

I shake my head, my throat too tight for words.

'Dorotea.' he says.

'Yes.'

I put my hand on his cheek and he brushes his fingers over my lips.

'Dorotea!' he exclaims, and he wraps his arms around me, squeezing me tight, whispering something again and again into my hair.

'*Grazie, grazie.*' The word echoes around the cave, like the sigh of the wind, like the reverberation of a desperate prayer suddenly answered.

He kisses me, his mouth hot on mine. His skin tastes of salt and smoke from the fire.

He holds my face in his hands and laughs. 'I think you are never coming,' he says. 'I think I have lost you.'

His face blurs, until I blink, wipe my eyes. 'Never.'

'They are looking for me? The guards.'

I shake my head. On the night of the storm, as I jumped into the sea, I saw the boat being carried through the barriers.

The sea takes everything north now.

'The cave,' I'd shouted, as I jumped. The wind and water swept away my words, but I thought he might have heard. I hoped he had. I hoped, somehow, he would find his way there.

I don't know if I truly believed it was possible, then, but we have made it true, somehow.

Sometimes love allows impossible things.

I curl into his body. He wraps his arms around me. And I do not feel whole, but I feel less shattered.

There will be time to tell him of Con and how the sight of her bloodless body on a stone slab had hollowed me out and left my mind feeling like an empty cave, where thoughts and sounds and memories endlessly echo in the darkness. There will be time to tell him about Angus MacLeod.

For now, there is his breath, his voice, his smile. His body, keeping me warm in the dark.

We stay in the cave all that winter, making plans. At first, these are no more than what we will eat that day, whether we will walk or try to swim in the cold water.

We catch fish and rabbits; we gather kelp and bladderwrack. We talk, or we make love, or we sit in silence, remembering.

Gradually, as our bruises fade and our wounds become less raw, we begin to plan for a future, after the war, when we will find his family in Italy. For the moment, while the Italians are still the enemy, a runaway prisoner of war would be given a death sentence and it is safer to stay hidden. If we had escaped to Scotland on that night in September, I'm sure he would have been captured and punished. But the war cannot last for ever: one day, we will be able to travel south together.

Sometimes, when Cesare is restless at night, he walks over the island to the old camp, to the chapel. Sometimes I go with him. The camp is deserted now, falling into disrepair. In a strong wind, the sound of moving metal sings out across the sea.

Behind the barbed wire, the camp looks lifeless, desolate, hopeless. But we know that it never was. A bare concrete yard can be the start of a life; an old metal hut can be a house of God, or a prison, or a place to remember.

Cesare and I walk along the beach, hand in hand, listening to the waves, listening to our shared breath. Beneath the sea, somewhere, are the struts and ribs of sunken ships – the shattered *Royal Elm* and a hundred others, resting in the quiet darkness. Under our feet crunch empty molluscs and the sloughed shells of crabs – hollow bone clothes. But it is possible to shed your skin and still live.

Cesare puts his arms around me. He pulls me in close and holds me to him until my tears stop. He doesn't ask me to explain. He kisses my forehead, my cheeks, my lips. He tells some joke to make me laugh. He presses a piece of driftwood into my hand. And then we walk on.

Sometimes, when Cesare and I lie down to go to sleep, we close our eyes, and we can hear the far-off growl of the planes, or we think we hear footsteps or the whispers of people coming closer. We think we hear our past coming to find us.

But then we realize it is the hush of the waves or the thud of our hearts, or our blood in our ears. It is the sound of time, which keeps going, and which is so precious, every moment.

We lie, side by side, holding hands, listening to the water, hearing life. One day soon, we will leave. We will take our boat and travel north, to Fair Isle, or south to Aberdeen, or further south to Moena. We will search out the places from our past lives, the places where our parents belonged. And we will not care how people look at us, or what they say, or if they whisper or tell stories about us. Between us is a truth only we know, a language only we understand.

For us, together, every place will be home.

This kingdom, too, is ours, and in our blood
Its passionate tideways run . . .
and the wild flood
Of winter haunts our ears with spells that bind
Sea, sky and earth in one.

From 'Orkney', Robert Rendall

Author's Note

The Italian Chapel on Lamb Holm, Orkney, is a real place, built by Italian prisoners during the Second World War. While I used this genuine (and wonderful) work of art as an inspiration for the novel, this story is very much a work of fiction, as are the events and people in it.

The people of Orkney, many of whom were incredibly helpful and generous with their time and advice, will be quick to spot that I have fictionalized both the historical timing of certain events and the geography of the islands – the bombing of the *Royal Oak* (rather than the *Royal Elm*) took place in October 1939 and the construction of the barriers took place between 1940 and 1944, originally starting with Irish workers. However, I wanted the love affair between my characters to be constrained by time and intensified by the precipitous and perilous nature of war, so I took many liberties with timings and action. This was a very conscious decision: I'm painfully aware of the difficulties in fictionalizing real historical events and people and selling them as 'fact', especially when this involves taking on the voices of 'real' people: I was very certain that I didn't want to do that.

I wanted to write about war, memory and art. There

are so many war monuments to the dead, so many battlegrounds memorialized, so many landscapes that have been utterly changed by conflict. But the Italian Chapel seems, to me, to be something different: it is an object of hope, made during a time of war and darkness; it was conceived and crafted by men who were prisoners in a foreign country and had no way of knowing when they would return home. It is a creation born of expectation and love. It still stands today and has been beautifully maintained – I'd encourage everyone to go and see it.

The metal heart is also a real object: it was created by an Italian metal worker, Giuseppe Palumbi, as a symbol of his love for an Orcadian woman. He had a wife and family in Italy, so left his heart behind in Orkney. While I used this as inspiration for Cesare's story, I didn't base my character upon any single prisoner, and his fate in the novel is very different from that of the Italian prisoners, who returned to their families. I have changed many other details too: the painter of the real chapel was called Domenico Chiocchetti and he did not have an affair with an Orcadian woman. The commander of the camp on Lamb Holm was called Major Buckland, and historical sources show him to have been kindly and intensely human, encouraging the prisoners to build a chapel, as well as a small theatre and even a concrete billiard table. Although the influx of hundreds of prisoners must have been a huge challenge for the people of Orkney, sources from the time say that they were both welcoming and kind to the foreign men: the brutal character of Angus MacLeod is entirely fictional. I have also made Selkie Holm much bigger than Lamb Holm, where the real chapel stands, and have changed other details for the purposes of fiction: Catholic Mass would not have been taken with both bread and wine until the mid-1960s and I've added the words 'Body and Blood of Christ.'

While researching *The Metal Heart*, I came across a story of a man who, in response to feeling increasingly trapped in his father's business, failed to go to work one day, then found himself in New York, with no memory of who he was or why he was there. This led me to explore the idea of a dissociative fugue, where, in response to stress or an injury, an individual loses all knowledge of their identity and often wanders far from home, sometimes having formed a new or different personality. These genuine cases have intrigued psychologists for years and are distinct from instances where, in attempting to escape the consequences of a crime, an individual may feign memory loss. Arguably, both responses are the brain's way of coping with trauma. I'm fascinated by the idea of how we respond to crisis and how very clever our own brains are at concealing information and hiding memories. I wonder, too, if this is something at which the brain becomes increasingly adept: a well-worn pathway of concealment. In the same way as I cannot recall large chunks of stressful times during my childhood, even now, after having an argument, I can rarely remember what was said afterwards.

Like many writers, I find that my characters reveal themselves to me slowly, and over a number of drafts. Gradually, I grow to learn their likes and dislikes, their desires and motivations and, as part of this process, a voice develops. This novel was different, in that the character's 'voices' made themselves clear very early on, as did their longings and animosities. But, as I wrote, I discovered that most of my characters were hiding things, even from me. I'm aware that this sounds irrational, but it led to a writing process full of surprises, and of the same theme of concealment and discovery occurring in different characters, as well as the idea of pairs, doubling and repetition. This wasn't something I'd intended but I was pleased to find, when I reread the whole of my first draft (much of which, ironically, I barely remembered writing), that similar ideas made themselves clear in each of the character's narratives. When paired with the ideas I'd started with, of twins, doubling and concealment, and of men creating art during a time of destruction, I felt I had something that was richer and more complex than I'd originally envisaged. It led me to question the extent to which we ever truly admit to (or even understand) our own motivations.

I wanted to write about how war, trauma and death affect people: the idea of someone being ripped out of the fabric of existence and how that changes every other thread. I've thought a great deal about how war often creates a hollow absence rather than a death, particularly when there is no body: when people are cut off from each other and simply 'disappear'. My great-uncle died at El Alamein; his body was never returned home. I know that his sisters (my grand-mother and my great-aunt) and his widow were all desperate to visit his grave, hoping it might close the raw wound left by his absence. But seeing the grave only made his loss more haunting. The inscription on the wooden cross that marks his grave reads, *Where the road breaks off and the signposts end.*

In some ways, he continued to exist because he simply disappeared. I don't think they ever stopped hoping for his return.

Which brings me back to the Italian Chapel, the barriers built in Orkney in the Second World War and the way that war changes people and landscapes for ever.

To the people of Orkney, who maintain their beautiful memorial, and to the Italian prisoners who built the barriers and the chapel: thank you.

Bibliography

Before starting this novel, I read widely about Orkney, its traditions and the chapel, as well as visiting the islands and spending hours in the wonderful, welcoming Orkney Library and Archives, which is a fount of information and the creator of the best library Twitter account I've come across.

For those interested in factual considerations and fictional explorations of some of the places and events covered in this book, this list provides an excellent starting point and I would begin with the superb books by Philip Paris and Donald S. Murray on the Italian Chapel.

Compton Verney, *Created in Conflict – British Soldier Art* (Compton Verney, 2019)

Dimbleby, Jonathan, *Destiny in the Desert, The Road to El Alamein* (Profile Books, 2012)

Dunn, Douglas (ed.), *The Oxford Book of Scottish Short Stories* (OUP, 1995)

Firth, John, *Reminiscences of an Orkney Parish* (Orkney National History Society, 1974)

Gardiner, Juliet, *Wartime Britain* (Headline, 2004)

Garfield, Simon (ed.), *Our Hidden Lives* (Ebury Press, 2005)

Garfield, Simon (ed.), *We Are at War* (Ebury Press, 2006)

Jamie, Kathleen, *Findings* (Sort of Books, 2005)

Liptrot, Amy, *The Outrun* (Canongate, 2016)

MacFarlane, Robert, *Landmarks* (Penguin, 2016)

MacFarlane, Robert, *The Old Ways* (Penguin, 2013)

Marr, Andrew, *The Making of Modern Britain* (Macmillan, 2009)

Marwick, Ernest, *The Folklore of Orkney and Shetland* (Birlinn, 2000)

Muir, Tom, *Orkney Folk Tales* (The History Press, 2014)

Murray, Donald S., *And On This Rock – The Italian Chapel, Orkney* (Birlinn, 2010)

Murray, Donald S., *The Guga Hunters* (Birlinn, 2015)

Murray, Donald S., *The Italian Chapel, Orkney* (Birlinn, 2017)

Paris, Philip, *Orkney's Italian Chapel* (Black and White Publishing, 2010)

Paris, Philip, *The Italian Chapel* (Black and White Publishing, 2009)

Tait, Charles, *The Orkney Guide Book* (Tait Publishing, 2017)

Walker Marwick, Ernest, *An Orkney Anthology* (Scottish Academic Press, 1991: edited by John D. M. Robertson)

Acknowledgements

This novel wouldn't have come into being without inspiration from my incredible editor, Jillian Taylor, who, when I said I wanted to write a story about wartime imprisonment, showed me pictures of the Italian Chapel and spent a lunchtime enthusing with me about the creation of art during war. Over the next two years, Jill has continued to be the most inspiring, exacting, wonderful and insightful editor, guiding me through the process of rewriting most of the novel multiple times, without ever losing her enthusiasm for my work. It's impossible to articulate quite how empowering it is to have an editor who believes in me so absolutely, and my thanks to you will always feel inadequate.

Endless thanks also to my equally brilliant agent, Nelle Andrew, who pushes me to find and write the best story I can, who always tells me the truth (however painful that might be), and who is fearless and utterly indefatigable on my behalf. Superwoman: I feel ridiculously lucky to have you in my corner.

Thanks to my first and most enthusiastic cheerleader, my lovely mum, Sue Lea, who fed my childhood reading obsession and continues to talk about books with me. To my sister Annabelle, who reads so much of my work and is so enthusiastic and kind; to my sister Sophie, who is so enthusiastic and sarcastic.

Enormous thanks to Bill Gurney, for brilliant and brutal advice and so many laughs. Sadly, your critiques are always spot on.

Huge thanks to my amazing friends Cathy Thompson and Sachin Choithramani for reading an early draft and being so kind, patient and perceptive over wine. And enormous thanks to the lovely Luisa Cheshire for providing such insightful advice on the draft and all my other writing woes. Thank you to Nicky Leamy for reading parts of this and being so encouraging, and to the rest of Gin Club, for being endlessly kind, funny and supportive: Laura Baxter, Jane Guest, Alison Hall and Adele Kenny. I adore you all.

I'm very lucky to have a number of wonderful friends, who provide constant support and advice. The alphabetization of your names is no reflection of who I love most. Thank you to Holly Alexander, Sandy Ameer Beg, Jen Bayley, Penny Clarke, Jo Davies, Andrea Docherty, Hazel Fulton, Anna Hardman, Jackie Hope, Bansi Kara, Sarah Lewsey, Luke Moore, Emma Ritson, Sarah Richardson, Duncan Vaux, Robert Ward-Penny, Claire Williams. And thank you to my book-club friends: Harriet Gott, Claire Revell, Jenny Mitchell-Hilton and Jane Tracey. Thank you to Helena Lönnberg for the lovely (fictitious) ritual of sprinkling a line of salt across the doorway. Thank you to Nana (Pam Lyddon) for all the love. Thank you to Liz and Doug Day for your constant love and kindness towards my lovely boys. Thank you to John Wood for all your support and co-parenting.

Thank you to all the bookshop owners who have been so tireless in supporting my writing, particularly Mog and Pauline at Warwick Books, Tamsin and Judy at Kenilworth Books and all the staff at Waterstones in Leamington.

Thank you to my Warwick Writing Programme friends: Gonzalo Ceron Garcia, Tim Leach, Sarah Moss, Lucy Brydon, Will Eaves, Maureen Freely and David Morley.

Thank you to Orkney Library, for letting me browse articles and photographs in the archives for hours, and for answering so many of my questions.

I'm hugely grateful to the whole talented team at Penguin, Michael Joseph – I feel so lucky to have such endless champions of my work: Laura Nicol, Jen Porter, Bea McIntyre, Hazel Orme, as well as Jane Kirby and the rest of the wonderful rights team; thank you all. And thank you to my brilliant US editor, Erin Wicks, and all the team at Harperbooks. I'm so very lucky.

The biggest thanks of all to the people who have to live with me: to my sons, Arthur and Rupert, who never (outwardly) resent sharing me with books and are always keen to talk about stories with me. You're wonderful and incredible: the best things I could ever hope to make. I'll try to be better for you.

And to Roger: confidant, cheerleader, tireless reader, best friend, lovely twat. Everything I write about love starts with you.

About the Author

Caroline Lea is the author of two previous novels, including *The Glass Woman*, which was nominated for the Historical Writers Association Debut Crown Award. Her fiction and poetry have been shortlisted for the Bridport Prize, the Fish Short Story Competition, and various flash fiction prizes. Caroline's work often explores the pressure of small communities and fractured relationships, as well as the way our history shapes our beliefs and behavior. She grew up in Jersey in the United Kingdom and currently lives in Warwick with her two young children.

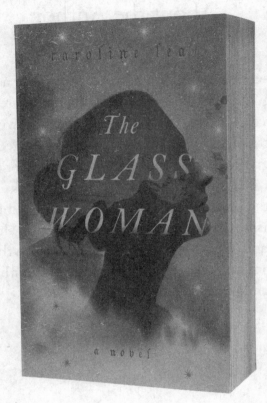